Sign up for our newsletter to hear
about new and upcoming releases.

www.ylva-publishing.com

PAYBACK

CHARLOTTE MILLS

DEDICATION

To C for her unwavering support, even though I haven't won the lottery yet.

ACKNOWLEDGEMENTS

Thank you to Astrid and everyone at Ylva Publishing for taking a chance on me. To Andrea Bramhall and Michelle Aguilar for all their guidance and support through the editing process when both my characters and I needed pulling into line. Thanks to Hayley Sherman for all her proofreading over the last few years.

PROLOGUE

RYAN TURNED THE WHEEL, TAKING the car from the well-worn service route through the woodland. The expensive suspension quickly sprang into action as the vehicle crawled through rougher terrain, cutting the headlights leaving only sidelights to light the way. The discreet markers left earlier soon came into view, revealing a snaking route through the trees, up the gentle slope, and towards the steep drop beyond. It wasn't meant to be like this. Two days of fear and panic, interspersed with the occasional rational thought, had led to this particular restored woodland. According to local websites, its exposed location kept residents away.

Work gloves went on over latex-covered hands. Tired eyes took a moment to adjust to the moonlight. The earthy scent and rustling sounds of the canopy overhead swaying in the gentle breeze drowned out all other noise. Sticks that had marked the car's route were removed. Loose soil and forest debris were easily kicked over the holes and tyre marks. The spade had been previously acquired from a stranger's unlocked shed, to be returned later to prevent any unnecessary attention.

Walking to the selected spot, away from some of the larger pine trees, Ryan began clearing an area of forest floor. Digging a hole occupied the mind, and focus and concentration were required in this darkness, lit only by an emergency head torch. A wandering mind could easily arrive at guilt.

The various layers of clothing were sweat-inducing, but removing any might lead to accidentally leaving evidence behind in the darkness.

Take nothing but memories, leave nothing but footprints. The long-forgotten quote suddenly came to mind. In this situation, however, Ryan wanted neither.

When the hole had reached shoulder height, the spade came flying out. Ryan followed it, then took a deep breath to prepare for the next step. The breeze had dropped, creating a painful eerie silence.

It was a short walk to the car. A lift of the boot revealed a form wrapped in plastic. In one long heave, gravity brought it to the floor with a muffled thud. Dragging the carcass to the hole was demanding on already strained muscles. The smooth plastic was difficult to grip with gloves, though it did ease the friction with the ground as it edged closer to what would be its final resting place. Ryan took a moment to stand up straight, stretching out body kinks that had formed during the strenuous process.

Grasping one end of the plastic caused the contents to shift and roll, revealing a figure slumped onto the forest floor. Dead eyes stared up into the night sky, their expression one of nonchalance, an indication how this man had lived his selfish life. Gathering the plastic, Ryan's eye was drawn to the ring finger on the man's left hand as it sagged across his chest. Glinting in the moonlight, the distinguished design of the ring was a harsh reminder of the devastation he had caused years earlier.

Thank God the bastard owned a vehicle large enough to fit both a body and a folding bicycle. Although the lengthy ride home would not be fun, it was the safest option. A sturdy boot shove was not quite enough to persuade the body to turn over into its earthy compartment below, so Ryan crouched down, rearranging the limbs into the recovery position, a small smile emerging at the irony as the figure rolled and disappeared out of sight.

Darkness made it impossible to see the dishevelled body that now lay at the base of the cavity, but Ryan flicked on the head torch again, the need for confirmation taking over. The bastard's arms had flailed during the fall, his face now covered by a forearm. The degree of satisfaction that pervaded Ryan's mind was sadly short-lived.

The screeching of car tyres nearby provoked an uncontrollable wave of panic, of hands shaking, of mentally preparing for cold metal cuffs slipping on limp wrists. A silence followed. Ryan stayed frozen to the spot, expectant ears waiting for the rumble of footsteps and voices that never came. A muffled whistle sounded, and the sound of crunching gears mixed with the sharp noise of a gunned engine brought some relief as a car sped off into the distance.

Ryan stumbled downhill towards the dry-stone wall edging the woodland, the desire to make sure the coast was clear taking over. From the protective darkness of the trees, it was possible to survey the road from the high banking. There was no sound or movement. A small sense of relief filtered through, until a dark shape on the road suddenly appeared in Ryan's cone of vision.

It had to be a deer. Moving to the wall to get a better look, Ryan instead found vague facial features waiting, visible in the moonlight but still not clear enough. The figure's position was right for neither an animal, nor a human out for an evening stroll. Scaling the wall and moving closer made it finally possible for Ryan to hear it: the infectious beat emanating from the prone human's earphones.

An unconscious woman dressed in running gear. Crouching, Ryan was unable to look at her face while removing a work glove to check for a pulse. Nothing. Bile threatened to emerge. Ryan stood bolt upright, head upturned to the sky in an attempt to prevent it, concentrating on a particular flickering star in the night sky until focus returned.

CHAPTER 1

Roused slowly awake from her slumber, she barely recognised the noise that had woken her before she grabbed the offending article from the makeshift nightstand. It was still dark as she fumbled with the touchscreen.

"Hello," she mumbled into the phone.

"DC Kate Wolfe?" The male voice on the other end had a caffeine-induced sharpness to it.

"Yes." Her mind came into focus.

"DCI Taylor has requested you at a scene; the address is—"

"What? I don't officially start till next week!"

"Don't kill the messenger. It's 14 Morley Lane, on the outskirts of Warner."

The phone disconnected in her ear. Kicking off the duvet, she scrambled for the lamp switch, knocking the *Blackstone's Police Manual* to the floor. She dug around in the box next to her for a pen and envelope to write the address she'd just been given. Sitting down on the edge of the bed, she tried to recall the information she'd compiled on her new boss.

Detective Chief Inspector Helen Taylor had worked in Manchester CID until seven years ago. She'd made a name for herself working several high-profile murder cases and one child abduction. Being a city girl herself, it made no sense to her why anyone would want to transfer to a back-of-beyond town like Warner. Not that it wasn't picturesque in its own way, but it wasn't the city life she was used to.

Close to the borders of Cheshire and Shropshire, Warner had a population of barely six-and-a-half-thousand people. It sat in the shadow of the Craven and Pendle Hills. The natural resources of the surrounding area had dictated the industries of the town, with mines providing materials for salt glazing in the potteries; a limestone quarry supplied local and national construction projects.

New developments had increased the size of the town in the 1960s to house the growing working population; new industrial estates were part of the new build, further expanding small business and commerce of the area.

Although the town still held a regular market day, some of the vibrancy had faded in recent years. Younger residents had moved away for study or work, reluctant to return. Dairy farming and cheese making continued to thrive in the area.

The address was easy to find—with a little help from the trusty satnav—although the flashing blue lights from the fire engines were a beacon in the darkness. While there had been no information on the call-out, it was pretty obvious from the presence of the firemen finishing the damping-down process that the call was a house fire.

Morley Lane was a short row of detached, cottage-type houses. The opposite side of the road looked barren in the darkness. The houses either overlooked a fantastic view across the countryside or a piece of wasteland filled with fly-tipped waste; it was difficult to see in the darkness.

She parked up in the nearest available space, then pulled a pair of latex gloves from the overstuffed glovebox before getting out of her lukewarm car. The cold chill was an unwelcome shock to the system as she made her way to the police tape.

Her path was cut off by a burly uniformed officer.

"No entry, I'm afraid. Are you a resident?" His thick Welsh accent was lyrical as he spoke.

Holding up her warrant card, she said, "DC Kate Wolfe." She watched him squint at her identification before pulling out a pen.

"Sorry. I didn't recognise you. Are you new?"

"Yes, on secondment from London." *And I can't wait to leave this two-bit dump.*

"PC Davies." He almost offered his hand, exposing his good manners. She glared at him; he offered her the clipboard instead.

"What can you tell me?" She started filling in her name on the scene report sheet.

"The house has been empty for over a year. Neighbour called it in just after 2 a.m. That's the fire investigations officer over there."

He pointed towards a darkened figure half sitting in his car under the intermittent blue lights. It looked like he was writing on his lap. Pulling the notebook from her pocket, she used the clipboard for support as she made notes on the page where she had already scribbled the Morley Lane address.

The house was at the end of a row, so there were only neighbours on one side.

"Residents around?" she asked, spotting the illuminated windows at the front of the adjacent house as she handed back the clipboard.

"Gone back inside, I think," the officer said in his sing-song voice. "No answer from the next one along. Neighbours think they might be away."

"Name?" she asked, pointing to the illuminated house.

"Goode, Mr and Mrs Goode."

Making a quick note before ducking under the tape, she headed for the dark figure that PC Davies had pointed out.

"Excuse me, are you in charge?" Holding her credentials in front of her like a shield to avoid a repeat of earlier, she offered them for inspection.

The fire officer looked up from his paperwork, giving her identification barely a side glance before starting his tirade. "No entry till the scene has been secured." His voice was harsh; he was obviously as happy as she was at being called out at three o'clock in the morning. He stood up and turned to face her. The white embroidered name on his jacket was difficult to make out in the low light: *Graham Brown, Fire Investigations Officer.*

He took off his safety helmet and laid it on the passenger seat. "The body's still inside, and will be, until we're sure it's safe."

"Body?" she repeated, trying to reign in the shock. The voice on the phone hadn't said anything about a body.

"Yes." His voice still held the dismissive, almost exasperated tone.

He looked tired and dishevelled as the blue lights illuminated his thinning hairline. Knowing the house was meant to be empty, she racked her brain, trying to recall what she knew about fires and arsonists.

"Any trace of accelerants?"

Graham Brown looked up from his notes as if weighing up how much to tell her. Feeling the scrutiny of his stare as he looked her up and down, she felt like the last ice lolly in the desert. She was quickly forming an opinion of Fire Officer Brown. "You're Richards's replacement." It sounded like a statement rather than a question.

She nodded her confirmation as the cold wind blew up her collar. She didn't have time to shoot the breeze right now, or ever.

He ploughed on, ignoring her lack of interest as he leaned against the side of his car. "Where are you from?"

Releasing a long breath as she moved her feet to keep warm, she prepared herself for the expected response. "London."

Graham Brown didn't disappoint, offering a raised eyebrow nod, as if the *Big Smoke* was another country, which in many ways it was to this particular town. His mildly relaxed demeanour seemed to evaporate before her eyes as he went back to all business.

"Fire started in the front room but spread up the stairs and into the back of the house. Petrol was used to start it. There are quite a few broken and empty bottles around the place… Could have been used to transport the accelerant, but we need to do some tests. Could just be kids, or vandalism."

She made notes as he spoke. "The house wasn't occupied. Which room's the body in?"

"Back room downstairs. There's a lot of damage to the rest of the house. What furniture was there was pushed together to make more fuel. No back door; it probably went up pretty quickly."

Suspected arson. She knew little of arson crimes, but what she did know was that the scene was deteriorating all the time, evidence being compromised by endless firemen traipsing through the house. With each physical step, they were making it impossible to find out what had actually happened and to bring the case to justice.

"Okay." Looking around for the scenes of crime officers, she expected to see a van, at least. They probably had to travel from a larger station, being out in the sticks. "How long till we can get inside?" she asked. She planned a visit to the neighbours to get out of the cold in the meantime.

"When it's safe." His irritated tone had returned. Maybe he realised that her only interest was the information he had.

"How soon?" she pushed, unflustered by his brash tone. She wasn't here to make friends; she was here to do her job.

"When it's safe," he repeated before turning his back to her, signalling the end of their conversation.

He focused on his paperwork once more. She figured Brown wasn't going to be any more forthcoming and headed off for the neighbour's house. Walking down the path to the front door, she saw the curtain twitch several times. She took a perverse pleasure in stabbing the doorbell, even though she could hear footsteps approaching on the other side. She pictured Brown's face beneath her finger.

As the door opened, she held up her warrant card. "Mrs Goode, I'm DC Kate Wolfe. Can I talk to you for a moment?"

The smell of stale sweat and cooking grease that invaded her nostrils was intense, making her use her forefinger and thumb to pinch them together.

The large, mature woman in the doorway was dressed in several layers, topped off with a bright-pink, fluffy dressing gown tied in the middle that emphasised her hourglass figure. Her once-matching slippers had now turned a shade of grey.

"Sure! Come on in." Standing back from the door, she continued, "Call me Gloria."

Caught between the icy cold and the warm house filled with stench, she wasn't quite sure how to proceed. "I don't want to impose."

"Don't be silly. You must be freezing."

Reluctantly, she stepped into the house. Her nostrils immediately responded with a series of leg-wobbling sneezes. "Jesus!"

"See? That cold air's bad for your chest. Got a cold coming, ain't you?" Gloria led the way into what looked like a sitting room at the front of the house.

Was she fucking serious? What about the air in here? She managed to keep a lid on it, her attention taken by a sausage dog heading towards her, his back end held in a harness with miniature bicycle wheels on either side of his body. He looked like a badly mended toy.

The dim light of the room made it look dingy. One wall was taken up by a long patterned sofa, facing the mock fireplace with a gas fire turned on low. An armchair nearby looked placed to suck up most of the heat. Shelving flanked either side of the fireplace each one filled with knick-knacks and books stacked horizontally.

"Tea?" Gloria offered.

The thought of having to spend any more time than necessary in this house made her feel a little sick. "No. Thank you." Manners maintained, she fired her first question in the hope that she would be back out in the fresh air as soon as possible. "You made the emergency call?"

Gloria Goode looked to be in her late fifties. Her hair had a Molly Sugden bouffant look about it, although it was flattened on one side, giving her a bedhead.

Gloria shoved her hands in her dressing gown pockets. "My husband did. He was up, saw the smoke and flames, called 999."

"The house has been empty for some time. Have you seen anything suspicious in the area lately?" Glancing down, she saw the broken dog sniffing at her boots.

"No. Don't think so." Gloria followed the detective's gaze. "Buddy, leave her alone. She's not come to see you."

"What about your…" She sneezed again. "Excuse me. Sorry. Husband?"

Gloria grinned at the young woman in front of her. "He had to go back to bed. He's ill. He hasn't said anything to me."

Aware of the ungodly hour, she relented. "Okay. Thank you, Mrs Goode." Quickly scribbling her name and number on a blank sheet of notepaper before tearing it off and holding it out, she said, "We may have to talk to your husband at some point, but if you think of anything else, please give me a call."

Gloria pocketed the piece of paper without even looking at it.

"I'll let you get back to bed." She made her way to the front door, happy to escape the persistent smell assaulting her sinuses.

"Not much chance of that with all this going on," Gloria said, taking hold of the door as the detective passed through it.

"Good job you're not in a terrace," she said, looking on the bright side, then realising that it was exactly the situation she lived in.

"I guess," Gloria said.

She felt eyes on her as she walked down the path until she was back along the road. The front of the damaged house was dark in contrast to the neighbours'. The front door was intact, but the large window had broken at some point, and dark, sooty stains covered the edges of the jagged glass. The upper floor had fared worse. Windows were blackened, although they were not broken. But the roof had a gaping hole, and the black smoke was escaping, intermittently lit by the blue lights.

As she approached the scene, she noticed a path to one side. It looked as if it led off into fields at the back of the row of houses. Turning on her phone torch, she could see a tall fence enclosing the garden. It seemed odd, considering there was little chance of being overlooked from nearby houses. This type of fence was expected in a cramped city, but surely out here you'd want to see the views of the countryside. Maybe the darkness hid an ugly view yet to be seen.

The large gate at the side of the building was wide open. From her position on the path, she could see the relatively small outside space at the back of the house, no doubt referred to as a "spacious, established garden" by an unscrupulous estate agent. Edging along the path, she could see a gaping black hole in the back of the building. The back door had been smashed in at some point. Graham Brown's words came back to her: the door was already open; vandalism was a possibility.

Flashlights began moving around inside as three firefighters made their way outside, carrying axes and large metal rods.

She took her phone out of her pocket and pretended to check on something as they made their way to the front of the house. Securing the scene was one of the most important aspects of police work; compromised evidence was no good to anyone. Taking her chance, she hurried through the gate, hesitating for a second as she approached the sooty doorway, almost overcome by the smoky, acrid smell that filled her lungs. She pulled the sleeve of her jacket to cover her nose and mouth before carefully making her way inside. The sound of dripping water in the dank room set her mind on edge; it felt like being underground.

She tapped the flashlight on her phone and began moving around what looked like a relatively small room. In one corner, she could see a doorway leading to the front of the house. She leant to one side and aimed her phone at the floor to prevent being seen. The flashing blue lights of a fire engine shone through a smoke-tinted broken window. The voices of the firefighters drifted through as the lights glared off the dripping walls.

Speed was of the essence if she didn't want to be seen; they could be back at any minute. Flicking on the camera option, she began videoing the scene around her. Once-decorated walls were now obscured with smoke damage. Partially visible, flowery wallpaper appeared along one wall as the flashlight danced along the surface. Panning around the room, she could see it was almost empty and moved to the internal wall separating the two main rooms downstairs. A number of boxes were stacked along the length. They looked damaged, but not extensively; partial words were still visible. It was the only place the body could be. She moved the light to the floor to avoid stepping on any debris or evidence; the last thing she needed was to trash the scene. Swallowing hard, she moved closer to the boxes, not knowing what she was going to find behind them. Dead bodies were something she'd seen before, but not charred remains. She prayed her stomach could take it.

Focusing on the screen, she hoped it would put some distance between her and whatever was there. Tilting the phone, the top of a dirty skirting board came into view, followed by a dark shape. It took a second for the image to come into focus. Sweeping the camera down helped put the form into context. Coal-covered legs filled the small screen. It wasn't clear how charred the legs were until patches of patterned material became visible below what looked like the knees. The legs were bent as if the figure were lying on its side. Further down, several layers of coloured thick socks were visible, as was a large boot on one foot; the other foot was covered by only a dark-green sock. She scanned around. The other boot wasn't in the immediate area.

Edging along the row of boxes, moving the camera along the body, she let the torso slip into view. It too was partially charred, the large dark coat still visible on one side, flapping open to the floor. One arm, the right, was trailing behind the torso; the other one looked like it was tucked under the body itself. The thick coat gave the figure a bulky look. She swallowed hard as she got close to the head and the shoulder came into view. She was expecting the worst but released a breath when she realised the hood was up, covering most of the head, saving her from that particular horror. What was visible was partially featureless as it faced the wall.

The images of smoke inhalation victims that she'd seen had not prepared her for this. They'd looked asleep for the most part.

She was just about to pan around the room once more to check the area around the body when she heard footsteps coming towards her.

"What the fuck! What are you doing in here? It hasn't been secured yet."

The gruff voice made her jump. Turning, she saw a large fireman with a metal prop in his gloved hand. It took her a moment to realise it was

Officer Brown from earlier. His coloured safety hat gave him away in the darkened room.

She resisted asking him what he was doing in there too, if it was that dangerous. "I'm documenting the scene in case it deteriorates. It's evidence!" Her frustration was apparent in her voice, even to her.

"I don't give a shit about that. Out now!" Brown replied with just as much vigour.

Glaring at him didn't seem to be getting her anywhere, though curiously, his eyes seemed to get further apart the angrier he got. "Just one minute," she spat in his direction.

"No! Now!"

He rushed across the room towards her, pushing her towards the door. He must have slipped as his full weight slammed against her, pushing her against the back wall of the room. For a moment, she thought the roof was caving in as debris began falling around them. The rod that he had been carrying smashed against her hip as he fell on top of her, sending a shockwave of pain along her hip bone. He seemed to be up on his feet in a split second as he pulled her out the back door with him.

"Are you fucking stupid or something? I said it wasn't cleared yet." He almost screamed in her face.

"Hey, it wasn't me that smashed up the place," she replied with equal venom.

Two other fire officers arrived on the scene, no doubt drawn by the noise and angry voices. Outnumbered, she backed away, not wanting to escalate the situation any more. Walking away triggered a shooting pain in her hip as she moved. Negotiating her way through the firefighters and their equipment, she felt their attention on her. Looking down at her clothes, she quickly tried to brush away the evidence of being found in a fire-damaged house.

Realising she wouldn't be able to enter the scene anytime soon, she hobbled back to her car. She was going to get the bollocking of her life for damaging the scene, whether it was her fault or not. The DCI wouldn't care. *Great first day, I'll probably get kicked off the case, sent back to London. Maybe not so bad after all.* She could quite happily get in her car and leave this place far behind her.

She arrived at her car, realising she didn't even know where the station was from here. As she let out a long breath and relaxed back against the headrest, a car passing by made her look up. Another patrol car. *Relief for Davies?* She watched as the officer got out of the car and chatted with Davies for few minutes before handing him the keys to the patrol car.

Lowering her window, she waited for the police car to get closer before sticking her hand out to get the officer's attention, waiting until the patrol car stopped parallel with her own. "Are you going back to the station?"

He nodded with a smile.

Great. "I'll follow you."

———◆———

Warner Police Station turned out to be a spacious, old-fashioned manor house set back from the main street as if it had once been surrounded by open land until the addition of modern roads had cut across the estate. Approaching the front of the building, she gingerly walked up stone steps through an ornate, carved archway. The inside was a little disappointing, crudely modernised to keep up with current policing requirements. Florescent strip lights replaced ornamental chandeliers, exposing every mismatched moulding or clumsily installed partition wall. After she had introduced herself to him, the desk sergeant furnished her with a swipe card that allowed her to access various parts of the building. She figured he was the one that had had the pleasure of calling her earlier, pulling her from her warm bed. Formalities over, he placed a call for someone to take her up to the offices.

PC Davies had apparently drawn the short straw once again, since he appeared through the security door. He rattled off a quick tour of the station before depositing her at a desk in a large open-plan office. She took in her surroundings: the office was empty of workers but full of desks, filing cabinets, and overstuffed folders. This would be her home-away-from-home, at least for the next six months. She saw a small office on one side of the room. She could just about read the name on the plaque: *DCI Helen Taylor.* With a bit of luck, she'd have a few hours to prepare for that confrontation.

Switching on the computer, she started work on her report.

CHAPTER 2

DCI Helen Taylor entered the large room housing her small team of officers. A hushed silence greeted her; not surprising after this morning's events. She briskly pushed open her office door and, a few moments later, the sound of the metal blind clattering in complaint broke the awkward silence.

Throwing her coat on the nearest chair, Helen fished out her mobile which had been silently ringing for the last ten minutes. She scanned the caller ID—Graham Brown again—then rummaged through the stacks of files on her desk, looking for DC Kate Wolfe's personnel file. It had been Mike's last job to provide her with the details of his replacement. She continued to sift through files. What do they call it—baby brain or something equally derogatory—when pregnant women get forgetful? No doubt Mike would say he had it by proxy. She immediately felt guilty when the file appeared in front of her.

Figuring she'd made Brown wait long enough, she finally accepted the call.

"Taylor. What's up, Graham?" she asked as she scanned Wolfe's file.

"You need to pull your new *officer* in line!"

Helen immediately took umbrage with his attitude and emphasis on *officer*.

"You mean my *acting* DS?" she asked loudly as she looked out through the blind at the large office beyond hers. A head bobbed up at her words. A head that belonged to a figure she vaguely recognised from Kate Wolfe's file was hunched over Mike's desk. Helen slumped back into her chair, looking up at the grubby tiles that made up the suspended ceiling of her tiny office.

"She's fucking crazy; running into a fire-damaged building before it's cleared…"

Graham's voice was full of bluster; maybe she should have taken the call sooner. She took a deep breath. It was going to be a very long six months.

Mike Richards had probably been the best DS she had ever worked with, reliable, and trustworthy. It had taken years to mould him just to the right shape; now he was a new father taking six months leave. Why couldn't she get another Mike instead of some crazy hothead?

"I don't know what to tell you. She's new…from London." She hoped that might go some way to explaining her actions. She closed her eyes to block out his whining voice, waiting for him to take a breath so she could respond, "Well, they breed them thick-skinned down there. Must be all the knife crime. Save money on stab vests or something."

From her seated position, she could only see the top half of DC Wolfe's profile; the rest was hidden by a filing cabinet. There was still a smudge of soot on her forehead. Nobody had bothered to tell her. *She needs a nickname.* Helen thumbed through Kate Wolfe's file again while she listened to Graham droning on in her ear. She'd already had a blow-by-blow account of the events at the scene via the desk sergeant on her way in.

She responded quickly to his silence, hoping he had finally run out of steam or maybe had a coronary, which he was surely heading for sooner or later.

"I know, I know. She's a bit wild…I'll reign her in, okay? Send me a copy of your report as soon as it's ready. And say hello to your lovely wife for me." Helen grinned at her own words, not waiting for a response as she ended the call. From her desk, she could see heads immediately bobbing down, pretending to be knee-deep in work. The veil of tiredness engulfed her again. The last few days had taken their toll on her energy levels. She struggled to understand how someone else's sickness could make her so tired.

Pushing away from her desk, she got to her feet and walked into the main office. She stopped at Mike's desk, resisting the urge to lean on it, to crowd her new officer. Instead she stood back, keeping her voice just loud enough for everyone to get the gist of her disappointment. "Well, *Virginia*, you've already made quite an impression with the Fire Department."

She watched as the young woman looked around the room in confusion before looking up to meet her gaze.

"Sorry."

The attractiveness of her new detective surprised Helen; the photograph on her file didn't do her justice. She felt the weight of Wolfe's stare as large brown eyes focused on her. They looked like perfectly formed chocolate drops, the same shade as her ponytailed hair. Her oval face looked flush with embarrassment, with more sooty smudges on her left cheek, like a child that had wiped at a snotty nose. The sight warmed her heart, and she resisted holding up a hand to clean off the dirty marks. Just.

"Don't worry, I've got your back. Brown's had a bug up his rear end since his wife left him three months ago."

Helen moved closer. She rested a hand on Mike's desk, remembering she needed to establish some authority over this rogue officer.

"Everyone gets *one* free pass…" she said, and lowered her voice as she locked eyes with Kate. "Next time I'll cut you off at the knees. Clear?"

Kate's throat twitched as she swallowed hard, like she was trying to swallow unwanted chewing gum. "Yes, DCI Taylor. Sorry."

Bollocking over for now, Helen made a start on the task at hand. "So, there was no ID found on the body, right?"

"That's right…"

Helen looked back at Kate, expecting an end to the sentence she'd started so confidently.

"Ma'am."

Helen gave her a second look to make sure she wasn't taking the piss before continuing. "Well, let's see this film you risked your life to shoot at the scene, as it's a little more inaccessible right now."

Helen watched with a little too much pleasure as Kate fumbled to plug her phone into the cable dangling from her computer. Her new detective obviously wasn't a stranger to technology as she quickly pulled up the video. Two uniformed officers made up a small group gathering behind her to view the footage.

The image was a little shaky as it panned around a dark, charred, and smoke-damaged room. The spotlight bounced off puddles of water gathered at the bottom of the wall. Remains of a once-domesticated environment were just visible beyond the smoke damage; remnants of partially charred furniture littered the floor on one side.

She tried not to grin as the sound of Kate swearing rumbled from the small speakers next to the computer. The image jolted as she had obviously stumbled over some debris while moving around the fire-ravaged room. The shaky image moved towards a smoky wall. In front was a series of what looked like tea chests creating a dwarf wall. The camera moved closer, peering inside an empty chest before peeking over the top. The figure on the floor was swathed in dark clothing as if hunkered down for a cold night. As the camera travelled down the lower half of the figure, a pair of legs blackened from the knee caps protruded to one side. The image came into focus; partial scraps of clothing became pin-sharp on the screen. The green- and red-checked material passed through the video, followed by one booted foot and then the other, with a thick green sock. *Pyjamas maybe*, Helen thought, although there was something familiar about it.

The image moved back down the body, darkening with every centimetre. Out of the corner of her eye, she saw Kate look away as a twisted, charred arm came into focus. Helen was glad to see she wasn't comfortable yet with the image of death right in front of her. In her time, she'd attended a number of fire deaths; thank God Smell-O-Vision never really took off.

"Wait, go back a bit," Helen said, moving closer. "There…pause it."

Helen reached out, almost touching the screen. She recognised the pattern. Only a week ago, she'd commented on his particular style to the wearer.

"It's Sandy." she said and rubbed at her face, genuinely saddened by Sandy's demise. She'd known him for years, pretty much since her arrival in the town. He'd become one of her faithful eyes and ears; he saw things others didn't.

"Is it…? Are you sure?" a uniformed officer asked.

Helen glared at him. "He had those trousers on the other day. I remember asking him about them. He nicked them out of the charity clothing bin by the supermarket, said he needed an extra layer."

"Who's Sandy?" Kate's voice piped up.

"He's a homeless guy, a vagrant from the area," Helen replied. She nodded back towards the screen. "Play the rest."

Almost immediately a loud voice boomed through the speakers as Fire Officer Brown entered the room, and the image blurred as Kate turned around with the camera to face him. Once again, Helen noticed Kate cringe at the muffled argument that ensued. Sniggers erupted behind her as the film came to an abrupt end.

Helen stood up straight, hands back on her hips. Turning, she glared at the two uniformed officers. "Right, you two, you find out everything you can about Sandy's last known whereabouts, friends, et cetera." She waited until they'd walked away before continuing. "Virginia, can I have a word?" she asked, nodding towards her office.

In her office, Helen retook her seat behind her desk and watched as Kate hesitated a moment before taking the seat opposite.

"Now then, Virginia—"

"Virginia?" Kate enquired.

Helen looked up from Kate's open file, eyebrows raised at Kate's tone. "Everyone has a nickname here. You're a university graduate, I'm sure you can work it out. Mine is Guv. I'm sure there are a lot of alternative names out there, but I only respond to Guv."

"Yes, Guv."

Helen responded to the grin on Kate's face with one of her own. She was relieved to see that she had a sense of humour underneath all that defiance.

"I can't have you going rogue on me. I need to be able to rely on you." It was time for the first layer of the shit sandwich she had to serve. "I've read your file." She looked up, seeing Kate shuffle uncomfortably in her seat. "You obviously have a lot of promise according to your last DI. Had a hand in breaking several cases down there."

Helen raised her voice to a level that the occupants of the outer office could hear.

"We work as a team here in Warner. I need you to be part of that team, Virginia, not upsetting everyone you come into contact with. I don't want to have to send you back home with *another* blot on your record. Am I making myself clear, Detective?"

Kate nodded.

Helen studied her new officer for a moment. She looked uncomfortable. She felt a tinge of satisfaction as she sucked in a breath, preparing for the final layer.

"As you're probably aware, you're replacing my current DS. So, after looking at your file, I think you have the experience to step up and temporarily become my new acting DS." She saw the shock on Kate's face and tried to backpedal a little. "It's not official, obviously, but think of it as an opportunity to show the boys back down south. Okay?"

"Thank you, Guv. I'll try not to let you down,"

The dimpled grin facing Helen made her momentarily reflect on the irony of what she'd just done—rewarded bad behaviour. She'd make a terrible dog owner. Shuffling through some files on her desk, she wondered if she'd just made an awful mistake, but shook it off.

"Now, back to the business in hand."

After selecting the file she was looking for, she handed it over to Kate.

"We've had a series of arson attacks in the area over the last seven months or so."

Kate flicked through the sparse file, scanning the reports and glancing at the glossy photos.

"As you can see, they have been pretty minor, starting with bins, until now."

Kate met her eyes over the top of the file. "You think this latest fire is an escalation of that?"

Helen raised her eyebrows. "Maybe. It's a pretty big jump, though."

Kate nodded. "Most arsonists are generally male, thrill seekers enjoying the chaos that they have created, or small groups of vandals having fun. This doesn't look like profit or terrorism, more like a serial offender; but this last one, it might not be connected. He was a tramp, right? Maybe he was just trying to keep warm, and it got out of hand."

Helen had been impressed by her new detective's knowledge until that last comment.

"Sandy wasn't daft. He wouldn't have started a fire with petrol. From your video, it looked like there were plenty of other things to burn to keep warm."

Kate nodded again, closing the file. She carefully placed it back on Helen's desk.

"When you were in there, did you see any sign of a trolley, like a small supermarket trolley, probably full of bags and stuff?"

"Uh…no, I don't think so. Why?"

Helen pursed her lips in response. "He never went anywhere without it." Rubbing her chin in thought, she knew there was something more going on here. "Maybe there's another scene out there we haven't found yet."

"You think it's a body dump?" Kate asked.

"Maybe. Okay, send me that video, and then get it to Forensics. And print some images of the room and the body." Helen made some notes as she spoke. Even with her vast experience of violent crime and death, she found it hard to use Sandy's name when talking about the blackened remains she had seen on the shaky video. He wasn't exactly a friend; more of an acquaintance—someone she would chat to a couple of times a week. He'd chosen an alternative lifestyle, but he'd been a good man. And nobody deserved that.

Focusing her attention back on Kate, she took in the large brown eyes surrounded by a slightly grubby face. "Do you want to go home and clean up before we head out?"

"No. Thanks, I'll be fine."

Helen shrugged. She obviously needed to be a bit more direct with her new charge.

"Okay. You might want to, er…" she looked away, not wanting to see the embarrassment on Kate's face, "splash a bit of water on your face before we go."

She saw the colour rise in Kate's cheeks without even looking directly at her. A reputation for insubordination, reckless at crime scenes, and so easy to embarrass: the next six months could be very interesting.

CHAPTER 3

"Where are we going?"

"First to the house, then we need to look for some of Sandy's friends." Helen led the way to the car park.

"Friends?" she asked, almost shocked at the thought that a tramp would have a string of friends and family to call on, and who would need to be informed of his untimely death.

"Yes, Virginia, even people like Sandy had friends. We need to piece together the sequence of events that led to his death," Helen said, quoting endless police manuals.

She flinched. Great. Now her boss thought she was a heartless bitch on top of being terrible at her job. "Sorry, Guv." The points she'd scored earlier with her arsonist research wilted before her eyes.

The early morning had taken its toll on her patience. This is not how she wanted her first day to go. She wanted to blend into the background, ride out the next six months until she could return to her real life.

Helen stopped abruptly as they entered the car park, and she almost barrelled into her back. "You can drive, to make up for that last remark."

Her gaydar was pinging uncontrollably as Helen stared at her. She had come to realise that it was far from the most reliable of her senses, after being pretty sure of the leanings of work colleagues in the past, only for them to talk of boyfriends later. But right now, if her gaydar were a Geiger counter, she'd need ear defenders. She'd always found older women attractive.

Not that Helen Taylor really fell into that category; she didn't look much older than her own thirty-four years. Her dark hair was loose around her shoulders. Dressed in a white shirt tucked into dark-grey suit trousers—ordinary, but she wore them well. The white shirt brought out the marble effect of her skin, and if the black smudges under her eyes were any indication of her tiredness, then she'd definitely been burning the candle at both ends. Her long coat smothered her small frame, gently swaying with her movement. Maybe that explained why she'd been called out instead of her new DI.

Considering her rank, she'd expected the DCI to be much older. Maybe her intrinsic skill had helped her climb through the ranks. Hot and good at her job. *Great. Just great.*

Getting turned on within ten minutes of meeting a woman, well that was something that hadn't happened in quite some time.

———◆———

Settling in Kate's car, Helen felt a twinge of amusement as Kate immediately turned on her satnav.

"You won't need that. I'll direct you," Helen said as she pulled a wad of paperwork from one of her numerous inside pockets. She knew she should have offered to drive, with Kate being new to the area, but something told her that Kate needed taking down a peg or two. Helen needed an acting DS that knew her place, not a cocky Londoner who dove headfirst into a scene.

"Right, Guv," Kate hesitantly agreed. "Which way are we going?"

Helen pretended to be engrossed in her paperwork, forcing Kate to get her attention by stepping sharply on the brakes as they stopped at the exit. She kept her voice even. "Take a left out of here, keep going till you reach some traffic lights."

"Okay."

She knew the route to Morley Lane was complicated and decided to have a little fun with it. The traffic lights were around a sharp bend and easily missed if you were not paying attention. She shuffled through her paperwork until a jolt made her look up. The lights were red. She was just about to make a joke about heavy shoes when she noticed they were in the wrong lane.

"We need to go right here," she offered before going back to her paperwork, covering her face with her hand. She could feel the grin on her face.

"Shit!" Kate barked as she flicked on her indicator to get into the other lane, pissing off several drivers behind her simultaneously.

The road took them to the outskirts of town, and before she knew it, they were in the countryside, flanked by dry-stone walls with muddy fields beyond, on both sides. The rougher road made it more difficult for her to focus on the reports she was trying to read. She'd never been a particularly good traveller, endlessly travel-sick as a child. Now karma was paying her back for tormenting Kate.

She focused on a stand of trees on the horizon. Kate slowed the car down as they came up behind a tractor and trailer taking up three-quarters of the road. Helen smiled at Kate's obvious frustration as she tailgated it instead of sensibly backing off like a normal person. The car was so close to the trailer, it forced Kate to swerve across to the other side of the road to see if the road beyond was free to overtake.

"Fuck!" Kate blurted out as an oncoming four-by-four quickly came into view. She turned the wheel quickly and slammed on the brakes.

Helen grabbed for the roof handle as the car swerved back behind the tractor.

"Jesus Christ, Virginia! Did you learn to drive with the Banana Splits?" She held in a laugh as Kate ducked when the driver of the four-by-four passed them and blasted the horn.

"Stupid bloody tractor taking over the whole fucking road!" Kate shouted.

"Get used to it, Virginia. You're in the country now." She looked across at Kate: her jaw was as tight as a drum; in fact, it twitched a couple of times. Maybe she'd pushed her too far—Kate's white knuckles were gripping the steering wheel. To her relief, they relaxed a little as the tractor turned off into a field.

At first glance, the only indication that they had reached their destination was the presence of a fire engine still parked outside the house. Shoving her paperwork back in a pocket, Helen took off her seatbelt.

"Maybe I should wait here?" Kate offered.

"Why? Not planning on making another exhibition of yourself with Fireman Brown, are you?" Any more infractions of the rules would have serious repercussions for the new detective, especially considering the past indiscretions in her file, but despite her best efforts, Helen could feel the slight grin threatening to overtake the frown she'd put there to worry Kate.

The officer on the scene grabbed his clipboard from the garden wall as they approached.

"Morning, Guv," he said before nodding in Kate's direction.

Taking the offered clipboard, Helen passed it expectantly to Kate while making small talk about the officer's family.

Approaching the house, they were met by a fire officer. Blessedly, it wasn't Graham Brown, she didn't want to have another fracas in front of Kate. Spotting the two crime-scene tech vans parked along the road, she was grateful there was progress being made in the house.

Her softly-softly conversation with the fire officer informed her that they'd shored up the building, allowing the body to be removed early that morning. Crime-scene technicians were currently processing the scene. She even managed to get him to clarify that the accelerant was most likely petrol, based on the smell that had been present when they arrived on the scene.

She caught Kate's smile as they walked around the back of the house.

"What?" Helen retorted, realising that the smile was directed at her. "Good manners don't cost anything."

Looking beyond the enclosed garden, Kate frowned as she asked the obvious: "Why would they have such a high fence?"

"The last known official occupant had a large dog that was prone to escaping and causing havoc in the local area," Helen supplied as she walked along the path, looking up at the back façade of the house.

"How do you know that?"

"Because, Virginia, it's my job to know these things. And the dog toys were a bit of a giveaway," Helen said as they continued walking to the front of the house. "Did you notice any spray paint when you went inside earlier?"

"Spray paint?" Kate repeated.

"Yeah. You know, that stuff kids spray on walls and call art, like cats marking their territory and what not?"

"Right. Er, no, I don't think so. Why?"

"There were a couple of cans of spray paint thrown in the back garden. Could be kids taking advantage of an abandoned house—or maybe something else."

"Spray cans." Kate half turned. "I didn't see them."

"Let's talk to the neighbours." She walked along the road towards the next house. With no CCTV in the area, they were relying on eyewitnesses, but without a timeframe it was going to be difficult.

"Maybe I should wait outside," Kate said, stopping by the path leading up to the Goode's house.

Helen turned to look at Kate square on.

"Not made an impression on them too, have you?"

"Uh no, it's…umm." Kate seemed to fumble for the right words. "It's the smell. I think I singed the inside of my nostrils last time I was in there."

Helen looked away to suppress a laugh. "I've got something that might help with that." She fished around in one of her inside pockets, producing a small tub of Vicks VapoRub. "Put some of this under your nose and you'll be fine."

"That's a bit *Silence of the Lambs*, isn't it?" Kate noted.

"My old boss in Manchester used it every time we went to the hospital. Hated the smell of the place."

Kate dipped a finger in the pot, then dolloped a hefty lump under her nose.

Approaching the front door, Kate jabbed at the doorbell twice, before stepping back.

Anger issues? Then Kate was behind her, probably trying to avoid the full force of the smell when the door opened, she realised.

Helen looked up as the warm, stale air wafted over her. Gloria's black leggings were stretched to their limit as they encased her ample legs in contrast to her baggy pink-teddy bear-covered T-shirt. "Hello, Gloria, can we come in for a chat?"

"Inspector Taylor, you come on in. Hello again," she directed at Kate as she walked past her into the hallway.

"Chief Inspector Taylor," Kate corrected in a harsh tone.

Helen mentally rolled her eyes. Was Kate really that petty or just a moron? *Why do the women I find even mildly attractive always have to be so fucking annoying the moment they start to speak?*

25

"What?" Gloria asked, confusion etched in her round face.

"It's Chief Inspector Taylor," Kate repeated irritably.

For the first time in recent memory, Helen wanted to disappear into thin air.

"It's fine, Gloria," she said and turned to glare at Kate, who looked totally unfazed. Did she really want to upset a potential witness before she'd had the chance to question her?

"Right," Gloria said, obviously still confused as to what was going on.

"Arthur not around?" Helen asked as she eyed the empty sitting room. She knew he never strayed far.

"He's just out with Buddy. Be back any minute I 'spect. Terrible business," Gloria said, nodding her head in the direction of next door as she entered the sitting room behind them both.

Helen nodded. "It certainly is. I just wanted to ask if you've seen anything odd recently."

Gloria wrung her hands together. "Tea?" she offered, ignoring Helen's question. "You'll be wanting one with your cold, Officer," she directed to Kate.

"Oh no. I'm fine, really."

She caught Helen's eye and raised an eyebrow from across the room.

The front door slammed, making everyone look in the direction of the hallway.

"That'll be Arthur now. I'll put the kettle on. He'll want a tea."

Arthur appeared in the doorway, his large frame almost filling the space. "Thought you'd turn up at some point."

"Hello, Arthur. How are you doing?" Helen kept her tone light, in contrast to Arthur's gruff manner.

Arthur struggled to move across the room with his walking stick. She hadn't realised how immobile he'd become compared to his wife. The small armchair squealed under the strain as he slumped his full weight down into it. She looked up to see Gloria's eyes watching her.

"He's got problems with his legs, like Buddy," Gloria offered by way of explanation.

The high-pitched squeaking of a rusty wheel broke the silence that followed as Buddy made his way across the room towards Arthur's chair, at a snail's pace. A pang of guilt immediately hit Helen as Buddy's back legs tried a walk and the wheels turned.

"Hey, Buddy." Helen crouched to rub the dog's ears, and his tail made a feeble attempt at a wag.

"Heard kids round there over the last few months, when I've been out for a fag. She won't let me smoke in the house." Arthur gave his wife the eye over the top of his glasses.

Gloria let out a snort before ducking into the kitchen.

"Over the last few months?"

His reply was more of a grunt.

"Anything over the last few days?" She nodded at Kate to take notes. "Anything yesterday or last night?" Gloria was coming back with a tray of tea-filled mugs.

"Someone shouting in the afternoon," Gloria said immediately after putting the tray down on a rickety coffee table near the window.

"Man or woman?" Kate asked, frustration evident in her timbre.

"Man. Young, I think, by his voice," Gloria shuffled the mugs on the tray.

Helen shot Kate a warning look for her tone. "What time was this?" she asked, taking over the questioning with a little more tact.

Gloria pulled at her bottom lip as she thought. "Mid-afternoon, around three, maybe later."

Focusing her attention on the seated figure of Arthur, Helen addressed her next question to him. "Recognise any of the kids you've seen going in or out, lately?"

"Some from the estate down the road. Don't know the others."

Helen continued her focus on Arthur. "You called in the fire at 2:12. What alerted you to it?"

"Had to get up for a piss. Saw it through the bathroom window," Arthur grumbled his reply.

"Seen your neighbours recently?" Helen asked, pointing to the occupied house next door.

"Doreen? Not seen her all week. Away at her daughter's, I think," Gloria said from across the room.

"What's her full name?" Kate asked, her tone a little more relaxed.

"Doreen Platt." Gloria covered her mouth. "It's not her, is it?" she blurted out between her fingers.

"He said it was a man, you silly cow!" Arthur grunted from his armchair.

He being a fireman, no doubt. Standing, Helen pulled a card from her pocket.

"Okay. Thank you both for your time, and if you think of anything else, give me a call." She slipped her card between the still full mugs on the tray.

<hr>

Helen blew out a long breath when they pulled into an empty space in the station car park.

"What's next?" Kate asked.

Helen looked across at Kate's profile in the dim light. It gave her an orange glow. They'd been scanning the streets for Sandy's friends most of the afternoon with no luck so far.

"You go home. You were called out at silly o'clock. I'll see you tomorrow bright and early. In the morning, get Uniform to check along Morley Road. See if anyone has security cameras that pick up passing pedestrians or traffic. I know it's a long shot, but we don't have anything else."

Helen thought she'd spotted at least one house where the owners were security savvy.

"Okay, I'll follow up with Mrs Platt, find out when she's back too," Kate offered.

Helen checked her phone before meeting Kate's eyes in the darkness. "Okay, good." She reached for the door release. Despite her obvious tiredness, Kate was far more pleasing to look at than Mike. "Get some sleep. I'll see you tomorrow."

Kate let out a long breath. "Night, Guv."

Helen made her way through the station car park, clicking her key fob to unlock her car. She'd promised to visit Julia this evening. The twenty-minute drive passed quickly as she thought about the events of her day, and the death of Sandy. She wondered how many people in town would actually mourn or even notice his loss. It was going to be a difficult case—she could feel it—not to mention a new colleague to break in. That looked a challenge in itself, if her first day was anything to go by.

The car park at The Oaks was quiet. From the glovebox, she grabbed the book Julia had requested and then headed inside. The nurse dutifully informed her that Julia had had a difficult day.

Undeterred, she persisted, informing her she would only stay a short time.

She followed the nurse down the corridor, the sound of a starched A-line uniform thwacking against her knees as the woman walked ahead of her.

Since when do they need a third party to smooth out my arrival? Is this what I have to look forward to?

Helen desperately wanted to keep the connection alive with Julia. Holding her fear in check each time she walked into her room was a big part of that.

The nurse tentatively knocked on Julia's door before entering. "Julia, you have a visitor."

There was a mumble from inside the room before the nurse returned.

"She's just waking up from a nap," the nurse announced before disappearing back along the hallway.

With a breath, Helen edged into the room, finding a sleeping figure sitting in an armchair. The relaxed face looked only vaguely familiar. Sharp eyes were hidden behind heavy lids. Her chest rose and fell with long, deep breaths. The spark of life was missing from the rumpled face.

Helen took a seat in the neighbouring armchair, placing the book on her knees. Her head rested back against the chair; the rigidity of the design made it hard for her to get comfortable. How Julia had managed to fall asleep she would never understand.

"Helen! How are you, my dear? Would you like some tea?"

She looked up, confused for a moment. "No. Thank you." Blinking, she realised she had no idea how much time had passed since her arrival.

Julia adjusted her position in the chair, grabbing her glasses off the small side table next to her.

"What's been happening today? The nurse said you'd had a bad day."

That seemed to have made Julia look away. Her gaze was now fixed on the view from her window. "They keep moving my things, giving me pills; it's not right, Helen."

Helen leant forward in her chair, taking the book in her hands. "They're just trying to help you, and keep you well. I'll talk to them about moving your things, though. That we can sort out." She knew from experience that Julia's grumbled reply meant that this particular topic of conversation was over. "I brought you that book you asked for." She held out her offering.

"What's that, dear? Oh, thank you." Julia turned the book over in her hands, her eyes scanning the back blurb. She placed it on the side table, then turned to give Helen her full attention.

Helen smiled. There was something different in the shape of her face, or perhaps it was the way she held it. Familiar intense eyes gazed at her through metal-rimmed glasses; this was the Julia she knew. Spotting the photographs on the wall behind Julia, she got up to take a closer look. "New photos."

"Oh. Yes."

Scanning the framed images, her eyes landed on a young Julia with another woman, standing next to an old black Mini. "Is this you? Who's that with you?" She turned to see Julia watching her.

"My sister Ellen with her pride and joy. She loved that car."

The next one was a little more recognisable. "Is that me?"

"Don't you remember? The birthday party we had for you, when we dressed you up as a pirate. You spent more time with me than the other kids. Every time they asked you to play with them, you said 'No, thank you' in that sing-song tone you had."

Helen grinned as she thought of her eighth birthday. She had been so pleased with her handmade outfit, eyepatch and all. "You were always doing something more interesting."

Julia chuckled to herself. "Wanted to be closer to the cake, more like."

"That too."

"And that curly moustache you wanted me to paint on your face."

"I wanted to look like a mean pirate."

"You looked so sweet with that plastic sword, even tried cutting the cake with it."

Julia's smile was wide, and the years fell away from her face. At times like this, she wondered what Julia was doing in this place. Then she recalled the angry confusion that took over her mind; she'd seen it with her own eyes.

"You look tired," Julia offered clasping her hand in her lap.

Helen turned back to the photographs. She didn't want to have that conversation. "I should go, let you get some rest. I'll come back in a couple of days." Turning, she bent to place a kiss on Julia's head before leaving.

Outside her house a little later, she slipped the keys from the ignition, resting her head back against the seat. Julia was right. She *was* tired. Glancing out the side window, the dark windows of her home held no comfort for her. She yearned for the days when Julia had lived with her, evenings spent cooking and chatting, days off spent setting up the garden just how Julia wanted it. Helen hadn't had the heart to set foot out there since Julia had moved to The Oaks. She'd be furious if she saw how untidy it had become. By then, the slippage had set in.

At first she wasn't sure if it was Julia's illness or her fierce independence—a trait Helen had acquired along the way—that had been the bigger issue. The days soon became filled with chaos, but, still, something was better than nothing.

Helen swiped at tears as she looked back at the dark, empty house. This was not what she wanted out of life. She didn't want to be one of those single, lonely coppers that fought retirement because their lives were barren away from the job. There had to be more for her than that.

CHAPTER 4

LOOKING THROUGH THE BLINDS IN her office, Helen watched her new detective as she moved around, making a cup of tea. She wore dark-grey trousers with a navy-blue shirt that caught the florescent lights of the office beyond, a silky material maybe, she thought. Her movements were confident. She was an attractive woman, if a little wilful, which, if Helen was honest, she found equally appealing. She contemplated tapping her mug on her desk as if requesting a cup of tea, just to see her reaction to it, with the added bonus of a closer look at her outfit.

The phone on Helen's desk rang, making her jump. She answered on the second ring.

"Are you in the business of promoting your own officers now? I thought that was my job."

Helen felt a half-formed smile cross her lips at the familiar voice in her ear. "Grace, or should I say Chief Superintendent Scott? It's good to hear from you."

The slight guttural sound she heard could easily have been mistaken for a fault on the line, but Helen knew she'd touched a nerve without even meaning to. Helen had been in line for the chief super's job. It was only her strong sense of duty that made her walk away from an all-but-guaranteed promotion four years ago in favour of a transfer out to Warner to look after her ailing foster mother.

Grace had been in the job for less than a year, and she often found an excuse to call. She had nothing but respect for her friend and colleague, but she still liked to tease her now and then.

"Well?" Grace let the question hang between them.

Helen grinned. "Wow! News travels fast uphill. Is my office bugged?"

"Not yet, but I do have my spies just like you, Helen 'Fagin' Taylor."

Helen smiled at Grace's quip, one she often made regarding her approach to community policing.

"So I see. I promise it's just informal. More of a carrot rather than the stick approach."

"Okay. Go on, let's hear it."

"I figured she'd had enough of the stick for now, so I thought I'd try something different, see if it helps. I'm just giving her a chance. She's knows it's not official. She's replacing a sergeant, so I made her one just while she's here."

Grace blew out a breath. "Leave it to you to try and help an insubordinate officer. Using rank as a motivational tool? That never seemed to work for you."

Helen let that slide. She knew her friend was disappointed in her career aspirations. Grace could never fully understand her reasons; she wasn't close to her family through her own choice, not theirs.

"So, what's she like?" Grace asked.

"Virginia?"

"What? I thought her name was Kate, Kate Wolfe. Oh, I see. Very good. Virginia Wolfe. You know, if you've named her, you'll have to keep her."

"University fast track," Helen mumbled under her breath, referring to Grace's educated background. Soon she'd be a minority.

Looking out of her office window, she saw Kate talking to what looked like PC Davies and wondered if there had been a break in their case when they left the office together.

"Come on, now. I'm sure Julia told you that you were just as bright as all the other girls."

Helen felt a surge of emotion as she thought back to her foster mother in her younger days. "She did, on numerous occasions."

"How is Julia?" Grace asked.

"Not great."

Grace was one of her oldest friends, but she didn't want to talk about it, not now. Work had become Helen's respite away from Julia's continued demise.

"I'm sorry, Helen. If you need some time off, I'm sure I can swing it for you."

"No. I'll be fine. Thank you."

Thankfully, Grace changed the subject, already well aware of her reluctance to take time off.

"So I hear you caught a murder. Must feel like old times."

"Umm, more of a mess than a murder."

"Sounds right up your street."

"Oh yeah, I remember those days filled with frustration, feeling like your hands are tied when the dregs of society are wreaking havoc and ruining people's lives because there's no real deterrent to make them think twice about their actions—yep just like old times." The silence on the line made her regret her outburst. "Sorry," she said in a small voice.

"Okay. Why don't you let me know if there's anything you need? And keep me informed of your progress," Grace replied as if trying to regain her position of authority.

"Yes, ma'am, thank you...ma'am," Helen said with a chuckle. The silence on the other end of the phone worried her for a second until her friend piped up.

"Is that insubordination I hear in your voice?"

———◆———

"DC—sorry—DS Wolfe."

She looked up from her computer, expecting to see a smirk on PC Davies's face but saw only confusion at her rank.

"Yep. What can I do for you?"

"There's a woman downstairs. She's wants to talk to a detective about her son. She's worried he's missing. He's not returning her calls. Can't get any joy with his employer." His voice was almost apologetic as he finished his sentence.

Not returning her calls; does that really mean he's missing? Reluctantly, she grabbed a pen and her notepad. "Lead the way," she said with a heavy sigh.

"It's Mrs Jarvis. She's just in there," Davies said as he pointed to the closed door on the right of the corridor.

Entering the small interview room, she eyed the elderly woman wiping her nose, eyes red-rimmed; she looked worked up. The thought of having to placate an old lady who had been dumped by her son made her groan inwardly.

As she introduced herself, she watched nervous hands fiddle with a carrier bag resting on the table that separated them. Opening her notebook, she mentally lined up the questions in her head.

"Can you give me your son's full name please, Mrs Jarvis?"

"Richard Arnold Jarvis."

Annabelle Jarvis's hand shook a little as she pulled out a photograph, still in its metal frame, and handed it to her.

She scanned it quickly, avoiding the man's face before setting it down gently on the desk. She couldn't afford to get roped into this, not...this, not now.

"Is he employed?" she asked, going through the motions. Gathering the information and not wanting to presume anything, she then remembered Davies had said she'd tried to contact them already. She was getting flustered. She needed to calm down, stay focused. Professional. She just needed to be professional and not get distracted. She sucked in a silent, calming breath as she waited for the woman to answer.

"Yes. At Dalton and Weeks in Manchester. He's an architect." A sense of pride shone through in the older woman's words as she revealed her son's occupation, her attention wandering frequently to the framed picture.

She ignored both the arrogance and the loving gaze on Mrs Jarvis's face and asked, "When did you last see or speak to him?"

"He called me two weeks ago, just before I went on holiday."

She nodded her head as she made notes. Checking the calendar on her phone, she plotted the day. "Was that the eleventh of February?"

Mrs Jarvis didn't take the time to think about her answer. "Yes," she said almost immediately.

"Can you tell me what sort of car he drives?" She kept her pen poised, her gaze fixed on her notepad.

"A red one, big. I'm not sure what it's called," Mrs Jarvis dabbed at her eyes with her tissue.

"Okay. No problem, I'll look it up later. And when did you last see him?" She asked, knowing a mother would most likely pick up on any obvious changes in her son's mood.

"I think it was a few days before he called me. He dropped off some shopping... He's a good boy."

She smiled. Everyone's good when they've gone missing. Everyone. She wiggled the pen between her fingers, quickly trying to dispel some of the energy in her body. Suddenly a missing person becomes a saint. All their annoying and destructive character flaws are overlooked. Happens every time.

"How often did you talk? Did he call a lot?"

"Maybe two or three times a week, just to check on me."

Nodding, she asked, "I understand you've already contacted his employer to see if they know where he is?"

Mrs Jarvis nodded as she wiped her nose. She had pulled out another tissue; the reality had hit her. She was officially declaring her son missing, a son she might never see again.

"They said he's at a conference in London till Friday. Normally he works from home a lot. I've called his mobile, but it just goes straight to the answer machine."

Blinking at the realisation of what the woman had just said, she made a note of his contact details before slowly closing her notebook. As much as she wanted to voice her true opinion, she felt sorry for the frail old lady in front of her.

Annabelle Jarvis pulled a set of keys from her handbag, pushing them into her hand.

"These are his spare keys. Please just take a look for yourself. It's not right. Something's happened to him."

She saw the pleading in the old woman's eyes and felt immediate guilt for the distress there. In silence, she watched Annabelle Jarvis leave the room and hoped she would never have to see her again.

———◆———

She barely made it back to her desk before Helen's voice stopped her in her tracks.

"Virginia!" Helen nodded to the open doorway before exiting through it.

Mentally rolling her eyes, she grabbed her jacket. "Where are we going?" She tried to put the thing on and walk down the stairs simultaneously.

"We are scouring the streets for Slim Jim," Helen offered as she checked her phone.

"Who's that? Did you, by any chance, have anything to do with his nickname?"

"I can't take that honour, I'm afraid."

She turned, giving Helen one of her best *Oh really?* looks as she crammed her notebook into her pocket.

With a grin, Helen relented. "I'm sure you're aware of what a Slim Jim is," she said and continued without waiting for an answer. "Yes, well, this particular chap has a penchant for sleeping in other people's cars when it's cold. He always carries some form of Slim Jim on him to make that possible, hence the name."

"And people don't mind this?" she asked, a little shocked. She knew full well what her reaction would be if she found a smelly tramp asleep in her car.

"I wouldn't say people are in love with the idea, but he's harmless. He doesn't steal anything. He just wants somewhere to kip down for the night."

Helen led the way to the small car park.

"I'd better drive, after yesterday's fiasco." They approached the black Volvo.

Looking up to the sky, her eyes rolled to the back of her head. She wondered how long she could stand this so-called promotional secondment. The smug grin on Helen's face was infuriating as she got in the car.

"Any news on the neighbours yet?" Helen asked as they pulled out of the car park.

"Uniform are still out checking. I got hold of Doreen Platt's daughter; she's on her way back today. I'll call around to see her today or tomorrow."

<hr />

She slumped into the passenger seat for the third time in an hour. In her opinion, they were wasting their time looking for some deadbeat who probably didn't even know what day it was, let alone anything about a possible murder. She snuck a quick look at Helen, who, annoyingly, looked as relaxed and serene as possible, although her eyes were firmly fixed on the wing mirror, no doubt scanning for her trampy informer.

A knock on her side window nearly sent her through the sunroof.

"What the fuck!"

"Calm down! It's just Jim," Helen said under her breath.

"Fuck! Is that a man or a fucking bear?" She just managed to resist the urge to lower her window to shoo him away.

The grubby man just stood there, oblivious to the reaction he had caused. He looked like a cross between *Teen Wolf's* dad and Animal from *The Muppet Show*. Dressed in dark, heavy clothing, his holey, woolly hat tamed what looked like a lion's mane of hair.

"You'd look like that if you lived like he does. I've seen his opposable thumbs; he's not all bad." Helen's low voice broke the silence in the car.

"Really? Coz he looks pretty bad from here."

"Calm down, Virginia. You'll give him a complex."

"Give him a complex? What about me?" she said to Helen's back as she exited the car. Watching them both walk to the back of the car, she lowered her window and took out her notebook to take down anything pertinent. *As if.*

"Who's that?" Jim asked as she saw Helen appear in her wing mirror next to the dishevelled man. Straining her ears, she was surprised by the shabby man's voice. It was sharp, not local at all. Sleeping in cars had obviously saved him from the gruelling effects of rough sleeping.

Helen's shoulders rose and fell as she sighed. "New colleague. Have you heard about Sandy?"

Jim nodded, looking at his hands.

"I'm sorry, Jim. I know you two were friendly. When did you last see him?"

She readied her pen, only to be disappointed.

"Not seen him for a couple of weeks." Jim shrugged his shoulders.

"Do you know his full name?" Helen asked.

He shook his head.

She blew out a long breath as she clicked the top of her pen. Without a formal ID, it was going to be hard going in terms of getting a handle on Sandy's background.

"What happened?" Jim asked as he wiped at his nose.

Getting out of the car, she made her way over to join them.

"We're not sure yet. Waiting for the doc to get back to me. I need to find his trolley. Can you help me with that? It'll help us find who out how and where it happened."

"I thought he died in a house fire," Jim replied with a frown.

"That's where he was found. Have you ever seen Sandy without his stuff?" Helen questioned.

She heard the caution in Helen's words, careful about what she shared with Jim; they didn't even know the full story yet.

Watching Jim closely, she spotted a barely noticeable shake of the head. The slight bunching of skin between his eyes told her the cogs were obviously turning.

"What do I get?" Jim enquired, obviously realising there was a profit to be gained from this discovery.

She had to look away. She knew she was grinning at the grifter.

"*If* you find it," Helen clarified, "what are you in the market for?"

Turning back out of curiosity, she followed Jim's line of sight to the shabby boots on his feet.

"New shoes. Nikes. Blue ones." Jim spoke in an excited bluster.

"No problem. Size ten, right?" Helen confirmed with a smile.

She couldn't believe what she was hearing from this fashion-conscious vagrant. She stepped halfway in front of Helen, sick of all the pussyfooting and bargaining going on. "Do you know how to drive or hotwire a car?"

Jim glanced in her direction, as if he was actually considering her question.

Helen released a frustrated breath. Maybe she shouldn't be muscling in on her boss.

Holding her ground, she waited for Jim's reply. The heat of Helen's eyes was burning into the side of her head. She took the vague shake of his head as his answer. Stepping back, she decided not to enquire where he had been around the time of the murder, not that they even knew when, let alone where that was, right now.

Helen leaned forward and handed Jim a card.

"Remember, if you find it, don't touch it. Just call me, okay?"

She balked as Helen walked back to the passenger side of the car, effectively ending the conversation.

She frowned as she watched Helen get in the passenger seat of her own car. *I guess I'm driving us back.* She caught the wry grin on Jim's face as she made her way to the driver's door.

Helen waited till they were both secured in the car before she began to vent, her voice loud in the confined space.

"What the hell was that all about? You really think Jim's a murderer?" Helen asked as she tossed the car keys into her lap.

Snatching them up, she rammed them home as her irritation grew.

"What? He could have done it. He sleeps in cars all the time; he had opportunity. Maybe they argued about something. He saw him passing by and snapped."

She had to admit she didn't have the background knowledge that Helen had, but people flipped out all the time, why not Jim? She angrily pulled out into the line of traffic, suffering a beep from the driver behind.

"Do you actually listen to what you're saying?"

"What?" Her irritation, growing by the minute, matched her boss's anger. Couldn't this woman be objective towards one of her so-called informants?

"Okay, pull over!"

"What?" She asked wondering where this was going.

"You heard me, DS Wolfe. Pull over!"

Helen's words were drenched in authority, forcing her to reluctantly comply. She swerved over to the side of the road, her annoyance evident in her harsh movement as she pulled up on a residential side street. She saw Helen grip onto the door as the car lurched to a stop.

"Are you always this angry?"

"What?" she asked in confusion. She was just trying to do her job. Looking straight ahead to the empty street beyond, *angry* didn't even scratch the surface. She was furious with herself for getting into the position she now found herself in. What was she doing? She didn't belong here. Out of the corner of her eye, she noticed Helen turn towards her a little.

"Look, forget that I'm your boss for a minute. Let me give you a bit of advice." Helen took a breath. "I know you're pissed off about being sent away from your regular post, out to the back of beyond. I don't know what your last boss was like, but for me, policing is essentially the same wherever you are. It's community based; you need to get the support of the locals. They are the eyes and ears of any place—town or city—and from what I've seen so far, you're not exactly a people person. Maybe you could actually learn something from being up here."

She opened her mouth to reply but was cut off by Helen holding up her hand to stop her. "Please don't say *what* again or we're potentially going to have a *Pulp Fiction* moment here, and in case you haven't seen the film, it doesn't end well."

Some of the tension left her body. She relaxed back against the seat. Why did her new boss have to have such a good sense of humour? How could she stay angry, faced with such wit? She realised how unfair she was being—none of it was even Helen's fault. The lopsided grin on Helen's face was already improving her mood.

"I'm sorry, Guv. I overstepped. I'm just finding it difficult adjusting to a slower pace of life, I guess. I'm not used to such civic-minded individuals." She made a stab at returning the humour. Her mouth now loosened, she continued to vent. "This case is driving me crazy; there's no CCTV, no phone or bank account to track. I don't know where to start." They had no sequence of events to follow, no formal identification, or next of kin.

"How do you know he didn't have a bank account? Just because he didn't have the same life as everyone else doesn't mean…" Helen's words trailed off as she took a breath. "In my experience, people often jump to the wrong conclusion about people and their private lives. People like Sandy become invisible to onlookers; they disappear into the background, with no expectations that they have a life. That's the city for you, Virginia. Makes you jaded. A few months with the wholesome people of Warner might just set you straight."

She released a laugh. *I doubt it. It's not like it had worked for Helen, had it?*

"Maybe you're right, although that's a pretty big ask. I think it'll take more than that to set me straight." She relished the chance to make a covert reference.

Helen rewarded her with a quick raised eyebrow. "Listen, I don't want to teach you how to suck eggs, but if you want people to open up to you, maybe you need to be less accusatory when you're talking to them. It's not enough to be as hard as nails like some of the men of our profession. We need to be better, smarter, if we're to get noticed."

"Yes, Guv."

"We're not all *Okies from Muskogee*. You need to give us a chance."

Helen's phone rang, and she sighed as she saw the name on the caller ID. "Sorry. I have to take this."

Curious, she adjusted her body to get a glimpse of the name—*Dr Thomas Oaks*. Was Helen sick? She wondered.

Helen got out of the car before accepting the call. Standing on the pavement, she moved to shelter under the nearest tree as light rain started to fall.

After watching Helen's animated arm movements as she spoke—she wished she'd learned how to lip-read—she then turned away to give Helen a little privacy. She took some deep breaths, needing to decompress from their argument. She was doing a pretty good job of royally fucking things up, but she had to make this work, to fit in. It was only for six months. The alternative wasn't worth thinking about.

Unable to resist any longer, she lowered the window a notch, hoping to pick up on the conversation Helen was having. A few words floated her way as the wind changed, something about medication being refused and a meeting later that night. She quickly clicked up her window as Helen ended her call.

"Sorry about that."

Helen settled in the passenger seat, massaging both eyes with her thumb and forefinger for several seconds before speaking. "What I was trying to say was we've all got a past; it's how you move forward that counts. Maybe it's time to make this a fresh start."

She let Helen's words sink in rather than bounce off her body armour as advice usually did. "Yes, Guv."

"And by the way, Virginia, listening to other people's private phone calls is not polite."

"Yes, Guv." The colour rose to her cheeks as she drove back to the station.

It was almost eight when she finally jabbed her key at her front door. She was still getting used to the quiet blackness of the countryside at night. After several attempts, the key slipped in the lock, and she sighed in relief when the catch snapped open. Her hand fumbled along the wall for the light switch. Click. Nothing. She tried again, as if that was going to help; still nothing.

"Shit!"

Pulling out her phone, she tapped the flashlight app, illuminating her dark hallway. Deciding it was too late to eat, she headed for the kitchen for a drink before bed. The beam of light moving along the wall reminded her of being in the fire-damaged house. It made the cottage look dingy; the only thing missing was the water running down the walls.

She tried the kitchen light in the hope it was just a blown bulb.

Nothing.

"Bollocks!" Her voice reverberated in the small space.

For some reason, she thought the light from the fridge might help, till she opened the door and the stupidity of that sank in. She gulped from the chilled two-litre bottle of water, then a knock at the door made her jump and spill water down herself. Wiping her chin with the back of her hand, she peered down the hallway. The glass top panels in the door gave little away of the darkness beyond. She hesitated until a second knock came. At the thought that it might be Helen with updates in the case, she picked up her phone, made her way to the front of the house, and pushed her booted foot behind the door, opening it to prevent it from being pushed open further. *Just in case.*

The light from her phone exposed a short, balding man with a transparent carrier bag in his hand. The dim light made it impossible to make out its contents.

"Hi, I'm your neighbour from just along the way." He waved his arm in the direction of the house next door but one. "Garry Burton." He offered his hand.

She stared at it for a moment before releasing her hand from behind the door to shake his. "Kate, Kate Wolfe."

He grinned at her. "I saw you come home. I figured, as you'd just moved in, you might not be prepared for a power cut just yet." He offered the bag in her direction.

"Uh, thanks." On closer inspection, she could see a small selection of candles in the bag. "Is it usual around here?" She wondered why he was so prepared.

"Power cuts?" he confirmed. "Afraid so. Didn't you get the letter from the electricity board?"

"No." She inwardly groaned at the thought of this being a regular occurrence.

"Oh right. It was probably before you moved in. They're doing some work on the power grid or substation, updating it apparently, over the next couple of months. There'll be regular blackouts while they work on it."

"Oh."

Great! Not only am I live in the middle of nowhere, there isn't going to be any electricity either.

What was next? Contaminated water?

Jesus Christ. I've never been more thankful that I'm a city dweller. How the hell do people do it? It's like being back in the Stone Age.

"Didn't the landlord tell you?" Gary asked, clearly unhappy at being the bearer of bad news.

"No. He may have neglected to mention that when I signed the rental agreement."

"Oops!" He grinned again. "Bastards probably won't even give us any compensation or discount for the trouble."

"Well, they've got to keep their profits up somehow, I guess." She tried to be congenial considering he'd gone to the effort to bring her candles to chase away the darkness.

He suddenly backed away from the door and said, "Well, I'll let you get on."

She was left wondering what she'd said, considering she had been doing her best to be affable.

"Thanks for the candles," she said to the retreating figure.

"No problem."

She watched him disappear into the darkness before closing the door. Maybe being agreeable to the general public was going to prove more difficult after all.

CHAPTER 5

THREE EMAILS SAT IN HER inbox. Not one. Not two. Three, all of them asking Kate to call home. To call her mother. She knew she needed to reply, if only to stop the constant bombardment. Grateful she wasn't texting and calling too, she quickly drafted a reply, saying that she'd been put straight onto a murder case and was working a lot of overtime. Then ended it with a promise to call when she could. Then she quickly closed the application, hoping no one in the office had seen her conducting personal work.

For the second morning in a row, her new boss had already been in the office when she arrived. She wondered what kind of life she must have, to be work before 7 a.m.

Quickly opening her final draft of yesterday's interview report—she wasn't sure what else to do—she read through the notes. After asking PC Davies for Slim Jim's real name, she had conducted an internet search for him, as well as for the previous residents of the burned-out house—nothing. Without Sandy's full ID, they were stumped.

However, this morning's visit to see potential witness, Doreen Platt, had provided a slight glimmer of hope. A slight woman, probably in her fifties, Mrs Platt had been shocked at the events happening on her street and seemed a little uncomfortable in her own skin. It was easy to see why her daughter had insisted on installing a security camera system. One camera pointed down the garden, while the other covered the front of the house. From the brief look she'd had at the Platt house, it had a partial view of the path and road. The system had been installed by her electrician son-in-law, who, after a short conversation, had offered to send in all the footage that had been recorded since the last system purge.

She clicked on her official email for a quick check, just in case the footage was something he could email. Deep down, though, she knew it would be too big and he'd have to post it or drop it off at the station.

"Virginia."

Helen's words pulled her from her contemplation, and she smiled to herself. Was she actually getting used to her new nickname?

"The pathologist is ready for us. Get your coat." Her thick overcoat was already in her hands as she made her way out of the main office.

Flustered, she made a grab for her belongings and tried to catch up. The fact that she would be face to face with Sandy's body once again had somehow slipped her mind. Now there was no escaping it.

"We might have some CCTV after all, Guv," she said as they both trotted down the steps to the ground floor of the station. She took a sideways look at her boss. She was dressed in a black shirt with matching suit trousers, and it was just possible to make out a small patch of exposed skin near Helen's hip that became uncovered as she walked, separating the waistline of her trousers from the curved cut of her shirt. She couldn't take her eyes off the patch of creamy skin. The desire to trace its outline with her fingertips made her hands twitch. It was only the addition of Helen's heavy coat as they got outside that allowed her to drag her eyes away.

Helen looked across the top of her car, clearly expecting more, and lifted an eyebrow to prompt it from her.

Realising she'd been staring, and all too aware that she'd only given Helen half the story, she said, "Uh, Doreen Platt's son-in-law set up security cameras at the back and front of the house. He's sending us the footage."

"Good. When it arrives, send me a copy and get Davies on it. Oh, and make sure you get the stuff from the back of the house too. The open fields at the back could provide a suitable access without being seen."

"Yes, Guv," she said, remembering their relationship dynamic. Subordinate. Not an equal. She wanted to know more about this woman, but she'd yet to figure out quite how she was going to make that happen.

Don't look at it. Don't look on the table. Don't do it. Just don't.

She would not look directly at the figure on the cold metal table. She didn't want to. *Who would?* Instead, she glanced near the body. Near, but not too near. Just close enough that she could vaguely make out the extent of his injuries.

The bright light of the room exposed the hideous discolouration of skin and limbs. They had been hidden by his heavy, blackened clothing when she had last been this close to him. She looked around the room for something else—anything else—to focus on. Across the room, Helen seemed almost distracted as she looked at the figure. Everyone had their own method of dealing with it. Their own unique way of coping, keeping their distance to do their job effectively. Especially when they knew this particular individual. Like Helen did.

The pathologist, Dr Henry Nicholls, began outlining his findings. He was a short, mature man with a thick crown of silver hair. His strong Geordie accent seemed to be accentuated by a permanent facial shrug.

"Formal identification is still in progress. We managed to get some prints from his right hand, which survived pretty much unscathed. The burns are superficial, from the smouldering clothing, but as you can see he sustained some major blunt-force trauma injuries."

She had to fight hard to swallow back the bile that threatened as she recalled the smell in the house when she had been filming. She'd been breathing in his burning flesh.

"Most importantly for you, there was no evidence of soot particles in his lungs, which means he was dead before the fire started." Nicholls finished with a smug smile.

"What?" Helen asked with two arched eyebrows directed at the man; to be fair, it was fully warranted.

Nicholls performed another facial shrug. He looked pleased with the reaction he'd gained from his bombshell. Placing his clipboard on a side table, he walked back over to the body. Using a gloved hand, he pointed to the flesh on the side of the body facing Helen. *Thank God she had opted for this side of the room.*

"You can see from the livor mortis he was lying on his side at the time or very soon after death, similar to—if not the same—as the position he was found in."

Curious she moved to look at the pale, yellowy flesh that had been in contact with the hard floor, as if his skin had been pressed against a glassy surface, the surrounding skin holding a purple glow. She felt for

Helen across the room. The thought of someone she knew and loved being murdered and dumped like a piece of rubbish made her feel vile inside. The condition of his body suggested he'd been dead for some time, which no doubt meant a long list of suspects, as the likelihood of starting a fire when you're already dead was pretty slim.

Questions. Those would give her something else to focus on, besides Sandy. "How long has he been dead?" The smell was beginning to get to her now; a mixture of chemicals and decay filled her nostrils. She lifted her hand from her notepad, absentmindedly touching her top lip until she felt the stickiness of the Vicks that Helen had offered her on the way into the morgue. Nicholls's voice brought her to her senses.

"More than a week. I should be able to tell you more after I've done a few more tests." Nicholls turned his body as if he was giving a lecture to the room. "Decomposition happens at different rates depending on what the body is exposed to. Immersion in water or burial slows the process. Casper's law states that one week in the air equals two weeks in the water equals eight weeks in the earth."

Ignoring the lecture, she scribbled down the information in her notebook, mentally counting back the days to find the timeframe. It took her a few seconds to realise it coincided with her arrival in the area.

Nicholls continued with the breakdown of his initial report. "Stomach contents show he'd eaten within an hour or two before death. Looks like ham salad sandwiches and jam tarts."

She allowed a little smile to cross her face as she imagined Sandy living it up on jam tarts, probably swiped from a supermarket waste bin. She could think of worse last meals. She blinked away her thoughts as she realised Helen was asking the ultimate question.

"So, if it wasn't the fire, what actually killed him?" Helen asked.

Nicholls looked over at Helen. "These particular injuries are consistent with typical hit-and-run, blunt-force trauma. Like over sixty percent of pedestrian victims, he was struck by the front of the moving vehicle."

She frowned and jumped straight in without thinking. "And the rest?" Logically, they had to be struck by the back or side.

"The rest are mainly side impacts, Detective, which result in different injuries to the pedestrian. This type of post-impact can be classed as a wrap. Primarily, the body is thrown against the front edge of the vehicle, striking the bumper, resulting in leg, pelvis, and chest injuries just as we have here. X-rays show the extent of the bone injuries."

He moved across the room to a large screen fixed to the wall and switched it on. The black screen was filled with grey-blue bones that were half-familiar to her. Luckily, Nicholls made an effort to place the mixture of rounded shapes into context, using his index finger to point out the damage.

"You can see the breaks here, here and here." He continued to put the injuries into perspective. "The body is thrown forward as the vehicle brakes. The body then strikes the surface of the road as it falls, resulting, in this case, in massive head injuries."

The sound of shuffling feet made her look up from her notes. Focusing her attention on Helen, she could see that she was visibly upset by Nicholls's explanation. Nicholls looked just as surprised by her reaction.

"I'm sorry, Inspector, did you know this individual?"

"Yes, I'm afraid I did. He was known locally as Sandy. Nobody knows his full name…yet." Helen plunged her hands deep into her pockets.

"I'm sorry for your loss."

To her surprise, his words of comfort seemed genuine.

"Thank you, Doctor. Please go on."

Nicholls waited for a few seconds before continuing. "I'll need some more time to determine the height of the car and if there are any particular models that are compatible with the injuries. The clothes have gone to Forensics and may contain some trace evidence picked up from the car."

She scribbled more notes as the doctor spoke, then glanced across at Helen; she looked a little paler than before.

"I've got some more bad news, I'm afraid. Unrelated to the trauma, I found massive tumours in his kidneys. He didn't have long left; maybe six months."

"Shit." She mumbled under her breath, Sandy was by no means a lucky man.

Nicholls seemed to ponder his next words as he hobbled from one foot to the next. "Putrefaction has started to occur, the body naturally breaking down. As I said, I need to do more tests to determine a more accurate time of death. If the body was placed in the house soon after death, the lack of central heating and exposure to cool air has slowed the process, reducing the smell, which might have alerted the neighbours sooner."

"The back door of the house was open." she interjected, remembering vivid images of the house.

Nicholls nodded in her direction at the snippet of information. "I noticed that at the scene, opportunist dumping, and poor concealment. In my experience, when a criminal tries to hide evidence, they do a pretty crappy job, and this was no exception. The body has started to mummify slightly due to the dry air, which explains the slowed process. And that's it for now." He dug his hands in his pockets.

The silence hung between them for a moment while they all took a final look at Sandy. Pulling her hands from her coat pockets, Helen looked as if she was going to offer Nicholls a handshake but then thought better of it.

"Okay. Thank you, Dr Nicholls."

"I should have more answers in a week or two. I have some maggot work to do first. I'll send a full report through when I've concluded the tests."

She nodded at the doctor before following Helen out of the room. She certainly didn't envy his job, messing around with maggots and dead bodies. Shaking her head didn't manage to dislodge the visual. "So, what are we saying here? He was run over then dumped in the house, and a few days later the same person or somebody else sets fire to the house to get rid of the evidence?" Seeing Helen cringe at her words, she felt guilty for her insensitivity; Sandy had been her friend, or acquaintance at least.

"Maybe. Whoever they are, they're local. They knew where to put the body, where it wouldn't be discovered."

"Until the fire," she reminded her.

"Exactly."

They walked in silence down the corridor to the car park.

"The body has remained more or less intact. It wasn't covered in petrol with the aim of getting rid of evidence," Helen mused. "So why would you draw attention to it?"

"Unless you wanted it to be found," she added as they approached the exit.

Glancing across at her boss and spotting the raised eyebrow again, she asked, "By the killer or someone else?"

"Who knows? We need to find the scene of the accident. Sandy always had a trolley of crap with him. It has to be somewhere."

Opening the door, she welcomed the fresh air into her lungs. She knew the scene would hold some of the answers, including skid marks which would help determine the speed of the car. She frowned. Didn't she mean murder? Not only did they not help Sandy; potentially they'd hidden the body preventing anyone else from finding it. Realising she still had an unsightly layer of what probably looked like snot under her nose, she dug into her jacket pocket for a tissue. Finding a balled-up, hardened lump that once had been a tissue, she attempted to peel it open as they walked, startled when a fresh tissue appeared in front of her. She looked up, meeting Helen's warm gaze.

"Thanks." Taking the tissue, she rubbed at the skin under her nose, scrunching it up to join the other one she had secreted back in her pocket.

Helen pulled out her keys as they approached her car. "We should get that arson report today; chase it up if it's not there when we get back. Actually, I'd better do that; don't want you falling out with your boyfriend again."

She gave Helen a sideways look as she got in the car.

"We need to start getting some answers, not more questions." Helen continued.

"Yes, Guv." A twinge in her stomach drew her attention to her watch. "Can we have lunch now? I'm starving," she whined as they put their seat belts on.

"What?" She asked as she caught Helen's eye.

"I was just about to ask if you are always this irritable, or just when you're hungry, but then I remembered who I was talking to."

She cast Helen another sideways glance, hoping she wasn't in for another bollocking.

"Okay, what about a nice, healthy salad from the deli?" Helen asked as they made their way out of the car park.

"I missed a meal yesterday. Can't we have something hot?"

Helen stopped the car at the exit. "Right. Well, we can't have that then, can we? How about the Wheatsheaf? They do a great vegetarian lasagne."

"Vegetarian!" she cried with what she deemed justifiable distaste.

She watched, pleased with herself as Helen seemed to supress a smile. She was beginning to enjoy the banter they shared, even if she was the butt of many of the jokes.

"Or horse-flavoured, of course, if you prefer."

"Oh, I definitely prefer horse and chips. I'm not a rabbit, you know," she said as she read the latest motherly email threatening to visit if she didn't get in touch soon. Rolling her eyes, she wondered how she was going to placate her this time.

"Okay! Last one inside pays for lunch!"

She looked up as Helen made a grab for her door handle. Her reactions were fast. But her progress was somewhat hampered as she eyed the large wooden pole rooted behind her door.

"What the fuck?" She turned to see that Helen had already exited the car—graciously leaving the door open for her. All she could do was watch in awe as Helen sprinted into the side entrance of the pub. Realising she'd already lost the bet, she sat back in her seat, her skull against the headrest. She hadn't seen this coming. She'd witnessed Helen's sense of humour, liked it even, but this was different; this was mischievous and deserved a suitable response.

Climbing out of the car, she noticed the keys still in the ignition. She made her way with them into the pub. As her eyes adjusted to the darkness, she spotted Helen sitting at an oblong, wooden table, a menu in front of her. She placed the keys on the table as she sat down opposite.

"Hey, slowpoke. Don't worry, I already ordered you horse and chips." Helen was grinning, looking far too pleased with herself as she organised the cutlery and condiments on the table she was sat at. "I hope you've brought your money with you. I've worked up quite an appetite jogging in here."

Returning to her desk after lunch wasn't a problem. Getting anything done, however, was. It was too hard to focus. All she could see was the grin on Helen's face as she had entered the pub. Looking across the room towards Helen's office now, she could see Helen engrossed in reading some paperwork. She took a deep breath, applying herself to the various tasks at hand, and began making enquiries about the missing person, Richard

Jarvis. Contacting his employers to get some background and checking if he had surfaced resulted in a big, fat nothing. She called the hotel where he was meant to be staying, to be told that he hadn't even checked in. All the other hotels in the area—she'd checked just to make sure—yielded the same result.

She was just about to go and talk to Helen about Jarvis when Sergeant Kirk appeared by her desk, a thick, padded envelope in his left hand as he tapped it on the palm of his free hand.

"Got a delivery for you," Kirk said, his eyes never straying from the level of her chest.

Noticing the slight whistle that accompanied his speech, she focused on him a little harder. It reminded her of something, a whistling kettle maybe. A sneer soon appeared on his face; the result of her staring, she thought.

"Thanks," she said, trying to keep her voice light as she reached out to take it from him. Realising that he was reluctant to let go so easily, she tugged a little harder, yanking it from his fingers. A grin developed on his face, but it didn't seem genuine, not like Helen's. Kirk's eyes were hard as they looked at her.

"No problem," he said before walking back out of the office.

Shrugging off the encounter, she read the words printed in black marker pen on the front of the envelope:

FAO DS Wolf

The *E* was missing, an easy mistake to make over the phone. The CCTV footage, she hoped as she opened the envelope, allowing a bunch of DVDs to fall across her desk. As she sifted through them, she could see they were labelled front and back and numbered. With only two disks per camera, either there wasn't much footage, or the resolution was going to be poor.

Finding some blank disks in a cupboard, she set up her computer to copy the first one before heading to Helen's office. She found her making notes from her computer.

"Guv, CCTV's arrived. I'm just making copies for you."

"Good. The arson report has arrived, too." Helen shuffled the paperwork, putting it in order before handing it over.

"Anything?" she asked, figuring Helen had already been through it with a fine-tooth comb. Scanning the report, she could see a layout of the ground floor showing the position of Sandy's body in relation to the point of origin.

"Burn patterns show that the point of origin was the stairwell at the front of the house. Petrol confirmed as the accelerant."

"So," she pondered, remembering the scene as she'd seen it several days ago, "the body was almost hidden behind those boxes." She checked the report. "There was no accelerant found near it. So, it was either hidden by the murderer or protected by the fire-starter." She looked at Helen for conformation.

"Two separate crimes, like we said earlier."

Nodding, she pursed her lips, appreciating Helen's recognition of her minor input, but it was a depressing thought that at least two people had known that Sandy was dead and hadn't inform the police. Looking back down at the report, she read aloud, "Cigarette butts found at the scene." She looked up and said, "We should get a DNA match…when we get a suspect that is," and then closed the file.

"We need the coroner to give us some kind of timeframe in which Sandy was killed."

Nodding again, she kept hold of the report to read it in more detail later. "I'll drop the CCTV disks off when they're done."

CHAPTER 6

She leaned against the doorway of Helen's office. The morning din of the officers behind her had obviously disguised her approach. Helen looked deep in thought as she read through some paperwork. How many hours of the CCTV footage had Helen watched last night?

She continued her scrutiny as Helen gripped the back of her neck. She seemed to be massaging, kneading the muscles as she read. She speculated at the number of inappropriate behaviour policies it would breach to offer her a neck rub.

It surprised her how attracted she was to Helen; she wasn't her usual type, if she even had one. She hadn't dated a lot lately, with only a couple of short-term relationships to speak of. They were mostly with women she had met during her misspent youth, before she found the straight and narrow, so to speak. Helen was intellectual, funny, and she had a presence, a way with people she could only wish to attain someday in the very distant future. She was out of her league, but it didn't stop her wanting to touch Helen, feel the softness of her skin against her own.

Helen shifted in her seat as she sifted through the reports on her desk. She must have finally felt eyes on her as she rummaged, a small, probably unconscious smile was on her lips as their gazes met.

"Virginia!"

"Morning, Guv. Couple of things to report: Richard Jarvis, a fifty-three-year-old architect, has been reported missing by his mother."

"Was that the woman in here the other day?" Helen asked, putting her paperwork down. "I've seen your missing persons' report. Is there a reason why you haven't requested Uniform take a look a look around his home address already?"

Nodding, she hesitated for a moment. Not only did this woman have eyes and ears on the street, but there were squealers in the station too. "His mother left me a set of keys to his house, so I figured someone should go take a look, see if there's anything suspicious. I've put out a request on Automatic Number Plate Recognition for his car and contacted the Met Police, circulating his picture to see if he's turned up anywhere in London."

"London? Why would he be there? When was he last seen?"

"The mother saw him almost three weeks ago before she went on holiday. When he didn't call or turn up after she got back, she went around to his house and called his work. They said he was at a conference in London, but when I called the hotel, they said he'd never checked in, so he could have been missing for up to three weeks."

"Shit! We're already on the back foot; three weeks is a long time. Someone must have seen him in that time, or at least missed him, apart from his bloody mother."

She nervously shuffled her feet. She didn't want to be on the end of Helen's anger.

"Any previous?"

Her jaw clenched. She didn't like being called out for her lack of attention when there were far more important jobs to be done. "Nope, nothing."

Helen nodded in reply.

"I'm waiting to get access to his phone and bank records to see when they were last used."

"Still? Bit slow off the mark, aren't you?"

"Sorry Guv. I got a bit distracted by the CCTV," she quickly deflected.

"Okay. Anything else?"

"Our firebug has been out again. Another fire reported—an abandoned car. No injuries or bodies this time."

Helen blew out a long breath as she sat back in her chair.

"I hate to say it, Virginia, but this place was pretty quiet till you arrived. Now we've got a dead body, an arsonist on the loose, and a missing architect."

Before Kate had a chance to reply, PC Davies came running up behind her, almost bowling her over as he stuck his head into Helen's office.

———◆———

Helen glared at the intruder.

"Guv, we've got a formal ID on Sandy from his fingerprints."

Helen saw the look of glee on the officer's face; she knew it was going to be juicy whatever it was. "Let's have it before you piss your pants."

"Full name Michael Thomas Sandwell, a.k.a. Tommy Sandwell, a.k.a. Sandy." Davies flashed the printout of the DVLA photograph before walking across the main office to the white board Kate had used earlier to note the main points that Dr Nicholls had given them yesterday, as well as to pin up stills from her unauthorised video.

Helen quickly moved to the main office, watching as the officer used a marker pen to write the various names below the new photograph he'd attached of Sandy. The DVLA image looked to be at least twenty years old. Sandy had been an attractive man in his day, before the streets had ravaged his body. He had the look of a young Harrison Ford in the seventies, pre-*Star Wars* stardom.

Davies turned for a second to make eye contact with the occupants of the room before he wrote more information on the board.

"Date of birth, 4 March 1961; date of death, 20 August 1996. Aged thirty-five."

"What?" Helen asked, looking away from the photograph. She was beginning to sound like Kate.

"Tommy Sandwell was declared dead by his parents after being missing for over seven years. The officer assigned to the case presumed he had committed suicide after he was questioned over accounting fraud, although it was never proven. Over three hundred grand went missing from the firm. He disappeared after being released on bail pending further enquiries."

"That's when his fingerprints were taken," Kate confirmed. "He doesn't have any previous?" She took the seat at her desk.

The officer shook his head. "Nothing, just the suspicion of fraud."

"Fraud? Where?" Helen asked as she rubbed at sore eyes.

"At the family business, County Biscuits. Sandwell's father owned the company, and Tommy had worked in accounting in preparation for taking over, apparently."

"County Biscuits? As in Treacle Dodgers and Lemon Creams?" Kate asked. "So you're saying that tramp was going to run a multimillion-pound company?"

"Yep," Davies confirmed with a slightly smug grin, clearly—and understandably—proud of his efforts.

"He wasn't homeless then!" Helen voiced her annoyance to both of them as she sat on the edge of the nearest desk, struggling to take in the information. She knew a police officer of her experience shouldn't be shocked by this kind of revelation; she'd seen it all, over the years—mindless violence, cruelty beyond imagination. But this time, it was someone she knew. It was hard to accept that the Sandy she knew was not only heir to the Sandwell fortune but had been declared dead almost twenty years ago.

"Are his parents still alive?" she asked, hoping to get hold of some solid ground.

"Mother, Diane Sandwell, died two years ago. The father, Johnathan, still lives in the family home." Davies handed Helen a sheet of paper containing the address.

She scanned the information on the page. The address was just outside Manchester. She looked over at Kate and said, "We need to pay him a visit," then got up from the table, directing her attention to the uniformed officer. "Good work. Now I want you to find everything you can on Sandy's disappearance, and the case against him."

Helen's upright position gave her an advantage. As she stood over Kate's desk, she could see the woman's shirt had flapped open a little, exposing the curve of her right breast encased in a light-blue, lacy bra. She reluctantly looked away, blinking as she feigned interest in the paperwork scattered around Kate's desk. Once her focus returned, she placed the address on Kate's desk and spoke in a low voice. "I need to make a couple of calls before we go. Don't want to upset the locals."

"O-Okay, I'll dig up what I can on the biscuit business. Give me a, erm, a shout when you're ready."

She frowned. Why was Kate fumbling over her words? Was her explanation unclear?

Helen returned to her office to gather her thoughts, not the least of which was the thought that this probably wasn't the best time to be ogling Kate's breasts. Had she caught her? Was that why she seemed freaked out? Their relationship seemed to have turned a positive corner since the blowout from the other day, but was Kate the right person to be getting involved with? Scratch that, was it right to even consider getting involved with her? She wasn't blind to the hints being sent her way, but Kate was only here on secondment; she'd be gone again before Helen knew it. That road was just asking for trouble.

Taking a seat at her desk, Helen realised she had another meeting at The Oaks this evening to discuss Julia's medication and treatment again. They'd never make it back in time. She couldn't miss the meeting, which meant delegating the trip to see Mr Sandwell, but she didn't want to do that either. A road trip with Kate could prove risky considering the way Kate looked at her sometimes, but what was life without a few risks? She wanted to know about Sandy and his life before the streets first-hand, not read it in a report when it landed on her desk.

Helen picked up the phone and called the Mossley Police. She let them know they would be paying Mr Sandwell a visit tomorrow to inform him that his son had been found dead. Next, she called her friendly fire investigations officer. She scolded herself to make sure she didn't mention his estranged wife; she needed to keep him sweet right now.

"Hello, Graham."

He released a long breath into the phone. He obviously didn't want to talk to her.

She pressed on. "The fire you were called to last night, does it look like the same arsonist as the house?"

"Preliminary findings show petrol was used as an accelerant, so looks like it."

She ignored his irritated tone as she made a note to ask Davies to access any CCTV in the area around the garage and to canvas the locals for any theft of petrol from sheds or cars. The petrol station at the supermarket was the obvious choice, but they'd already checked their CCTV after the first few fires, and asked them to contact the police if they noticed anything suspicious.

Helen tried a little bit of charm. "Could you maybe send me a copy of the report as soon as you're done?" She felt a little queasy at having to sweet-talk him, but she knew there'd be pressure to close this case soon.

"You'll get it when I finish it."

Helen swallowed back the desire to call him the arrogant prick that he was. "Thanks."

The phone went back down in its cradle. Helen looked out into the main office, her gaze finding the board they'd all just been looking at. She'd moved to Warner for several reasons, one of them being a lower crime rate. Kate walked in front of the board, breaking her staring contest. She visually travelled the length of Kate's body, dressed in snug-fitting dark jeans and a white shirt. Her hair was held in a loose ponytail; she looked sexy. Helen covered her mouth, only just preventing any drool from escaping on to her desk. She thought back to yesterday. After seeing Dr Nicholls, Richards probably wouldn't have eaten for the rest of the day. And although she'd gotten used to it over the years, it was never easy. It was actually refreshing having a different sergeant, someone a little less conventional, even if she was prickly. Attractive, but prickly.

She mentally berated herself for continuing with the nickname, but ribbing Kate was fast becoming her favourite pastime.

CHAPTER 7

"Ready?" Helen had returned to Kate's desk. This time, she managed to keep her gaze on the computer screen. Kate had done a map search for the Sandwell address.

"Sure. According to Google, it'll take us a couple of hours to get here." There was a little too much glee in her voice.

"I figured it would. I said we'd go tomorrow. I have to be back for a meeting later."

"Okay." Kate frowned. "So, where are we going?"

"The Jarvis house. Remember our missing architect?" Helen flashed her another grin.

"Right, right," Kate answered somewhat less enthusiastically and pulled a set of keys out of her desk drawer.

The satnav said this was their destination. Helen gave the house a once-over. Richard Jarvis was obviously not short of a penny or two, judging by the size of his large, double-fronted house with attached garage. It had its own double-gated driveway, allowing cars to pull round to the front door like all the upmarket hotels.

"Someone's done well for themselves," Kate said as she released her seatbelt.

Helen caught the frustrated tone in her words. She also noticed her avoiding her eyes, choosing to focus on the keys she'd just pulled from her pocket instead as they approached the front door with the overhead porch.

Helen held up a hand, gently gripping Kate's elbow.

"Wait. Let's check for a break-in first."

"Right, Guv. Sorry."

Helen looked at Kate for a long moment. She didn't know her very well yet, but she could see from the heavy frown forming on her forehead there was something on her mind.

"What's up? Do you think we're wasting our time here?" Her tone was a little sharper than she intended.

"No." Kate held her position near the front door. She took a breath, then relented. "It's just... I spoke to his mother, and she seemed like the overbearing type, like maybe he just needs a break from her and doesn't want to tell her where he is for a while."

"Okay," Helen yielded. *So maybe they were wasting their time, but they still had a duty to do their job.* "So, we'll just take a quick look and be on our way."

"I'll check the back," Kate offered, handing Helen the keys before making her way along the front of the house.

Helen watched as Kate passed a stray green wheelie bin in front of the garage. The other two bins were more ordered to the right of the garage. Kate disappeared down an alley between the garage and a high timber fence. Returning her focus to the façade of the house, Helen scanned the windows and door, making sure they were all still intact. Nothing stood out to her.

Once she'd moved back to the door, she selected a Yale-type key. Pushing it into the modern lever lock, the door opened effortlessly. Inside, the house was cool, the hallway spacious, with closed doors on either side; a pile of mail and menus from various takeaways had been pushed through the letterbox. She detected a slightly musty smell as she made her way down the hallway towards the light coming from the back of the house. She came face to face with a large kitchen window exposing the expanse of garden beyond. The warm spring sunshine bathed the terraced borders and shrubbery. The garden was one of those that seemed to disappear into infinity as the trees and shrubs mingled, obliterating any sense of neighbours beyond. The first flush of spring was visible with the flashes of colour in the flowerbeds. Jarvis was obviously green fingered—or maybe his gardener was—as Helen realised it wasn't the sort of garden that could be left for a couple of weeks at a time. Someone had definitely been here.

Out of her peripheral vision, she saw Kate focused on the windows and doors, squinting at the plastic frames, checking for any forced entry. Plastic frames for an architect's home? Wasn't that a bit off the peg? Shouldn't he have something a little more eco-friendly, made out of recycled car tyres or something?

She caught Kate's eye and nodded for her to join her.

Inside, looking around the large room, she could see it had been designed much like the garden, terraced with two different levels, with the kitchen essentials on one side and an open-plan dining room on the other, divided by two wide steps.

"Guv!" Kate called out.

"In here!" she called, her words echoing in the large room.

"Anything?" Kate entered the kitchen.

"Can you smell something?" Helen asked, not waiting for Kate to ask another question.

Kate sniffed.

"There's something…stuffy, but something else too."

Kate quickly scanned the room as if she was looking for something. "No sign of a struggle, nothing. Looks normal enough."

"It does. I don't like it. It's too tidy."

Helen snapped on her gloves as she continued to look around the kitchen. There was a notepad attached to the fridge; she could see it was blank—except, as she tilted her head towards the light, she saw an imprint from a top layer. Could just be a shopping list. In the fridge, there were just the essential sauces and condiments. Jarvis had gone away, or at least it was made to look like he had. She needed to check the bins before they left to see what exactly had been thrown away.

"Well! Maybe he's a neat freak or he's got OCD or something…" Kate trailed off as she moved into the dining room.

Helen scanned the space around Kate. It was a large area with a dark tiled floor that made it look like the timber dining suite was rising out of the floor. The walls were a cream colour with only a couple of framed exhibition posters on the walls.

Leaning against the solid timber worktop, she watched Kate take a pair of latex gloves from her pocket and smothered a grin at her struggle to put them on.

"I'll take a look upstairs," Kate offered, almost running out of the room.

Helen looked across at the empty doorway, hearing the footfalls on the stairs. She opened the dishwasher, saw that it was clean and empty. Even the whiff of cleaner was evident, as you'd expect if someone was going away for a few days. She could understand Kate's lack of interest in this case, if it even was a case. She had been in her position not so many years ago, eager to make an impact, wanting the big cases. Who wants a possible missing person when there were the more pressing issues of an arsonist and a murderer on the loose? But did she have to be so impatient about everything?

The kitchen bin was hidden behind a built-in cupboard. Helen wasn't surprised to see it was empty. She stood upright. Her eye caught the door on the far side of the room—the entrance to the adjoining garage? To her surprise, it was open. The coolness of the large space hit her as she entered. She could see there was no car present. Two small, elongated letterbox windows high up on the back wall of the garage provided enough illumination for her to find the light switch. Footsteps behind her made her look back at the doorway, waiting for the approaching figure to appear.

Kate's head peeked inside. "Hey! Nothing upstairs. Well, nothing besides maybe some clothes missing. It's a big house for one person, don't you think?"

Helen's attention was still focused on the garage floor. She heard Kate blow out a breath, no doubt from all her rushing around. Helen thought of her own living arrangements. *Is that what she'd think if she saw my house? Granted, it's too big for me.* But, then, she hadn't intended on being the only one living there when she'd bought it.

Is that what this mood is all about, a dislike of rich people? She hoped her raised eyebrow would indicate her need for more information.

Kate shrugged. "Empty hangers in the wardrobe. No car then?"

"I knew I was right to bump you up to sergeant, if only for your ability to state the obvious." Helen glared at her for a moment before focusing her attention on the garage's concrete floor. She could see from the stains left in the centre near the front, maybe from the air conditioning, that Jarvis's vehicle tended to be parked in the same position. Looking further afield, she could see two faint drag marks going from the door they had both entered to the front of the garage. Moving furniture or rubbish maybe? Or, if the car pulled straight in as normal, moving something or someone to the boot of the car.

Helen inspected the interior of the garage; the walls were blank; the breeze blocks hadn't even been painted. The only storage was at the back below the windows; three shoulder-height cupboards lined the wall, designed exactly for the space, Helen figured. "What type of car does he drive?" She asked without looking around.

"Umm, a red Audi Q2."

An SUV. Perfect for moving bulky objects or bodies. "See these marks?" she asked as she took out her phone, snapping several photos before returning it to her pocket.

Kate squinted to see what Helen was photographing. "Erm…"

Spotting the confusion on Kate's face, she called her over to the doorway. Resting on her haunches, she encouraged Kate to do the same. Down the length of the garage, two faded parallel lines became more noticeable as her gaze travelled the length of the floor surface. "You see those marks there?"

"What are they?"

"Drag marks, maybe," Helen said.

"Heels of shoes?" Kate rubbed her forehead.

"Could be. Is it all carpeted upstairs?" Helen asked as she headed for the door back into the kitchen.

"Yeah." Kate got to her feet, hot on her heels. "Why?"

Helen went to the other two reception rooms at the front of the house. She took a quick look inside, checking under scatter rugs before returning to the kitchen.

"You think something's happened to him?" Kate asked. "It's the easiest floor to clean if something did." She regarded the floor as she considered phoning the crime scene techs to give the place the once-over, but she knew the budget would never stretch to it, not without more evidence of a crime. The satin-black tiled floor had been sealed with black grouting; it looked spotless as it sucked in the light from the bright walls.

"We should check the bins," Helen said, trying to break her scrutiny of the tiled floor, then left the room, hoping Kate would follow her. Finding the nearest bin, she pulled up the lid to check the contents. A waft of sickly-sweet aroma filled her nostrils as she stared down into darkness.

"Empty?"

She met Kate's gaze. She hadn't heard her approach. "Yep. Check the others." Helen let go of the lid, letting it drop back into place as Kate walked to the other bins.

Helen followed, voicing her observations. "Someone's been here. The garden's been tended to, and there are no outbuildings for tools. I didn't see anything in the garage either."

Kate murmured her agreement as she lifted the lids on the remaining two bins. "This one's got garden waste, shrivelled but still green."

Helen peered inside the last bin, half-filled with recyclables. Kate made a grab for the closest thing to the surface. Pulling out part of a newspaper, she found the date in the top right-hand corner.

"Fifth of February."

She mentally added up the days. It was over a month old, and if Jarvis has been gone for over two weeks he could have put it in there any time before then.

"Why would someone with an upmarket house leave their bins out like this?" Kate queried.

"Maybe he wanted to catch the bin the day after he left. Gardener could have moved it back for him," she offered.

"I'll find out the bin days for this street. Check with the neighbours, see if they know who the gardener is."

"Okay," Helen agreed.

With no vehicles present in the closest driveways on either side of the house, she offered some advice, not wanting Kate to have wasted her time.

"You might want to come back later in the evening. Maybe one of them saw the gardener's van."

"Yes, Guv."

"And chase up the phone and bank records."

Kate nodded as she took her gloves off, scrunching them up into a ball.

They were destined to end up just like the tissue she saw the other day, Helen figured as she watched her stuff them into her jacket pocket.

Looking back at the house one last time, Helen spotted a ceiling-mounted CCTV camera on the underside of the porch overhang. She stepped closer to get a better look. The plastic housing had been treated to blend in with the surrounding dark wood; it was only the sunlight glinting off the bubble that had caught her eye.

"Well, it might not be all bad, Virginia."

Kate joined her under the porch. "'Can we be that lucky twice?"

"Get the techs to see if they can pull any footage from it."

———◆———

Viewing the CCTV from outside Doreen Platt's house was certainly keeping her busy. Just not the good kind of busy. The resolution wasn't great. In fact, *crap* was a better description. And all the excessive squinting was giving her a headache and very little else. She wondered why she hadn't been deployed with Davies to do the Sandwell interview. It would be nice to think it was due to her charming company, but right now she wasn't sure which way the chips would fall if she actually asked the question.

"Virginia, Davies has sent through everything he could find on the fraud investigation at County Biscuits."

Keen to make a better fist of the afternoon after her obvious lack of enthusiasm at the Jarvis house, she was on her feet before Helen had finished her sentence. The fact that she wanted Helen's respect, as well as her body, was a surprise to her. Not the body part. That wasn't surprising in the least. She was a gorgeous, intelligent, witty woman. Of course she was attracted to her. The respect part—that was new. And now was so not the right time for that. Everything here was temporary. Six months and gone. Back to her real life.

Entering Helen's office, she heard the printer whirring into life as it sucked in another sheet of paper.

"I printed you out a copy already." Helen stood to hand her a wad of paper across her desk.

The whiny beep from her printer made her half turn as she grasped for the offered paperwork. "Shit!" She attempted to juggle the slipping papers as they slithered to the floor.

Helen stepped around her desk and eyed the scattered papers. "Oh, erm, sorry, Kate. I thought you had hold of it."

"No problem," she said as she crouched down. She gathered the sheets, trying to place them into some semblance of order.

Helen knelt next to her and helped her pick up the papers.

Looking at the pages she'd scooped up, she scanned for the page numbers to put them in order. "Okay, I've pages four, seven, nine, and ten," she said and looked up. She released a small gasp, unaware of how close she was to Helen. She focused on her profile; it was shapely. She had such full lips, such smooth skin, with a light flush to her cheek and neck. Was Helen was as self-conscious as she felt at their close proximity?

Feeling the heat rise in her cheeks, she stood to lay out the paperwork on Helen's desk, fumbling to leave gaps for the missing pages. As much as she wanted to be near Helen, it made her nervous as hell. She was her superior in so many ways, including rank. Reluctantly, she turned to her, retrieving the sheets of paper she had collected without making eye contact.

Helen broke the silence. "I can't help thinking there's been some kind of role reversal here," she said, still kneeling.

She was once again grateful that Helen always knew what to say, a skill that was definitely going to keep her on her toes. "I have to admit it usually takes a little longer to get a woman to fall at my feet these days." She gave the unruly sheets of paper a newsreader shuffle to tidy the stack.

Helen seemed to be struggling to hold in her laugh and used the edge of her desk as a lever to get to her feet. "I find that hard to believe. What with your infinite charm and all."

"I know, right?" she said in her best teenage American accent as she met Helen's eyes. The lopsided grin on Helen's face enclosed her in its warmth.

She stood toe to toe with the woman in her small office. Helen seemed as reluctant as she was to break their near contact. Boisterous voices in the larger office beyond forced apart the static connection between them. Taking a breath to steady herself, she took her seat, placing the desk between them for safety. To busy her fingers, she flicked through her assembled copy of the case file.

Helen cleared her throat, effectively breaking the awkwardness before she said, "So, there's a list of employees at the time. We'll need to see who's still around."

Not daring to look up as Helen spoke, she nodded. She couldn't—absolutely could not—get involved with this woman, no matter how much she wanted to. Not only was she her boss, but Helen was tied to her job, and Warner.

She had plans; she was only staying as long as she had to, then, finally, she could get on with her life. Resolved in that final thought, she began to focus on the words in front of her. Her brain had other ideas, however, as she recalled the gravelly tone in Helen's voice when she had spoken to her earlier. It had made her body quiver when she'd looked into those dark eyes. She nervously bit on her bottom lip as she tried to read.

"It doesn't look like there was much evidence against him, certainly not enough to charge him. It could have been a number of people. They all had opportunity. Why did they only arrest *him*?" Helen stated.

Skimming through the interview transcript that the detective on the case had conducted with Sandy, she saw it. "Ah. It looks like there was access to the computer accounting system. Everyone had their own login. Sandy's was used to access the money and transfer it to another account. The money was never recovered."

"So either he did it, or someone used his password," Helen confirmed.

"Looks like it, Guv," she replied, briefly making eye contact.

Helen picked up her phone and glanced at the screen. "Right. I've got to go now." She rose from her seat, then piled up a stack of files.

She stood quickly. Watching as Helen slipped her arms into her coat and picked up the stack of files, she was surprised by the slick movement. She hastily shuffled her own report back into order.

"So I'll see you tomorrow, Kate." Helen grinned as she moved towards her office door.

She tried to hide the surprise on her face. Helen had just called her Kate. Not Virginia. Kate.

"I-I'll check with Jarvis's neighbours about the gardener and bins on my way home."

"Okay, good. We'll see what Sandwell has to say tomorrow."

She nodded. "Night, Guv."

CHAPTER 8

STARING OUT THE PASSENGER WINDOW, her eyes fixed on the horizon, she barely took in the rolling open countryside around her. Helen had been ready to leave as soon as she arrived at the station; they hadn't even taken the time to get a cup of tea. She cleared her throat, ignoring the parched feeling as she pulled out her notebook.

"I managed to catch a couple of Jarvis's neighbours yesterday. One of them has the same gardener, so I've got his details and a rundown of the bin days," she said and flicked through her notebook to find the right page. "Bin day is on a Wednesday. Two days after he's meant to have left." She closed her notebook. "I'll ask the gardener if he moved the bin when I talk to him later. There was no answer last night. There's been no activity on Jarvis's bank accounts since 12 February. His accounts look healthy; no evidence of money worries."

Helen kept her eyes on the road nodding. "I've called in a favour with a friend who's a crime scene tech; he's going to pick up the Jarvis keys from the station, see if he can get a look at the CCTV."

"Is he going around today?" she asked, a little surprised.

Helen let out a little laugh. "You're not in the Big Smoke anymore, Kate. Depends on his workload. It's probably nothing, but I just want to be sure." She flashed a look in the rear-view mirror before continuing. "I got the report on the latest fire from your mate Brown."

She looked over at her, her lips pursed at the smirk on Helen's lips. "My mate!" she said, scornfully. "The man's a…turd." She discreetly pressed her hand to the bruise on her hip. The pain had mostly gone, although the dark mark on her skin had turned a colourful shade of yellow. She thought back to his angry face that night. "His eyes are too far apart; he looks like a fish."

"That was a bit restrained for you." Amusement coloured Helen's voice.

"I'm trying," she said and smiled at Helen, relieved that the awkward tension that had developed between them yesterday had evaporated.

"Anyway." Helen continued. "Petrol was used as an accelerant, so it's likely it was our firebug again."

"I asked Davies to check through any CCTV in the area, and Uniform are doing a door to door, but it's a bit out of the way, not many witnesses." She turned the notebook over in her hands. About the only thing they did know for sure was that whoever it was, they were local. How else could they get around without being seen each time?

"Good. We need to catch him before he really hurts someone or worse."

"I got the phone records back for Jarvis too." She flipped through her notebook. "His phone was last used at 5:37 p.m. on Sunday, 12 February at or near his home, according to the pings of local masts. Nothing after that. They think it was turned off or ran out of battery—whichever."

A heavy frown appeared on the profile of Helen's face. "That's bad news. When was he due in London?"

"On Monday, 13 February."

She waited for a reply, but after a few moments, she realised there wasn't going to be one. Holding her notebook in her lap, her gaze drifted to the far side of the windscreen, where her eyes found Helen's delicate hands softly holding the steering wheel. She knew that if she had been making this journey on her own, the driving would be much more erratic, with a smattering of frustrated swear words. In contrast, this felt almost sedate. Was that the journey or the company? She immediately thought of the saying about lovers and partners making people want to be a better version of themselves. Although they weren't lovers, it didn't stop her from wanting to make a better attempt at her so-called life.

She continued her perusal up Helen's arms. The cuffs on her long-sleeved grey shirt had been turned up to just below the elbow, revealing elegant, pale forearms. Her shoulders were relaxed, as was her profile as she looked out ahead, occasionally flicking a quick look in the rear-view mirror. Her almost blank expression changed occasionally with a slight furrowed brow or twitch of the lips, giving the impression of cogs turning as she considered ideas and possibilities.

"You're quiet." Helen said with a quick look across at Kate. If she was surprised by her observations, she didn't show it.

"Sorry, bit tired. Too much CCTV watching," she lied. She'd barely scratched the surface of the footage. Another power cut when she arrived home had put paid to that.

Johnathan Sandwell lived on a small private estate. The two-storey stone house was set in acres of open countryside. The edge of the estate was lined with large oak trees. It was well kept. *No doubt by a team of gardeners.*

Helen stopped in front of the entrance to the house, and its large timber front door, and looked over while she performed her angry doorbell pressing. The grin on Helen's face told her she'd expected it, and well…who was she to deny the lady?

The sound of the chiming bells could be heard from their position. Helen pulled her warrant card from her pocket, and she followed suit. A heavy sound behind the door piqued her interest as she imagined a large plank being removed from brackets either side of the door, like a medieval castle.

The door opened only a few inches before an elderly face appeared in the gap. The man looked to be in his sixties at least. His thinning grey hair had receded, leaving a bulbous shiny forehead. His thick, black, plastic glasses covered small, dark eyes. He held an expectant look as his gaze travelled between the two of them.

"Good morning. We'd like to talk to Mr Johnathan Sandwell," Helen said in what must have been her best friendly voice.

"Is he expecting you?" the man enquired. His tone sounded cautious.

"No. We're police. I'm DCI Helen Taylor, and this is Acting DS Kate Wolfe." Helen held up her credentials for the man to see. "We need to talk to him about his son, Tommy Sandwell."

She might not know Helen that well, but she knew one thing for certain: the woman wasn't about to be fobbed off after driving all the way up here. The old man barely glanced at Helen's credentials, although his expression flickered at the mention of Sandy's name and he opened the door wider.

"I'm Richard Lees. I work for Mr Sandwell."

She noticed the glum expression on Lees's face, and his reluctance to step aside. Common sense won as he allowed them in to a grand hallway. After he shut the door, he turned to face them.

"I'll let Mr Sandwell know you're here."

In the bright entrance, she saw the man was slight as well as elderly. He obviously wasn't employed as a protector. She worried for them both, living in this remote location. She hoped there was someone a little more youthful on hand.

She took in her surroundings as she half-watched the man disappear towards the back of the house. It felt like she had stepped back a hundred years in time. The large entrance hall was painted white and had a beautifully tiled floor. An ornate timber staircase in the centre provided access to the left and right of the upper floor. There were several timber-panelled doors leading off the ground-floor space. She imagined a large library with leather wingback chairs behind one of them. She glanced at Helen, trading raised eyebrows at the time warp they'd walked into.

Looking across the vast space, she watched as Helen arched her back—fatigued from the long drive, she guessed—and stared at the ornate ceiling above them.

"Nice bust," she offered playfully from across the room.

Helen's head snapped back in her direction, a look of surprise on her face.

Grinning at the reaction she'd gotten, she nodded to the white ceramic bust of a woman behind Helen, just to the right of the staircase.

"Nice bush." Helen countered.

She smiled as she briefly looked down to her crotch before catching the mischievous look that danced in Helen's eyes. "Thanks. I try and keep it pruned."

Helen's eyes darted to a space to her left.

Oh, the painting. "Right… I thought you had X-ray vision for a minute." Apparently, Helen wasn't one to be outdone. She liked that. Really liked that. She knew she was pushing her luck, but she couldn't resist a bit of harmless flirting.

Approaching footsteps prevented her from voicing her inner thoughts of butlers and their supposed criminal behaviour.

"Mr Sandwell is in the conservatory," Richard Lees announced by way of explaining their necessary journey through the house. No doubt, his walk had slowed over the years, the urgency of youth long gone.

"How long have you worked for Mr Sandwell?" Helen asked.

"Thirty-four years," he replied.

"You knew Tommy too?" she asked as they passed along a dark corridor behind the stairs.

Lees slowed his pace even more. He seemed to want to look at them. "Of course. It broke his parents' hearts when Tommy vanished."

"Why do you think he disappeared?" Helen continued.

Exiting the dark passageway, they entered what could only be described as a sunroom occupying a small corner of the house. The two exterior walls were made up of windows with large metal stanchions to support the upper floor.

With his gaze fixed on the route ahead, Lees held his position. "He couldn't stand the thought of letting his parents down. I remember he was so upset at the thought that they would think he had done it."

"Done it?" she asked.

Richard blinked a couple of times before answering. "Stolen the money," he offered reluctantly.

Obviously no secrets in this house. "You don't think he did it; stole the money?"

Lees tried to straighten his weary frame. "No. I thought he would come back when it all died down, but…" Lees shrugged his shoulders. "He had a few problems in the past, but he had sorted himself out." He fixed his stare at the floor, his stature losing its form. He stooped a little before moving towards the large glass door that led to the conservatory.

She considered the man's words. Tommy hadn't been known to the police until the fraud allegations; any earlier problems must have been kept within the family. Which brought up two questions: What were those issues? And—more importantly—how would she find out about them?

The heat of the conservatory surprised her. Condensation covered the windows that were visible behind a variety of plants lining the long sides of the oblong room. Several rows of tables topped with plants occupied the far end of the room. The curved structure of the roof looked delicate against the cool blue sky beyond.

She scanned the room for Johnathan Sandwell until a man, whose face she recognised from the file on Tommy, stepped out from behind the distant greenery. As he walked towards them, she could see that he was well dressed, wearing what looked like a smoking jacket atop a white shirt and patterned cravat. Tall and slim with wire-rimmed spectacles and his grey hair slicked back, he looked elegant despite his elderly years. He was still holding a pair of secateurs in one hand and cuttings from one of his plants in the other. He placed them both on a nearby potting bench before saying something she couldn't hear to his employee.

"Mr Sandwell, I'm Chief Inspector Taylor, this is Detective Sergeant Wolfe. We're from Warner Police station." Helen took a breath. "Can we sit down?" she asked.

With a slight wobble in his hands, Sandwell nodded, offering an open hand towards the small suite of wicker furniture on one side of the room.

"Please."

She wondered if Sandwell had ever given up hope for his son. Declaring somebody dead as soon as technically possible seemed so clinical.

"I've ordered us some tea?"

"Thank you," she said, taking out her notebook as she took a seat opposite. It finally dawned on her that they were delivering a death notification; she felt the smile disappear from her face.

"I hope you're not parched. It might take a while," he said quietly as they watched Richard shuffle out of the room.

She caught the warmth in his smile as she made herself comfortable and focused on his enlarged eyes behind the glasses, knowing what Helen had to tell him, she wanted to check his reaction.

"Sir, I'm very sorry to have to inform you that we've found the body of your son, Tommy Sandwell."

"In Warner? Where's that?" he asked with a frown.

"It's on the Shropshire border, a few hours from here."

She worked hard to keep the smile off her face, knowing exactly how he felt; Warner was in the middle of nowhere, and in many ways a perfect hiding place for Sandy.

Helen waited for Johnathan Sandwell to nod in reply before continuing. "Tommy had been living in the area for a number of years before he died."

If he was surprised, it didn't show.

"Tommy was declared dead in August 1996," Helen said, letting the statement hang in the air.

"Yes. His mother wanted some closure, and it was necessary for the business. He was due to take over in a few years." Sandwell shook his head. "When did he die?"

"Several weeks ago. We're waiting for more tests to confirm exactly when."

Sandwell's eyes grew even wider behind his thick glasses and he covered his mouth with a shaking hand. She found herself grateful that they were sitting down.

"Weeks! He was only a couple of hours away all these years? What was he doing there?" Frustration coloured his voice.

"He did odd jobs now and then, cash-in-hand stuff. He had a few close friends, but he mainly kept off the radar. I became acquainted with him over the last few years and helped him out when I could. He was a good man."

"Thank you, Inspector." Sandwell wiped away a tear.

She was more than happy for Helen to take the lead as she quietly took notes. This was one interview she had no intention of butting in on. Besides, she didn't have long to wait for the question that was at the forefront of all their minds.

"How did he die?"

Helen took a second to reply. "We think he was hit by a car. The driver failed to report it. No witnesses have come forward so far." Helen waited few beats before continuing. "His body was found by firemen when they answered a call to a fire at an abandoned house. We were investigating his death when his fingerprints revealed his identity. He was just known as Sandy in Warner. We had no idea of his background."

She waited patiently for Helen's words to be absorbed. The fact that Helen knew Sandy must have made this interview quite difficult for her too.

A sniff drew her attention back to Sandwell, and she looked up to see him nodding. "Then you learned about the fraud at the company."

"Yes," Helen confirmed. "We need to know about the circumstances of his disappearance. I know it's a long time ago, but can you tell me when you last saw Tommy?"

The number of times he must have gone over his last meeting with his son, looking for any hint of what he'd been planning. The fact that Sandy had been alive until very recently had to be a jab to the ribs, but she understood why Helen needed to ask.

The old man clenched his hands together in his lap. "The day before he went missing, he came here to see us, his mother and me," he clarified, "after the police released him."

"And how did he seem?" Helen asked softly.

"He was…angry."

"Looking through the case file, there didn't seem to be much evidence against him at the time. Do you think he took the money?"

Sandwell shook his head. "No. He had access to money if he needed it; he didn't need to steal it. It never made any sense to me."

"Did anyone leave the company under a cloud around the time of the money going missing, or shortly after, maybe?"

"Not that I can think of. It was a long time ago. You're better off talking to some of the people that worked with him at the time."

"We're in the process of tracing them," Helen confirmed.

"I got the feeling he was involved with someone. He seemed…happy before it all happened. There were odd phone calls that he always ended when someone entered the room. I could be wrong. I mean, no one ever came forward or anything."

Married, an affair? She jotted in her notebook.

"Was he living here at the time?" Helen queried.

"No. He had a flat a few miles from the factory at the time. He'd moved out a few years before."

No doubt cleared out after Sandy was declared deceased.

"I see. Do you have any of Tommy's belongings from his flat?"

Sandwell shook his head. "No. There wasn't a great deal of personal stuff… He was never very materialistic."

"Do you have any questions you want to ask me?"

Sandwell shook his head. "For the first few years, we were so hopeful, but hope gradually fades. His mother was much more practical. She found a way to move on. I'm not sure I ever did. Maybe now…"

Helen held a mournful expression. "Thank you for your time, Mr Sandwell. I'm sorry for your loss. We'll do our best to find out what happened to your son." She stood, indicating it was time to leave.

"Thank you, Inspector."

Helen pulled a card from her pocket, stretching her arm to hand it to a still seated Johnathan Sandwell. "Here's my card. If you think of anything else or have any questions, please don't hesitate to contact me."

The opening of a door behind them made everyone look around, watching as Lees returned, wheeling a small trolley into the room. The uneven tiled floor made the china clatter as it moved towards them.

"Would you like some tea before you leave?" Sandwell offered.

"Thank you, Mr Sandwell, but we should get back." Helen replied.

"I'll see you out," Lees said to the police officers.

She waited until they were back in the dark corridor before asking any questions. He continued to walk towards the front door, obviously keen to eject them. She had other ideas. "Do you know if Tommy was in a relationship with anyone at the time he disappeared?"

Richard frowned as he released the catch on the front door. "I'm sorry, I don't know. He didn't bring anyone here."

Helen smiled. "Okay. Thank you for your help, Mr Lees. Someone will be in touch with Mr Sandwell to make arrangements for Tommy."

Richard nodded before closing the door behind them.

"I guess I should be grateful you didn't accuse him of running Sandy over."

"Who me? Just getting a bit of background info, Guv."

"Really."

"I'll drive back, Guv. Give you a break," she offered as they walked towards Helen's car.

"Sure?" Helen asked, before she cautiously held out her car keys.

"Yeah," She took the keys, knowing she had to be in the driver's seat to put her plan into action. "Lunch?" She spotted the time on the dashboard as she started the car. "I saw a pub not far from here."

"Lead the way."

She noted the subdued look on Helen's face as she plugged in her seatbelt. "I-I think he appreciated what you said about Sandy being a good person."

"Thanks."

Helen closed her eyes and let her head fall back against the headrest. "It's the shittiest part of the job," she said quietly. "And certainly not one

I've missed since leaving Manchester. Not including Sandy, I've only given two notifications here, both due to accidental or natural causes."

She slowly directed the car out of the Sandwell estate.

"Not that it will make you feel any better, but I think you're very good at it."

Helen opened her eyes to look at Kate. "Two compliments in the space of five minutes, Virginia? Have you had a bump on the head?"

She pursed her lips at Helen's response. "Let's put it down to light-headedness due to lack of food." She didn't want to mention the fact that they'd left Sandwell's before getting that cup of tea, on top of missing her morning cuppa at her desk.

Helen smiled in reply.

"It's a shame there aren't any more old company workers in the area. So far, the others we've located are in the opposite direction."

"A job for another day," Helen said.

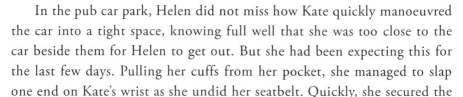

In the pub car park, Helen did not miss how Kate quickly manoeuvred the car into a tight space, knowing full well that she was too close to the car beside them for Helen to get out. But she had been expecting this for the last few days. Pulling her cuffs from her pocket, she managed to slap one end on Kate's wrist as she undid her seatbelt. Quickly, she secured the second cuff to the steering wheel, trapping Kate in the car.

"Fucking fucker!" Kate yelled.

Helen pushed the passenger seat back and tried to contain her laughter as she slipped off her big coat to make her escape. Kate was fishing into her pockets with her free hand, trying to find her handcuff key, while Helen made her way into the back seats and out through the passenger door behind her.

"No key?" Helen asked with a laugh as she straightened her clothes.

"I can't fucking find it."

"I know where you can borrow one from. But it'll cost you," Helen shut the back door carefully to stand just out of Kate's grasp should she try and grab her.

Kate thumped the steering wheel with her free hand and sighed loudly. "What?"

Helen smiled, toying with her a little longer. "Lunch, for starters."

"Fine," Kate said as she blew out a long breath.

Helen pulled the key from her pocket. "Here!" She tossed it to Kate, who wore an anxious expression as she tried to catch it with her free hand across her body.

Helen sauntered off into the pub, leaving Kate to fumble with the key.

"You do realise I'm not just here to supplement your expense account," Kate said three minutes later as she tossed the handcuff key across the wooden table where Helen sat inside the pub.

"Of course. You're here to drive me around and come up with inspirational ideas too."

Kate sniggered. "No, no, inspirational ideas are way above my rank."

"And mine."

Two tall glasses of Coke were deposited on their table.

"Thanks," Kate said before taking a long drink.

Helen waited for the waitress to walk away before saying, "I called Davies while you were larking about." She waited for Kate to meet her eyes. "He's texting me Sandy's old address so we can take a look before we drive back."

Kate grunted her acknowledgement.

"And I've ordered you lasagne and chips."

Kate's face brightened. "Really?"

Helen nodded and sipped her drink.

"Perfect!"

It didn't take much to make Kate happy. What intrigued her more was how content it made her that Kate was happy. She was just a colleague, wasn't she? Although she couldn't ever recall trading such charged comments with anyone else she'd worked with before, let alone someone she'd been intimate with. This woman had stormed her once-quiet police station, forcing her to feel things she hadn't considered in some time. Yet it was only a temporary situation. A dampening disappointment filled her stomach. She had a feeling Kate Wolfe would be quite the person to know on a personal level, away from work.

But not for her.

CHAPTER 9

"Morning, Guv." She had knocked on Helen's door as soon as possible after making her customary cup of tea. She needed it this morning; her eyes were sore from all the hours watching the CCTV recordings. Thankfully, the time had paid off, or at least she hoped it had. Trawling through endless hours of the footage of Doreen Platt's back garden had provided a couple of incidents of a figure moving back and forth through the end of the garden and heading towards the burned-out house—the first two days before the fire and the last about an hour before the fire was reported. It had to be their firebug. Who else would be creeping about out there after midnight?

So she'd taken the initiative employing her skills to help identify their skulking figure. Although it had proven a lengthy process, they now had an image of a suspect, albeit slightly blurry.

Helen looked to be already deep in work with papers scattered across her desk as she scrutinised her computer screen. But she looked up and nodded. "Morning, Virginia."

She'd given up trying to beat Helen into work, resigned to the fact that she would always be second to arrive.

"Is that a fresh cup of tea you have there?" Helen asked.

"It is. Would you like it?" They drank it the same way, a little milk, no sugar.

"Sure you can you spare it? You look tired."

Taking a deep breath before walking around to Helen's side of the desk, she held out her hand and offered Helen her mug. "Well, I might have something on the Platt CCTV from the back of her house." That should explain her tiredness.

"Really?" Helen took a sip of her newly acquired tea and smiled over the top of her cup. "You've been busy."

"It's a little blurry still, due to the quality of the original footage, but I used a computer enhancement programme to clean up the image. At least it's something. I figured, with your knowledge of the locals, you'll probably know his inside leg measurement at the very least," she quipped, recalling Helen's familiarity with Slim Jim's shoe size.

A sparkle danced in Helen's eyes. It was impossible not to be engulfed by it. She was close enough to touch her. If she had reached out a hand, she could have felt her firm thigh before it disappeared under her desk.

Standing abruptly, Helen had a slight height advantage over her even as she leaned on Helen's desk. She wondered whether Helen would have answered the challenge in her eyes if the cup hadn't occupied her hands. Either way, the arrival of another officer in the outer office prevented any further thought on the subject.

Helen raised an eyebrow. "Let's see this work of CCTV art, then, shall we? Oh, and by the way, Forensics says it looks like the security footage from the Jarvis house has been wiped from the server."

Kate led the way to her desk in the open-plan office, taking her seat she grasped the mouse clicking on the image she'd uploaded earlier. "Shit!" She met Helen's gaze. "Do they know if it was done from the house or remotely?"

"They're still working on it, apparently." Helen frowned as she looked down at her. "I didn't realise you were such a tech geek."

She returned her attention to the screen. "Ah, well, that'll be my hidden depths, Guv."

Clicking on the small picture icon, it took a couple of seconds for the image to flash up on the screen. With fresh eyes, she found herself a bit disappointed; she remembered the image being more impressive than it seemed now. For a moment, she thought she'd gone too far, built this up too much. She turned to see a slightly flummoxed-looking Helen before her expression changed to thoughtful as she stared at the computer screen.

She shook it off, returning her attention to the image on her screen. It was dark, but there were lines of definition outlining the face and its features. She was genuinely hopeful. "This guy was caught at the back walking towards the house shortly before the fire was reported. So, the question is, do you recognise him?"

Helen squinted at the fuzzy image. "Erm…he looks a bit like one of the Whiting lads off the Sanford estate."

"The Sanford estate? Is that the same estate Arthur Goode was referring to?"

The crash of a door opening against a wall with force drew both of their attentions away from the screen.

"He copped a fucking plea!" the uniformed officer announced, realising he had the attention of everyone in the office.

She looked up, seeing Helen's raised eyebrow. She wasn't sure if it was for the officer's swearing or something else.

"Johnson?" Helen asked.

"Yep!" the officer said with an equal amount of glee.

"Yes!" Helen threw her hands in the air.

She'd never seen Helen quite so animated, not even when they'd argued. She waited until the officer had disappeared out of sight, and on hearing him pass on his mirth to another colleague nearby, she asked the burning question, "Who's Johnson?"

"Anthony Johnson. He's a plasterer from Leeds who assaulted a former police officer from this station. Now she won't have to go through a court case, and I won't have to testify against the prick."

"Pub later?" PC Davies said as he passed.

"Absolutely," Helen stated matter-of-factly before leaning on Kate's desk to scrutinise the image on the screen.

She felt the warmth from Helen's arm as she leaned close to her. Reaching to grab a pen, she brushed her arm against Helen's, relishing the spark that flowed through her body.

Helen cleared her throat. "There are three Whiting lads: Curtis, Kyle, and Dominic. There's only a year or two between each one, which makes them quite hard to tell apart sometimes, especially in the dark." She scribbled a note of the names to check out on the database. "They've been in trouble for minor stuff, mainly drinking, fighting, car theft. Get Uniform to check out their whereabouts recently."

"Yes, Guv." She knew she could at least cross-check their arrest photos against her scrubbed-up image.

"Okay." Helen stood to her full height, holding out her left hand as she listed off jobs. "We need to speak to some of Sandy's old co-workers, if they're still around. Chase up Nicholls, see if he's got anything else for us yet, and I'll call the crime scene techs, see if there's anything more on the Jarvis house."

She twisted her lips as she thought of Dr Nicholls and his maggot tests, and swiftly changed the subject. "I've located one or two, but unfortunately a lot of them have either moved on or passed away now. I've still got a couple more to check up on."

"Okay. Let me know when we have solid contacts on people to interview."

"Yes, Guv."

Helen disappeared back into her office, leaving her to search for her missing County Biscuit employees. It didn't take long as her methods were a little less…orthodox when compared to those of her colleagues, no doubt. Being a computer geek had its rewards.

"Any luck?" Helen asked, when she approached her desk half an hour later.

"I found Sandy's secretary from back in the day, and the bonus is her husband also worked there, in the marketing department. It's how they met, apparently. They live just outside Sheffield." A quick route-check had told her it was at least an hour's drive. She was looking forward to another road trip with Helen.

"Great work. You'll have to take Davies with you. I need to update Superintendent Scott," Helen replied. Was that a hint of disappointment in her tone?

"Oh. Well, it won't be as much fun locking him in the car while I tuck into my delicious pub lunch."

"You don't really think you'd get away with that, do you? I've got your number, Virginia." Helen replied with a wide smile.

"I bet you do," she responded in a low tone, testing Helen's resistance. She held Helen's gaze as she waited for a witty retort.

The seconds dragged as Helen failed to respond to her salacious comment, the sound of Davies's loud, sing-song voice in the outer office released her of that burden.

With the moment gone, she looked down at the sheet of paper in her hands, skimming over the addresses of Sandy's ex-colleagues.

"I could interview them over the phone, save the petrol."

"No. It's generally harder to lie to the police when you're sat right in front of them. Most work places have a gossip network; we need to find a way to tap into it. It's also a long time ago, so we can't take any chances with anyone we find."

The weight of the case rested on her shoulders, and she realised suddenly how unsuited she was for these delicate interviews. This was Helen's territory. "Are you sure you don't want to do it?"

Helen looked at her, clearly amused by her discomfort. "You'll do fine," she said, then quickly amended her statement. "Just don't get angry."

"Yes, Guv."

"Or frustrated."

"Yes, Guv."

"Or stab the doorbell like a demented woodpecker."

"Yes, Guv," she said, deploying a wink as she turned to leave the room.

<hr />

The Plume and Feathers pub was boisterous when Helen arrived. The large screen showing football dominated the front bar. She recognised several locals as she strolled through to the back lounge. She spotted Kate talking to PC Davies as she made her way to the bar, offering her a warm smile as Kate raised her half-full glass in her direction. The sexual tension between them had been threatening to boil over in the last few days, so she was relieved to have been called into a progress meeting with Grace. Leaving Kate to her own devices was a risk, considering her recent behaviour, but she hoped Davies's calming influence had had its desired effect. She knew she was playing with fire with Kate, but she couldn't help herself. Despite their differences, she enjoyed every moment she spent in her company.

After slipping the barman some cash to cover at least one round of drinks, she turned, sipping her red wine as she faced her fellow officers.

Her gaze lingered on Kate a little too long as she traced the outline of her figure. Her mind drifted to the thought of what it might feel like to do the same thing with her hands. She recalled Kate's comment about her hidden depths and swallowed hard. Oh, how she wanted to know all of Kate's hidden depths in detail.

She mentally scolded herself for inquiring after her sergeant's well-being after seeing her fatigued state. What she got up to in her spare time was nothing to do with her. Yet she did care. It mattered to her that Kate was okay. She had never worked with anyone for such a short time that she'd developed such strong feelings for. It worried her. That was the whole reason that relationships with colleagues were frowned upon, but at the same time she had no idea of how to deal with the issue without drawing attention to it.

As the boisterous crowd parted, giving her a view of Kate, familiar stirrings settled low in her belly. She found it difficult to drag her gaze away, even as Davies, next to Helen, appeared to be trying to show her pictures of his recently born niece. Helen glanced at the image of a plump newborn, making the appropriate noises as she kept one eye on Kate, who was quickly flanked by several more officers, clearly passing judgement on today's courtroom events. Helen wanted to go across and talk to her, even if it was only to inquire about the information she had gained from her interviews with Sandy's old colleagues.

Helen quickly zoned out of the conversations going on around her as she focused her attention on Kate once again. Davies had been replaced by Sergeant Terry Kirk, who was giving Kate far too much attention as the evening dragged on. Helen had never been a big socialiser; even in Manchester she had often left gatherings, preferring to celebrate successful case closures with a glass of wine at home, alone.

She gripped her glass a little tighter as Kirk's hand dropped dangerously close to Kate's backside. Kate quickly grabbed for the offending hand, gripping it as she spoke calmly close to his ear. Helen was instantly amused. Whatever she had said, it apparently had the desired effect. Kirk walked away with a sneer plastered on his face.

"How are you getting home?" Helen asked as she placed her empty glass on the table next to Kate's.

"Who knows?" Kate replied in slightly slurred speech.

Having already witnessed the scene with Terry, Helen wanted to make sure he didn't get his way, although, considering Kate's rebuff earlier, that wasn't likely to be the case. Deciding to do the right thing, she pulled out her phone to call a local taxi.

"What's your address, Virginia?" she asked as she held the phone away from her face.

Kate narrowed her eyes at her as she mumbled her answer before finishing her drink.

"Come on, let's get some fresh air while we wait for your taxi." Helen steered Kate as best she could down the steps and into the front beer garden, heading towards a picnic bench in a darkened area. From that position, they had a good view of the road.

The cool air must have been a shock to Kate's system. She wrapped her arms around her body. "Do you need a taxi too?" She took a seat on the outside edge of the wooden picnic bench.

"No. I live just over there." Helen pointed to the dark road almost opposite the pub that led to her hidden-away home. She took a seat next to Kate, aware of her close proximity to Kate's thighs as they jiggled a little in the cold air.

"Where?" Kate squinted across the road and into the blackness where Helen had pointed.

She looked at Kate, smiling at her confusion. "You can't see it from here."

"Are you as drunk as I am?" Kate asked as her eyes squinted to adjust to her new surroundings.

"No. I don't think so."

"Why am I so drunk?"

"I'm guessing you skipped lunch again. Plus, Terry's been buying you doubles in the hope of getting a grope of the new girl." Helen fiddled with her phone in her hands to give them something to do.

Kate suddenly turned to look at Helen.

"Oh! Oooh! That dirty bastard tried to touch me up earlier."

"I saw that," Helen said with a laugh, although she had actually wanted to drag Kirk out to the car park and pummel him at the time.

"I don't like the way his face whistles when he speaks. Maybe I should arrest him."

"For whistling?" Helen questioned, trying to hide the amusement from her voice.

"No. For being an obnoxious prick!"

Helen laughed out loud. Kate certainly had a way of hitting the nail on the head.

Kate shivered, her hands clamped between her thighs as she continued. "He called me 'virgin'. Said he wanted to pop my cherry."

She turned to look at Kate's profile and then looked out towards the road. She realised how much she'd missed spending the day with her, regardless of the consequences. "God, I should arrest him for that kind of talk." Although she made light of it, she planned to have a quiet word in Sergeant Kirk's ear regarding his conduct with female colleagues.

"Were you watching me?"

Helen thought there was a little more confidence in Kate's voice. She ignored the question, deciding to reply with a question of her own. "What exactly did you say to him?" The look of pain on Kirk's face had certainly been memorable.

Kate grinned. "I told him I'd make him into a eunuch if he touched me again." She adjusted her position and straddled the wooden seat, resting her left arm on the table. She centred her body, sitting upright, and began singing in a low, tuneless voice. "*Who's afraid of Virginia Woolf?*"

Helen smiled as she heard the words. "George sings that at the end of the film." She was tempted to say more but didn't want to give the impression that she had been waiting for an opportunity to discuss Kate's nickname, even though she'd watched the film recently, specifically in case the topic came up.

"I know," Kate replied confidently as she sang the words again.

There was silence for a few moments before she finally had the courage to speak. "I am, Kate, I am," she said quietly, changing the final words of the film slightly. The couple of drinks she'd had seemed to have loosened her tongue, but the looks and signals that had passed between them were unavoidable. She'd purposely put distance between them today, fearful of her own feelings, but somehow Kate always had a way of getting around her defences, absence the latest tool in her arsenal.

"What?" Kate asked, surprise evident in her tone.

There was no going back now. Helen steeled herself before continuing. "I'm afraid of Virginia Woolf."

"Are you? Why?"

"I think you know why."

They were getting into dangerous territory, and how the hell was she going to close it down now that she had opened the door for more questions? She should have kept her mouth shut. Why? Why did she have to say that?

Kate reached out and slipped her hand into Helen's, preventing continued fumbling with her mobile phone.

"Is it because…?" She paused.

Helen risked a quick look over at Kate, trying to hide the concern she felt for her intoxicated state. Kate was already a hothead. God alone knew what was going to come out of her mouth now. Helen was grateful for the dark solitude surrounding them. She found herself praying for the taxi's delayed arrival.

Kate leant towards her as she spoke in a low voice. "I want you. And you think it's a mistake, and that I'll screw everything up and hurt you."

Her eyes flickered closed as Kate's words burned their path into her bloodstream all the way to her heart. Helen turned her upper body around to face Kate more squarely, their bodies only inches apart. "I see you've thought about this a bit." Her fiercely contradicting heartbeat was throbbing in her ears as she realised that Kate still held her hand. A thumb danced along the skin on the back of her hand. The softness of Kate's touch broke through her final line of defence. Even in the darkness, Kate's lips looked full and tempting as they parted slightly under her scrutiny.

The silence stretched between them.

She couldn't wait any longer. She needed to know how those lips felt against her own. Throwing caution to the wind for the first time in years, Helen leant forward. Stopping only a couple of inches short, she heard Kate's startled intake of breath. The slight upturn of Kate's lips forced her to close the final few inches that separated them. Soft, warm lips pressed against hers. After a few seconds, they parted a little. A hand made its way to the side of her face, deepening the kiss. The heady taste of alcohol filled her mouth as she ran her tongue slowly along Kate's bottom lip before tentatively pushing inside. She swept her tongue deeper still and was relieved to hear the low moan of approval escape Kate's throat. She wanted this to last forever, to take Kate home with her right now, to feel her body against Kate's, but something cut through her, holding her back. This wasn't right. She couldn't risk getting attached to a *temporary* officer. She needed to take a step back before it was too late.

Pulling back, she caught her breath before pressing her forehead against Kate's. "Your taxi will be here soon," she whispered. She could hear the disappointment in her own voice. The thought of Kate leaving now filled Helen's stomach with turmoil. She brought their lips together again. The warmth of Kate's mouth sobered her, bringing her body to attention. A throbbing heat flowed through her body even as Kate pulled back. She wanted more of Kate Wolfe. It was too late already.

Helen stood abruptly. Without taking her eyes off Kate, she straddled the wooden seat, mirroring Kate's position.

"Come here," Kate murmured as she reached out to grasp the lapels of her coat.

Their lips collided, parting almost immediately. She wanted this, wanted to feel Kate's desire for her. Kate's hands slipped to her thighs, thumbs following the inner seam of her trousers. The additional dimension of Kate's hands on her pushed away any thoughts of ending this moment. Lifting her hand, she cupped Kate's cheek, pulling her closer, but nothing seemed to be quite close enough. Kate's hands felt electrifying on her body. She knew if they didn't stop soon there would be no need for the taxi.

The sound of an approaching car made them both pull apart, creating a yawning distance between them. The headlights of the taxi flashed across Kate's face as Helen stepped over the seat, walking towards the car as it pulled up next to the kerb beyond the garden. She waited for the driver to lower his window before speaking.

"Evening, Malc. New car?"

A sinking feeling developed in the pit of her stomach as she focused on the wonky, magnetic taxi sign attached to the driver's door proclaiming *Malc's Taxis*.

What exactly had she started here tonight?

"Traded up. Thought it was about time. Other one kept breaking down, started losing business," Malc Walters said from inside the waiting car.

Her voice had regained its regular timbre as she tried to make conversation with Malc. "One to take home," Helen said, indicating Kate, still sitting on the bench.

She heard footsteps approaching from behind as she reeled off Kate's address. She didn't want to risk Kate making a scene; she wasn't ready for that yet. She opened the rear passenger door and nodded for Kate to get in, stepping up to close the door behind her. The expression on her face was unreadable, which only worried Helen more. She'd basically kissed Kate, then dismissed her. She hadn't expected the evening to take the turn that it had, but, equally, she wasn't ready for the conversation now that their feelings were out in the open.

Helen held out a 20-pound note from her pocket towards Malc, adding, "Wait for her to get inside before you leave." She waited for him to nod in acknowledgement before letting go of the money.

Back on the pavement, Helen watched the taxi drive off around the corner. She couldn't help thinking that she'd made a mistake acting on her feelings towards Kate. They worked together. The whole thing was a terrible idea. She was only on secondment for five more months, then she'd be off back to London and back to her high-flying life in the Met.

She scolded herself. She was Kate's boss; how could she expect to have any control over her now? She was edging towards feral as it was; God knew what she'd be like now Kate was aware of Helen's feelings. The woman had a sell-by date, and she wasn't suitable relationship material. Not that Helen would know with her track record, or lack of it. She hadn't had a relationship in, how many years now?

She quickly blamed the alcohol for loosening her tongue, but now she would have to deal with the fallout. Crossing the road, she headed up the short, cobbled road to her house, hoping that sleeping on the whole thing would reveal some answers.

CHAPTER 10

THE INCREASING VOLUME OF THE clock radio roused her from her slumber, pulling a pillow over her head did little to stem the flow of horrendous thuds and beats that attacked her ears. Realising it was pointless to continue to try and sleep, she rolled over, stretching to turn off the alarm.

"Fuck off!" she breathed into the empty room. *Who the hell listens to that shit at this time in the morning anyway?* A persistent throb began at the front of her head.

Relaxing back on the bed, flashes of last night's events went through her mind. She recalled the kisses she had shared with Helen. The nervous flutter returned to her stomach just thinking about it, not to mention the rush of blood to her crotch. Turning over, she pressed her thighs together. A jolt of electricity flowed through her body at the thought of Helen's lips on hers, tentative at first, but soon revealing her desire. Her hand quickly moved between her thighs, ready to relieve the tension, but the ringing of her phone broke the reverie as if scolding her for impure thoughts.

She pulled her phone from the nightstand. Helen's name flashed across the screen. She wondered how they would handle it today, now that it was all out in the open. Helen was her superior.

She considered not answering it at all for a moment. There hadn't been any discussion of their feelings or about how they would act around each other after their kiss. Instead, she'd been shoved into a taxi and sent home. Reluctantly, she accepted the call.

"Morning, Virginia. I've sent someone to pick you up and bring you into the station."

Her mind slowly came into focus as she remembered having a word in Terry's ear after he tried to feel her up.

"Shit! Was I that bad last night?" Surely it wasn't an arrestable offence.

"Terry will be there shortly. You've got about twenty minutes to get ready."

"Fuck! Please tell me you're kidding." The pain in her head began to escalate.

She had a feeling Helen barely heard her reply over her laughter. She had to wait several seconds before there was a suitable gap.

"Seriously?"

"Okay, okay! It's not Terry, but PC Davies will be passing your house in about fifteen minutes, so get cracking."

"Where are we going?" she asked as she walked back down all the steps that she had just expended energy climbing.

"We're going to meet Slim Jim. I hear he's got some good info for us. But first I'm going to buy you breakfast, Virginia."

"Seriously, Guv?" she asked, a little surprised.

"Yes. I think we need to…talk," Helen said quietly, preventing any ears in the vicinity from picking up their conversation.

Any hope that their relationship had been upgraded to a more intimate level faded with Helen's tone. Helen was softening the blow as she shut the door on any chance of anything happening between them.

"Oh, right."

They left the station, walking up the street in silence, towards a short row of shops. She thought for a moment they were going to Helen's house for a *tête-à-tête* but quickly realised that wasn't the case when she saw a sign for Bobby's Café come into view.

Entering the café behind Helen, her stomach churned a little at the smell of grease floating in the air. The café was small and relatively busy, with three of the five tables occupied. A small queue of people stood at the counter where a young man took orders. It had been so long since she'd had a hangover, she had no idea how to make it better. She felt listless as she took a seat opposite Helen.

A woman sidled up to their table, notepad in hand, and they both ordered tea and breakfast cobs. She wasn't quite sure what it included, but the thought of reading the various foods on the laminated menu in front of her made her feel queasy.

Mugs of tea quickly appeared in front of them. She made a grab for hers, hoping it would be the answer to settling her stomach. She felt Helen's gaze on her as she sipped her tea.

"How are you feeling?"

Reluctantly, she looked up, meeting Helen's eyes, forcing what she hoped was a smile onto her face. "I feel a little tatty around the edges but otherwise okay." She tried to skirt over her embarrassment. "Thanks for getting me home last night. I'm sorry. I don't normally get in that kind of state."

"No problem." Helen grinned. "If that's what happens when you spend a few hours in Davies's company, then I should be issuing a restraining order to one of you. Don't worry about it, Virginia. We all need to let our hair down every once in a while."

Was that what she'd done? Let her hair down? This case was definitely getting to her. It wasn't meant to be this hard. She needed her wits about her now more than ever.

Helen filled the silence. "Anyway, I wanted, well, I thought we should talk about what happened in the beer garden."

The uneasiness in Helen's posture as she struggled to maintain eye contact for more than a second or two made her feel compelled to help her out. She wanted to reach out and touch Helen's hand as it gripped the mug in front of her. She imagined the soft, warm skin underneath hers, but the shadow of someone walking by their table made her change her mind.

"Look, I know we have to work together and I'm sorry if I went too far. It was inappropriate. It won't happen again."

"Okay. Erm… Good."

Helen looked away, gulping down her tea.

Helen softly placed the mug on the table, her eyes still cast down, and said, "I've got to make a couple of calls before we meet Slim. Can you wait for breakfast, and I'll meet you back at the station?"

"Sure."

Shocked by her own actions, she watched in surprise as Helen rose from her seat and deposited some money onto the counter before briskly leaving the café, and was glad to be on her own for a while. It hurt to look at Helen, knowing they couldn't be together. She hadn't planned on letting her off the hook, but the sight of her anxiously fiddling with her mug, as she had her mobile phone the night before, was too much. She had done it for both their sakes. It wasn't fair on Helen; she had no intention of sticking around in Warner, and she couldn't see Helen leaving on her account.

Breakfast in hand, she took a slow walk back to the station. She wanted Helen to be her normal, impressive, confident self, not the apprehensive woman that had left her in the café earlier.

Approaching the entrance to the station, she saw Helen emerge, phone jammed between her shoulder and ear as she jotted a note on a scrap of paper. She decided to wait at a respectable distance for her to finish her call; it could have been personal for all she knew.

"Ready?" Helen said, as she joined her in the car park.

"Yep," Her tone was probably a little too cheerful as she handed Helen one of the bagged-up breakfast cobs.

"Our firebug was out again last night, set fire to some garages off Green Lane. One of the owners tried to fight the fire and ended up with smoke inhalation. I've asked Uniform to canvas the area and check any CCTV."

"Shit!" She was almost relieved that Helen was all business as she reeled off the latest updates. Although, if she was being honest, she was a little disappointed that she had been so easy to get over. Not that anything had really happened between them. She certainly didn't come up here searching for a relationship, or whatever it was, between them.

Helen pulled her keys from her pocket and nodded for Kate to follow. "Jarvis's mother was just in the station."

"Really? What did she want?" She mentally chastised herself for asking such a stupid question as she got in the passenger seat. "Sorry."

Helen looked across at Kate with a raised eyebrow. "Well, apart from her son, she wanted to know what we were doing to find him. I told her we'd been to his house, and apart from the missing CCTV footage, we didn't find anything suspicious."

"Did she know about the CCTV?"

Helen pulled out of the car park. "No, which means she didn't know that he had cameras inside his house too."

"What?" she almost dropped her cob. Her stomach began to churn like it was on a spin cycle.

"I know. Every room downstairs apparently. The question is, why? Was he scared of something or what? I just spoke to the crime techs; they didn't find anything at the Jarvis house, no blood, nothing. The drag marks could be perfectly innocent with nothing to compare it to."

"How did she take it?" She asked, her stomach still spinning.

"Um." Helen manoeuvred around a parked car. "Not great, but we don't have anything else yet."

Relief flooded her brain. "He'll turn up sooner or later." She took another look at her cob. She needed to fill her stomach with something to stop the feeling of it eating itself, but now wasn't the time. At least they weren't about to launch another murder inquiry. She made a mental note to check with Uniform about those Whiting lads.

"So, Davies said the secretary was pretty useful yesterday?"

Caught a little off guard, she stared at Helen blankly. Her brain was certainly lacking a few necessary cells this morning. It took her a few moments to realise that she must have seen Davies in the station earlier.

"Uh, yeah," she mumbled and pulled her notebook from her pocket. "Turns out they were pretty friendly, got on well," Scanning her notes, she clarified her statement. "She thinks he was having an affair with someone who worked at the factory at the time he disappeared. Sandy was a bit of a ladies' man, apparently."

"She didn't say who it was?" Helen asked, hopefully.

"Well, he'd had relations with several women at the factory, often staying behind after hours to meet them in his office. She gave me a few names to check out, but she couldn't say who his latest squeeze was."

"Squeeze?" Helen laughed. "Have you been reading James Ellroy or something?"

"Who?" she asked.

Helen looked across at her. "It doesn't matter. It's probably not highbrow enough for you."

After turning the car down a side street near the canal, she turned to Kate again and asked, "What about the money? Does she think he took it?"

"No. She said some people knew each other's passwords. Sandy often wrote his down so he didn't have to remember it. So, basically, a lot of people could have done it, like we thought."

"What if it wasn't the money that made him run away?" Helen ruminated out loud.

She thought for a moment about the company finances that had been gathered in the original case.

"Well, three hundred grand is a lot to an ordinary employee, but maybe not so much to Sandy, whose dad owns a very profitable company. What are you thinking?"

"Not sure yet."

Helen parked up in a layby, giving her a good rear view of the path leading down to the canal. She considered revisiting the conversation they'd had earlier, although "conversation" was a stretch, considering Kate had done all the talking and she had just made an escape. It certainly wasn't the conversation she'd been playing over in her head since waking up early this morning, still thinking about the kiss they shared. She had been expecting a little more resistance from Kate during their conversation, hoped for it maybe. At least then she could have listed all the reasons why it would be a bad idea for anything to happen between them. She knew she'd let Kate down, encouraging something to happen between them, then immediately backing off. She sneaked a look at Kate, who had already zoned out, her head resting on the side window, then looked around at the semi-residential area; it was quiet, just a couple of people with shopping bags from the mini-supermarket around the corner.

After what felt like hours, the silence was killing Helen. She needed something to distract her.

"Do you want to play the alphabet game?"

"The what?" Kate's voice was barely audible in the restricted space of the car.

Sensing the need for encouragement, she tried to garner Kate's interest. "You know, the alphabet game; you chose a subject like cars or something and take it in turns to name one using the letters in the alphabet."

"Okay... films?" Kate offered, sounding livelier.

Helen twisted her lips, showing her distaste. "Um, what about chocolate bars?"

"Chocolate bars? Figures; you probably haven't watched TV since the *Banana Splits* were on."

Helen pushed out her bottom lip. "Hangovers make you mean."

Kate laughed out loud. "Okay," she relented. "Chocolate bars. You start."

Helen smiled gratefully. They were back in their usual conversational rhythm. This was going to be fun.

"Aero."

"Bounty."

"Crunchie."

"Erm..." Kate was quiet for a moment. "Dime."

"Echo."

Kate turned, glaring at Helen. "What the hell is an Echo?"

"Google it if you don't believe me. It was a bit like an Aero, if I recall correctly."

Kate busied her fingers as she searched before releasing a loud groan. "Okay," she said in a defeated tone. "Finger of Fudge."

"Galaxy."

Helen prepared herself for the response to her next answer, but hours of surveillance with various partners had honed her skills at this type of game. "Hanky Panky."

"What? Are you fucking kidding? What the hell is a Hanky Panky?" Without waiting for an answer, Kate busied herself with her phone. "Bollocks. Chocolate drizzled caramel corn with peanuts," she read from the screen of her phone. "Shit." Fingers tapped furiously at the small screen, her leg jiggling in time with her fingers. "Ice Breaker Bar."

Helen giggled as she studied Kate hunched over her phone and said, "If I didn't know any better, I'd say you were cheating, Virginia."

"I don't know what you're talking about, but I do know it's a chocolate bar with mint chips in it,"

Helen smirked at Kate's attempt at innocence. Could she really maintain a purely professional relationship with this woman? Then she offered, "Jazzies," through her grin.

"What? That's not even a bar. Okay, that's it. I'm done!" Kate shoved her phone back in her pocket. "I should have known better than to play a game like this with you."

Helen stifled a laugh at Kate's obvious frustration and said, "It could be a bar on a hot day." Helen blew out a long breath as she settled in her seat. "Someone's a sore loser," she added, glancing back at the wing mirror.

Helen noticed Jim appear in the rear-view mirror, closely followed by another younger man that she didn't recognise. She looked across to Kate to see if she was still awake; she looked lost in her thoughts as she stared out through the windscreen.

"He's here," Helen said quietly before getting out and making her way to the rear of the car. She waited for the two ambling figures to join her.

"Got any food?" Jim asked as his friend dumped his tattered army rucksack on the ground at their feet.

Helen pursed her lips before turning to Kate as she joined them.

"Could you pick up some sandwiches from the Mini Mart around the corner?" she asked Kate, pulling a twenty-pound note from her pocket. She really wasn't in the mood for this today. She couldn't stop thinking about her earlier conversation with Kate. What if she was making a terrible mistake in pushing her away?

Kate tutted lightly, her eye brows knitted together as she glanced at Jim before turning back to face her.

"Are you sure?"

Helen nodded confidently without even giving it a second thought. Even if Jim still looked like the wild man of Borneo, she just wanted this over so she could bite the bullet and talk to Kate properly. The new sidekick didn't look much better; his sinewy figure and patchy facial hair gave him a weaselly look.

Kate took the money from her, and crossing the road, she headed towards the shop.

"No salad!" Jim's sidekick shouted at Kate's back.

Helen watched Kate turn around, she saw her mouth *fuck you* before continuing on her way. Apparently she wasn't the only person to press Kate's buttons today.

Helen kept an eye on Jim's new friend as she made small talk. "So, you're in the market for some new trainers. It better be good, Jim," she said firmly.

Jim grunted as he parted his lips, exposing corn-on-the-cob teeth that looked as if they'd been on the barbeque a little too long.

"New friend?" Helen asked, nodding towards the now-pacing figure behind Jim.

Before Jim could answer, the wiry figure pushed forward a sneer on his face as he spat out his words. "What's it to you?"

Helen took a step back, instinctively making a grab for her baton as Jim moved in front of the wiry figure, holding his hands up to placate him. A passing car prevented her from hearing what Jim said to calm him, but it seemed to work, as he moved away, giving her and Jim space to talk.

Helen felt her patience wearing thin as the agitated figure began to pace vigorously behind Jim. She worried Kate's return would spark him off, make him react. He looked like a junkie waiting for his next fix, and that made him volatile.

"This is Paul. He's got a few…problems," Jim said as if it explained his friend's behaviour.

The shrill sound of Helen's phone drew her attention away from Jim's thin explanation. She knew exactly what Paul's problem was. Declining the call from Davies, she placed her phone on top of the car and got out her notebook. She prepared to write down the information she needed from Jim. As soon as she had what they needed they could go their separate ways.

Before she had a chance to speak, weaselly Paul piped up, asking for money. He jostled Jim, forcing him to try and placate the man again.

Then Jim turned his attention back to Helen. "I've told him there's no money," he said quietly, rolling his eyes before continuing. "I'm pretty sure it's Sandy's trolley on Rutland Lane. It's down the banking. You can't see it from the road."

"And you haven't touched it, right?" Helen clarified as she searched for a fresh page to write down the details while Jim continued to articulate the position of the trolley with hand gestures.

Jim merely shrugged, shaking his head at her question. Which meant he'd probably rifled through it.

Since Paul had backed off a little, Helen rested her pad on the top of her car to jot down the details. She was thankful when a passing car drowned out Jim's continued chatter and Paul began another rant. A familiar loud voice and a rustling sound drew her attention as the car noise abated.

She was surprised, not only to see Kate had returned but that she was pushing a bag of sandwiches against Paul's chest as if fending him off. Paul stumbled but didn't fall, lunging at Kate as he tried to stabilise his body position. Helen caught a glimpse of Jim on the floor behind Paul. What the hell was going on here?

The commotion confused her until she spotted the knife in Paul's hand. She grabbed her baton, snapped it to life, and lunged forward, striking Paul's hand.

Kate ducked at the close proximity of the knife. Losing her footing, she dropped to her knees as the knife skittered along the tarmac out of reach.

Unfortunately, Paul wasn't about to give in. Seeing Kate on the floor, he kicked her hard, his army boots connecting with her torso before Helen could restrain him, her movements hindered by flailing arms and bodies littering the floor.

Kate barrelled towards the pavement. The side of her head cracked on the edge of the kerb just as another crushing foot struck her shoulder. The shriek Kate released made Helen's blood run cold. This was her fault, and she knew it.

She finally managed to slap the cuffs on the man's whirling arm, briskly yanking it around his back and gripping his shoulder with her other hand, effectively restraining him. Shoving him away, she secured him to the metal railing next to the layby. Resisting the urge to give Paul a pummelling, Helen rushed back to Kate and Jim. She helped Kate sit up, resting her back against the side of the car nearest the pavement. Discomfort was evident on Kate's face as she settled back against the car. Panic rose to the surface of Helen's normally serene equilibrium at the sight of blood seeping through Kate's fingers as they pressed against her head. How could she let this happen? She was meant to be the senior officer, turning her back on a potential suspect how stupid could she get.

"Shit! Kate! How bad is it?"

"Uh, I'm okay I think. Are you okay?" Kate asked, fear evident in her voice.

"I'm fine." Helen quickly surveyed Kate's body and swallowed hard when she moved Kate's hand, seeing the deep gash on the side her head just below her hairline. "Fuck!" She quickly grabbed her phone to call in the incident, requesting an ambulance and backup, pulling a wad of tissues from one of her many pockets. "This might hurt a little," she said as she pressed them against the wound on Kate's head.

With her hands full, Helen could only watch as Jim scooted along the floor to rest back against the car next to Kate.

Kate's gaze became distant as she ended her call. Helen dropped her phone and reached out with her free hand to cup the side of Kate's face. Her skin was cool to the touch, and thankfully the contact seemed to bring her focus back as concerned blue eyes looked back at her.

"How's Jim?" Kate asked, looking at the slumped figure next to her.

"He's fine. Just a bit dazed, I think." She said glancing quickly at Jim, she noted the array of sandwiches surrounding them, no doubt that was what Kate had slipped on during the melee.

A slightly faraway look came over Kate's face, rattling Helen's fragile calm. "Kate! Kate, stay with me. The ambulance will be here any minute."

The sound of sirens made Helen finally start to come down from her adrenalin rush. Now all she felt was guilt. She'd made the decision to send Kate off to get bloody sandwiches instead of having her back. Now Jim had been assaulted, and Kate had a sizeable gash on her head, not to mention getting a kicking.

A wry smile appeared on Kate's face.

"What are you grinning at?"

"If I didn't know any better, I'd say you're freaking out."

Out of the corner of her eye, Helen spotted the knife lying on the ground. The blade was long and dirty. The thought of Kate being stabbed with it made the bile rise in her throat.

"I guess this isn't a good time to tell you I don't like the sight of blood. Especially my own," Kate mumbled.

Helen forced a smile on her face before she slipped back into work mode informing the arriving uniformed officers of the situation. She stepped back and watched the paramedics as they attended to Kate and

Jim. She gave Paul the dead eye as he was dragged away to the comfort of a police car.

Realising that the ambulance was preparing for departure, she knew she needed to see Kate before they left. The thought of anything else happening to her was terrifying. She just managed to duck inside before the paramedic closed the doors. Jim was stretched out on the gurney while Kate was trying to dodge the paramedic's probing hands. The fact that Kate was fighting back brought a little warmth back in her heart.

"Hey! Don't let her give you any trouble, Doc." She tried to sound buoyant despite her inner turmoil.

Kate looked up, offering only a grin in reply.

"I'll meet you at the hospital," Helen said as the paramedic encouraged her to remove herself from the doorway he'd opened again.

Kate held her grin, nodding quickly as the door closed.

CHAPTER 11

She stood in her small kitchen, hands gripping the edge of the worktop with all her strength, while all she could feel was the throbbing pain in her shoulder and head. Unwelcome souvenirs of the day's events. As soon as she had arrived at the hospital, she'd quickly made her escape, signing herself out once her wound had been treated. She hadn't wanted to face any awkward questions.

Looking out of the kitchen window to the farmland beyond, she noticed for the first time that there were no glazing bars interrupting the view. The modern window had been crudely fitted, not in keeping with the other Georgian windows in the cottage. *Maybe the landlord had employed the same sloppy tradesmen that had worked at the station in Warner. Square pegs in round holes.*

A knock at the door pulled her from her thoughts. She considered not answering it, but whoever it was, they were persistent as the letterbox flapped violently, echoing in the hallway.

Reluctantly opening the door, she fully expected to see her neighbour informing her about yet another power cut. Instead, a concerned-looking Helen was on the other side.

"Hey! I called the hospital. They said they'd released you already. I wanted to check on you. I brought us some pain relief." Helen brandished a bottle of vodka in one hand and a small blue box in the other.

"Is that official departmental medication?"

"Oh, that's not for you, these are for you." Her hand revealed a box of aspirin. "The vodka's strictly for me after the day you've had."

Stepping aside, she allowed Helen into the small hallway. She wanted to ask what she was doing here but opted for a different question altogether. "Weren't they a bit funny about you purchasing those two items together?" She shut the door and then headed for the kitchen at the back of the house.

"Yes is the short answer to that question. Nice place. A little out of the way but very nice. Very you."

"Thanks." She directed as she entered the kitchen. "I think."

"As long as you overlook the scorched wiring, that is," Helen said as they passed the dark-brown line leading to an old rounded light switch.

She certainly doesn't miss much.

There'd been little choice for her place of residence. Had it been her choice, she certainly wouldn't be living in a pokey cottage in the middle of nowhere.

"Is that safe?"

She ignored the question. She didn't want to think about ending up like Sandy right now. Had Helen just driven out here to check on her well-being, or was there something else on her mind? The warmth and concern Helen had shown seemed to go far beyond just colleagues or friendship.

"How did you get home?"

"I got a taxi back to the station. I didn't see your car in the car park, so I drove home. Am I in trouble?"

Swallowing hard, she hoped the hospital hadn't divulged the fact that she'd discharged herself against their wishes. A taxi had been her only option as she'd figured Helen would be busy. Considering what had happened, she didn't want to get in the way. In truth, she had just wanted to shower and change after rolling around on the floor.

Helen softened her tone. "No. No, not at all. I was worried about you, that's all. I thought they'd keep you in for observation. No concussion?"

Turning away to avoid Helen's concerned eyes, she plucked a glass from a cupboard to prepare Helen a drink. "Nope. Hard head, apparently." She wanted to say she was fine, but the words wouldn't come out. Her mouth was almost watering at the prospect of vodka. She desperately needed something to take the edge off the day.

"Listen, erm…" Helen took a breath. "You were right about that guy today; he was dangerous. Thank you for having my back and protecting me."

Helen's voice was starting to acquire that husky tone she loved. When she turned to face her, her jaw was clenched. She pulled the ice tray from the freezer, trying to hold it together. She needed Helen to be angry with her for getting hurt, not kind and caring for saving her.

"No problem. Just doing my job." She quickly released the top off a vodka bottle. She wanted to take a swig from it. Instead, she attempted to pour Helen a generous amount, but the wobble in her hand prevented that. She closed her eyes to prevent the tears from flowing freely.

A warm hand relieved her of the bottle, pulling her into an embrace.

"Hey, it's okay. I've got you." Helen spoke tenderly as she held Kate's trembling, chilled body. "I've got you," she repeated as she kissed the side of Kate's head. She buried her face in Kate's hair, and the scent of coconut shampoo filled her lungs.

"I saw the knife, I tried to shout, but the traffic was too loud; I didn't know what else to do."

She held Kate firmly, but there was still a tremble in her body. The guilt at her actions frustrated her yet again. Every time she tried to distance herself from Kate, something happened to make her rethink her priorities. It was time to stop fighting it. She wanted to feel the same passion Kate had for her last night. She needed to let her in. Considering Kate's current track record in Warner, she couldn't put it off any longer. She needed this; it was time to make changes in her life.

"I'm sorry," Kate mumbled. She pulled back slightly, leaving Helen's arms slowly.

"It's okay, you've got nothing to be sorry about. You saved me. He could've—" She stopped, not wanting to finish her sentence. Tears stung the back of her eyes as she looked up at Kate's injury.

"Killed you," Kate finished. Her voice was barely above a whisper.

Helen nodded. "Does it hurt?" She raised her eyes to Kate's forehead.

"A little."

"We've charged Wilson with assault, amongst other things, so…" She didn't want to dwell on the details. She stepped closer, looking up to meet Kate's eyes. She saw fear, fear for what she was about to do. Spotting the butterfly stitch poking out of the side of Kate's dressing, she reached up, gently brushing her hair aside to get a better look at the injury.

She locked eyes with Kate again. "I'm so sorry you got hurt."

"It's nothing."

Trailing her hand down the side of Kate's face, the soft skin was warm under her touch. They were both still for a moment. Before Kate could say anything else, she leant forward and pressed their lips together.

It was such a relief when Kate reached out and pulled their bodies together. Wrapping her arms around Kate, she slowly parted her lips, inviting Kate inside. The kiss was languid as their tongues met, and a fire seemed to spark in Kate as Helen felt herself being pushed back against the worktop. Kate was all around her, overloading every sensation she had. The heat from Kate's mouth made her light-headed as she pushed away any lingering doubts she had, her muscles relaxing into Kate's warm, firm body pressing against her. There were no thoughts of consequences, only want and need, as the intense heat flooded her body, the scent of coconut lingering as she circled Kate in her arms, relishing the bubbling fervour. With a single, audible breath, Kate rested her forehead against hers. Helen didn't want to stop. She moved her lips to the side of Kate's face, trailing kisses down her neck, savouring the scent of her freshly showered skin.

"Can you stay?" Kate whispered after she broke the embrace.

She had no intention of letting this slip away from her now. Her body was aching to be touched, to feel Kate's skin against her own. She took Kate's hand and brought it to her lips kissing the palm before nodding her head.

Kate kept hold of Helen's fingers all the way upstairs to her bedroom. When they passed the bathroom, Helen stopped in her tracks, forcing Kate to do the same.

"Could I take a quick shower? Someone was a little too free and easy with their blood earlier today, and I haven't had time to change." A smile appeared on Kate's face.

"Sure. Let me get you a fresh towel."

Stepping to one side, she pulled at the flaps of a cardboard box next to the wall of the bathroom and pulled out a large floral towel and handed it to Helen, who frowned at the gaudy offering. "God! You really haven't unpacked at all, have you?"

"I've been a little…busy."

Helen removed her coat and handed it to Kate before she made her way into the bathroom.

As she removed her clothes, she could hear Kate moving about. The sound of crockery being piled up and drawers being slammed shut made her chuckle. She couldn't afford to think too much about what was happening here. For a change, she needed to let go, enjoy the moment for what it was, regardless of the consequences.

One shower later, wrapped in a towel and feeling refreshed, Helen moved towards the noise in the next room. She stood for a moment, watching Kate plumping up pillows and straightening the bed sheet.

"Would you like a hand with that?"

Kate spun around to face her. "Nope. All done."

Helen moved from the doorway to within Kate's reach. "Thank God. I've never quite mastered the hospital corner." She stood there transfixed.

Her bare feet dug into the rug surrounding Kate's bed. She'd thought about this moment so many times in the last few days, and now she wasn't quite sure where to start. Her inner temperature rose, and yet, goosebumps broke out on her bare arms as she moved closer, her hands reaching for Kate's waist.

Helen wanted to regain the closeness they'd had downstairs, feel the warmth of Kate's body as her arms circled a firm waistline. Their eyes locked, and she had an overwhelming need to be honest with her.

"I haven't been able to stop thinking about the other night."

A hint of a grin appeared on Kate's face, almost forcing Helen's eyes to roll back in her head. When would she learn to temper her comments in front of this woman?

Helen's hands gripped lower as she steered Kate backwards towards the bed. No more talking. Approaching the bed, Helen felt warm fingers on her cheek before pushing damp hair from her shoulder.

They locked gazes. "I didn't mean what I said in the café."

"I know." Helen's eyes focused on the parted lips in front of her.

"Ouch!" Kate flinched at Helen's roaming hand.

"What? More injuries?"

She pulled up Kate's T-shirt, exposing her left side. A dark yellow bruise sat just above Kate's left hip bone.

"Is that from today too?" Helen asked, confused; it looked older. She turned Kate's body around to face the window to get a better look.

"No. Last week. Courtesy of Fireman Sam."

Kate pulled up her T-shirt more.

"Shit!" Helen ran a finger around the outline of the bruise. She looked up, meeting Kate's gaze. "He caused the collapse, didn't he?"

Kate nodded. "He found me filming and rushed towards me, carrying a big metal rod thing. He caught it on the ceiling as he came at me."

"He hit you with it?" Graham Brown quickly went to the top of her shit list.

Kate shook her head. "He tripped and fell against me with it in his hands."

"Arsehole. You've been here less than a month, and I've already nearly broken you."

"It's fine. It only hurts if you poke it."

With a last look at the bruise, Helen let her hand move up Kate's torso. It reached the swell of her exposed breast, and Helen took her time, exploring the soft skin with her thumb, circling the hardened nipple. She held Kate's gaze, enjoying her reaction. Kate's lips parted slightly. She moved her hand between Kate's breasts. Slowly, it moved up to her neck, removing Kate's T-shirt in the process as Kate lifted her arms up to assist in the removal. She did flinch a little as she raised her right arm.

Helen let her hand roam over Kate's body. She basked in the softness beneath her fingers, circling the darkening bruise on Kate's shoulder. The thought it provoked made a tinge of guilt stir in the pit of her stomach.

When Helen stepped closer, Kate pulled at the tucked-in end of the towel. She it slip to the floor. Helen grasped for Kate's hips, pulling them together. She felt her body react immediately as she slipped her thigh between Kate's and pressed her body firmly into hers. She couldn't wait any longer. She fumbled with the waistband of Kate's trousers. They slipped easily over her hips, but Kate's strong hands were already pushing her back onto the bed.

So Helen lay back as Kate stepped out of her joggers. Helen quirked an eyebrow as Kate climbed on the bed straddling her hips. She'd had no underwear on.

But she had no time to dwell on that. Helen felt her vulnerabilities rise to the surface as Kate ran her hands up her torso and she hovered over Helen, resting her weight on one arm. With her free hand, Kate traced the length of Helen's body, cupping a breast on the way up to her face.

Kate's gaze found hers. "I love your eyebrows."

"You do?" Helen replied, unable to stop one of them from rising at Kate's words.

"I do. They're so *expressive*." Using her thumb, Kate traced the curving shape as she settled her body on top of Helen's.

"I love your arse," Helen said as her hands roamed lower, skimming over glutes before cupping both her cheeks, pressing Kate's body firmly against her again.

"I know." Kate grinned down at Helen, her hand caressing the side of her face.

Helen felt the flush of embarrassment on her exposed skin. "How?" She couldn't believe she had been caught ogling.

"I've seen you looking. Why do you think I stopped wearing my long coat? I've risked getting pneumonia just to keep your eyes occupied."

Helen blinked a couple of times, recalling the short jacket Kate had been wearing lately despite the cooler weather. "Seriously?"

Kate nodded as she adjusted her legs, pressing her thigh tight against Helen's hot core, sending a heatwave through her body as she felt her arousal paint Kate's thigh. She wanted to explore every inch of Kate's body before leaving this room.

At the connection, Helen groaned, raising her head to bring their lips together in a crush even as Kate continued to grind against her. She raised her hips in time with Kate's actions.

She was so enjoying the contact. She felt a loss as Kate pulled away, then caught the look in her eye; she could tell Kate had other plans. Payback for handcuffing her to her car, no doubt. But she was powerless to resist anymore.

Kate moved down her body, sucking a nipple into her mouth as fingers traced the line of her stomach, moving lower. Her thighs were pushed apart. Helen obliged, watching Kate settle between her legs, her anticipation growing as the scent of her own arousal filled the room. The warmth of Kate's tongue on her delicate lips was almost enough to send her over the edge. It forced her to grip the sheet below her as she struggled to hold on, her head falling back against the bed.

Kate was relentless in her progress, surrounding her clit, making Helen reach out blindly for her, tangling her hands in Kate's long hair. Every stroke lit the blue touch paper stoking the fire inside her. She rocked her hips, encouraging Kate to take more.

Helen clenched her hands tighter. Her orgasm was firmly claiming her, pushing her hips forward a final time as she came against Kate's lips. Yet she was one gasping for air, and she collapsed back on the bed.

Balancing on her knees, Kate wiped the juices from her chin. The grin of accomplishment on her face hadn't escaped Helen's notice. Still panting, she watched Kate edge forward, her hands skimming up the sides of Helen's thighs towards her breasts.

Her composure returned. Helen reached for Kate's hands, pulling them towards her, forcing Kate on top of her. The aroma of arousal had woken up a primal need to have this woman completely. Throwing a hand around Kate's neck, she quickly brought their lips together, their tongues battling for authority as she tasted her own arousal on Kate's lips. In an effort to gain control, she turned the tables, flipping them over. A wide grin plastered on her lips as she moved forward, covering Kate's body with her own, enjoying the feel of Kate's body moving below hers. Their thighs seemed to part naturally as their bodies entwined.

Kate wrapped her legs around Helen's hips, pressing their bodies together.

After guiding their lips back towards each other, Helen then pushed her tongue deep into Kate's willing mouth. A push of Kate's thighs back towards the bed exposed her fully. Helen slipped a confident hand between them and caressed Kate's mound, groaning at the rush of wetness on Kate's parted lips. She pushed a finger deep inside and felt the tight walls surrounding it. Helen relished the shocked look on Kate's face. She removed it briefly, then added another, slowly both in to the hilt. Kate's hips thrust to meet her movements.

Helen pressed her hot centre against Kate's right hip bone, grinding against her in time with the thrust of her own fingers. She knew it wouldn't take long; she was so close to orgasm just being inside Kate. She pulled away from Kate's wanton lips.

"You feel so good. You're going to make me come again."

Kate growled in response as her fingers continued to thrust. Only moments later, her body gave in. Her entire frame shivered as she pressed against Kate's hip, a throb emanating from her core as she came.

Finally at long last, Helen got her breath back. "I want to taste you," she whispered against Kate's lips. Rolling them both over, she spotted the slightly confused look on Kate's face as she hovered above, no doubt at the brisk change of position.

"I think you like being on top, so…" Helen raised her eyebrows, encouraging Kate to climb up her body. "You need to…" She nodded her head upwards.

Springing into action, Kate got to her knees, allowing Helen to adjust her position while she moved higher up, stretching an arm out to grip the flimsy headboard at the top of the bed, settling her knees just above Helen's shoulders.

She gripped Kate's thighs, pulling them further apart as she flattened her tongue to run it along Kate's entire slit. There was no time to go slow; she wanted to give Kate exactly what she needed. Her tongue firmly circled the hardened clit before sucking it fully into her mouth.

Kate began rocking her hips, pushing herself against Helen's mouth. Releasing Kate's clit allowed Helen to inch lower, pushing her tongue between moist folds. Helen stiffened her tongue, pushing it deep inside as Kate continued to rock her hips, encouraging Helen to go deeper. She hummed at the flutter of muscles around Kate's entrance as she pushed inside her hot centre.

"Oh God," Kate said between ragged pants. Her hips bucked, forcing Helen to hold her firmly as she rode out her orgasm. She lapped at the flood of juices then, reluctant to let Kate escape her clutches. She was far from finished with this woman.

Panting, Kate removed herself. She lay back, slumped against the headboard, her hand reached for Helen's, caressing a breast as she caught her breath.

It revived her. Helen rolled over, climbing on top of Kate's torso. Slipping between her spread thighs, she used her fingers to separate wet lips, exposing the jewel beneath. She then zoned in on Kate's clit once more, teasing it with her tongue. The raspy stutter that emanated deep in

Kate's chest encouraged her even further. She had never been with another woman that made her want to fuck as much as Kate did. She climbed up the bed and stretched her body out over Kate's, grinding her hot centre against Kate's hardened clit.

With the effect this woman had on her, Helen didn't plan on sleeping anytime soon.

CHAPTER 12

THERE WAS MOVEMENT AROUND HER, and she stretched out in search of Helen's body. She felt the ache in her muscles from last night's activities, but that wasn't about to stop her. As her eyes focused in the shadowy room, she saw Helen kneeling on the side of the bed, fully dressed. She swallowed back her disappointment, but the warm smile on Helen's face went some way to ease the sting.

Helen tenderly ran the back of her knuckles down the side of her face. "Morning. I made you some tea." Helen nodded towards the side table.

At the gentleness in Helen's voice, she reached out and stroked her hand along Helen's thigh. "Thanks. Why don't you come back to bed for a bit?"

Helen sighed. "I can't. I have to go home and change before work." She moved closer, kissing her softly on the lips. "I had a really great time last night." She stayed within kissing distance.

"Me too," she croaked out.

Depositing another kiss on her lips, Helen reluctantly dragged herself off the bed. As she moved around the room towards the door, she turned back to Kate. "Don't be late. I need my wingman."

Chuckling at Helen's words, she watched her leave, then turned over. She needed five more minutes to think about this new development. So this could be considered another corner turned in their relationship. How many more corners might there be?

When she arrived at the station, she found Helen had been called to a departmental meeting. She couldn't remember Helen saying anything about it before she'd left her place earlier.

She took the initiative and got to work on her incident report for yesterday before trying to make up for the time they had lost thanks to Paul Wilson. The list acquired from Sandy's secretary, plus a couple of hours research, and she'd located the three women she had mentioned in her interview. Unfortunately, the first of Sandy's women, Karen Hill, had died a month after Sandy had disappeared. A second had also died, two years ago, of breast cancer. The third was living with her wife in Devon. After a quick telephone conversation, she decided to cross her off the list, although three hundred grand would have gone some way towards buying a decent house down there.

Frustrated, she worked the list again, looking deeper into the death of Karen Hill. The woman had not only been married at the time but had also committed suicide by stepping in front of a train. The secretary had said Sandy liked married women. After making a request for the original file, she began searching for Hill's next of kin. Scanning the text on the screen, she read under her breath, "Survived by her husband of three years, Martin Hill, aged thirty-two." Making note of his name, she moved on.

The second woman, Frances Moody, had also been married at her time of employment at the factory, but was widowed some years later, leaving two sons, Lawrence and Julian—both had been in their twenties. She wrote down their names for a more extensive search. There was only so much she could do without a time of death. She checked her inbox in case Dr Nicholls had sent his report through. Nothing.

Approaching thuds on the stairs made her look up from her computer. PC Davies entered the office, heading in her direction.

Davies stopped near her desk. "DS Wolfe—"

"Kate," she interrupted. They had had this conversation the other day, yet he seemed to have forgotten already.

Davies took a breath and started again with a slight smile. "Kate, the DCI just called; she wants you to head out to Langdale Woods. The local PADI diving club has reported a car dumped in the quarry lake. They think it's a..." Davies looked at the large sticky note attached to his right forefinger. "Could be a red Audi—SUV, they reckon—but there's no plates on it."

Shit! She felt the prickly heat of panic break out on her skin as Davis's words sank in. Jarvis's car. "What?" she asked, struggling to make sense of what Davies had just said. "What were they doing out there?"

"Checking the lake out in preparation for running courses later in the year. There's a tow truck and CSI on the way to see about retrieving the car. The Guv wants you to oversee the operation. Said she'll meet you there shortly." Davies offered her the sticky note, containing the information.

Her eyes glazed over as they scanned it. She wasn't sure what to do first. "What's this?" she said, pointing to the scrawl at the bottom of the note.

"Oh, the DCI said you might want to use the old quarry road to get on the site. Takes you straight round to the lake," Davies said, still hovering.

She looked up, about to ask him if there was anything else when he beat her to it.

Pointing to her head injury, he asked, "How are you feeling after your brawl? The DCI was quite worried about you."

The comment took her aback, she'd seen Helen's concern first-hand, but hadn't expected her to let anyone else see it too. "There's no rest for the wicked, at least, not according to DCI Taylor." She replied with a wink as she waved the sticky note.

Davies smiled at her before turning to leave.

Sticking the note to her desk, she waited for Davies to disappear before quickly writing up her notes on the search she had conducted for Sandy's lover. Opening another window on her computer, she pulled up a map of the area, finding the service road she needed. She gathered her stuff and left for the quarry.

❖

Walking up towards the lake, Helen spotted Kate leaning against her car, arms folded across her chest. She looked deep in thought, her chin almost touching her chest. From the description the divers had given, it sounded like it could be Jarvis's car. She figured it was playing on Kate's mind after her response to his disappearance.

"You found it alright, then," she said as she rounded Kate's car.

Kate turned, a now familiar smile on her face before she said, "Have satnav, will travel! How was your meeting?"

Helen let out a long breath as she took up her position next to Kate. The fresh air of the forest was doing little to quieten her inner thoughts.

"As expected. All budget cuts and pressure to close murder and arson cases before we've even got any key evidence, let alone suspects." Helen was worn out by the bureaucracy and was considering a lobotomy prior to the next meeting. She was even more annoyed that it was a little too much reality, taking the shine off a perfectly good morning, after the night before.

Kate's hand came to gently rest on her forearm. "Don't let them grind you down, Guv."

Helen looked into Kate's eyes. She was comforted by her touch, even though she was the spark that was edging her towards a change in her life. "I told them our mini crime-wave was probably only temporary, as it only started when you arrived; so to give it a few months and it'll disappear." She looked away, wanting to bite back those last words. Why was she taking it all out on Kate? It wasn't her fault she was only temporary, and she certainly wasn't responsible for the inner workings of the police service. She must have been more depressed by her meeting than she first thought.

Kate ignored her dig. "Well, maybe I should stick around then, and keep you in work."

The words had barely left Kate's mouth before a loud booming voice in the distance prevented Helen from responding. They both turned towards the voice, calling Helen.

Walking in unison around the lake towards the gaggle of people, no doubt discussing the best way to extricate a vehicle from a flooded quarry, Helen tried to process Kate's last words.

"DCI Taylor?"

"Yes," Helen replied to the white-suited man. She wondered at his outfit, but she knew that you couldn't take a chance at knowing where the crime scene started and finished in his job.

"Jim Delaney, senior scene investigator." He reached out a hand in greeting. "It's definitely a red Audi Q2—no tags, but there's quite a lot of crap down there. Might take us a while to get it out. Windows are open, so whatever was in the car is a total loss. Don't know about the boot till we get it out."

Helen looked out at the water, watching the divers as they took a break. "How do you think it got there?" she asked, hoping he wouldn't go with the obvious, sarcastic answer.

"Well. From its position, facing out in this direction towards us…" Jim motioned with his arms. "It looks like it came from up there somewhere," he said, and pointed towards the high side of the quarry.

Helen looked up to where his hand rested. The layered quarry face stretched out a good fifteen to twenty metres above the surface of the water.

"Okay. I'll get Uniform to sweep the area, see what turns up." She turned back to see the colour had drained from Kate's face at some point during this conversation. She frowned, giving her a second look as she asked her next question. "How long do you think it'll take?"

"Hard to say. There's some other debris in the way that we need to move first. Few hours, at least." Jim said.

Helen checked her watch. They probably had around four hours of daylight left. "Thanks." It was almost two in the afternoon. Hopefully they would be able to secure the vehicle today. She turned to leave, not wanting to delay their progress.

Kate jogged to catch up with her. "It's Jarvis's car!"

It sounded like a statement rather than a question. Helen knew it was far too much of a coincidence, but she didn't want to make Kate feel any worse than she already did.

"Do you think he's in the boot?" Kate asked, anxiety evident in her voice.

"Could be, or someone's gone to a lot of effort to get rid of the car." Experience told Helen that you don't just steal a car like that to dump it. As they neared Kate's car, she slowed, waiting for Kate to appear next to her. She didn't want to make Kate feel guilty for her lack of enthusiasm for the Jarvis case. She knew she'd be beating herself up enough already.

"It's not your fault, you know."

Kate struggled to make eye contact with her.

"He's been missing for weeks," Helen continued in a softer voice.

Kate let out a long breath. "I know." She met Helen's gaze. "I'll organise the search up the top."

"It's fine. I'll do it. I need some air after this morning." Helen looked around to make sure they were still alone before she continued. "We, erm… we didn't get much time to talk yesterday." Helen waited for the officer walking over to the crime scene team to get out of earshot. Turning back to

Kate, she saw the infectious grin on her face. She couldn't resist referring to it. "We were a little too preoccupied to talk shop."

"Far too occupied," Kate replied, still smiling as she leaned against the side of her car.

"I took a quick look at Rutland Lane, the place Slim gave us yesterday where Sandy's missing stuff might be," Helen clarified. Kate had missed out on this part of the conversation she'd had with Slim. "Looks like it's all there. Could be the place we've been looking for. Crime scene techs are checking it out."

Even thought it had been several weeks, Helen had everything crossed that they might find something that would lead them to the vehicle and driver responsible. She was certainly blowing the Forensics budget this month. Now she needed results to justify the expense.

"You owe someone a pair of Nikes, then."

"He's already left a message to remind me," Helen said. It was a little surprising, considering his friend's antics yesterday.

"Cheeky bastard." Kate offered.

Helen smiled at her indignation. Although if it weren't for his mate, Kate wouldn't have a gash on her head, and then maybe she wouldn't have spent the night with her.

"Whereabouts is it? Any potential witnesses? CCTV?"

Helen scrunched up her nose as she leant on the car next to Kate. "No, it's just a quiet backroad, but there's coverage in nearby streets." She'd already planned to get Davies to look through it as soon as possible, as soon as they got a rough time of death. "Anyway, how are you feeling today? Your injuries, I mean," Helen clarified, knowing Kate would more than happily give her a rundown on last night's antics.

Kate released a giggle. "Not too bad. The dull ache has subsided; it's only painful when I move around too quickly."

Helen smiled. "I guess I should have offered to give you the day off."

"Would you have kept me company?"

Helen stepped closer, almost invading Kate's personal space. She kept her voice low. "I would've loved to have stayed longer. Maybe next time you could stay at my place as it's a little closer to work."

Kate's eyes widened at Helen's words. "Next time? So you think there'll be a *next time*?"

Helen kept her eyes firmly on Kate's as she forced a small smile on to her lips. There was definitely going to be a next time—many next times, if Helen had anything to do with it. Maybe it hadn't been a good idea to get involved with Kate, but that didn't change the way she felt about her. It didn't change the way she'd felt in her arms last night when they'd made love. Made love. Yes, that's what had happened. And it scared and exhilarated her at the same time. Standing there, looking into Kate's eyes, Helen hoped that what she was seeing was a reflection of her own feelings.

The ringing of a phone gradually pierced the bubble they were both in. Realising it was hers, Helen reluctantly dragged her gaze from Kate's. She loved playing verbal tennis with Kate. She wasn't just physically attracted to her; it was more than that. They clicked.

"Taylor," Helen said into her phone. "Okay, thanks." Helen glanced up from her phone. "Nicholls has just sent through his report on Sandy's injuries, possible vehicles and time of death."

"Great. At least we'll get a window of opportunity."

"With a bit of luck."

"I've done some digging on the women Sandy might have been involved with, tried to narrow it down."

"Anything?" Helen asked hopefully.

"Well, one is living with her wife in Devon, so I crossed her off the list. The other two are dead: one only a month after Sandy disappeared, the other a couple of years ago. I need to do a bit more to track down their various next of kin. And I've requested the report on the first one that committed suicide."

"Suicide?" The cogs started to turn in Helen's head. "Okay. I'll stay here for a while. See if we actually get the car out today. You go back to the office and go through Dr Nicholls's report. Use your amazing IT skills to try and generate a list of possible cars in the area so we can start narrowing down the search."

Kate nodded, pulling her keys from her pocket, she began moving around to the driver's side of the car.

"And Kate," Helen followed her closely, waiting for Kate to turn around. "There will be a next time."

Kate's left eyebrow rose as a smile spread across her face.

Without waiting for more of a reply, Helen strolled off towards a uniformed officer.

CHAPTER 13

DISSECTING DR NICHOLLS'S REPORT WAS taxing. It took several attempts to isolate the information she was looking for. According to Nicholls, Sandy had died between nine and ten days before he was discovered. She imagined Nicholls conducting his maggot experiments and shivered at the thought. She opened a calendar and counted the days: Sandy died between Tuesday the fourteenth and Wednesday the fifteenth of February. The house fire was started at approximately 1 a.m. on Friday the twenty-fourth, according to the fire investigation; fire services were called at 2 a.m., and Sandy's body was discovered at 3 a.m. The vague timeframe was a little disappointing; forty-eight hours was a pretty big window. She mapped out the timeline on the wipe board to show Helen later.

It also posed another question. When had Sandy been moved to the house? She tried to recall how far back the footage from Doreen Platt's CCTV went. She flipped through her notebook; she knew she had made a note when she started reviewing the material.

The recordings started from the beginning of February. At least they had a chance of capturing the body being dumped—if the killer had passed the Platt's house.

Moving through the report, she found the excruciating, detailed description of Sandy's injuries and skimmed over it. There were diagrams relating to the impact of the body against the vehicle. According to Nicholls, the vehicle had some form of skirt below the bumper, preventing Sandy's legs from bending underneath. He estimated it to have a lower bumper height of around 230 millimetres and an upper bumper height of around

485 millimetres. Thankfully, he'd provided a list of possible manufacturers and vehicle types. Volkswagen, Toyota, Hyundai, Seat, and BMW, most of which looked to be large family cars, manufactured over the last fifteen years.

Blowing out a breath, she knew that was going to be one hell of a long list. A search of such vehicles registered in the surrounding areas alone resulted in a list of almost four hundred possibilities. *Shit.* She needed to find a way of narrowing it down. She made a mental note to call Forensics to see if they had pulled any paint flecks from Sandy's clothing. At least then they would know what colour vehicle they were looking for.

Putting a call out for PC Davies, she asked him to check with the local garages for repairs to the types of cars on Nicholls's list, just in case. Pushing back from her desk, she realised that she was finally alone in the now-quiet room. She looked around, wondering when exactly everyone had left. The events of the day had filled her head with so many questions, but she had still found time to think about last night. Leaning back in her chair, she could see that all the blinds were down in Helen's office, but the door was ajar, inviting her in. She hadn't even realised that Helen was back at the station.

The room looked dark, but as she got closer, she could see that there was a desk lamp on. Pushing the door open a little, she leaned against the door frame, watching Helen read a report as she perched on the front of her desk.

A few moments passed before Helen looked up, meeting her gaze. They had kept their distance from each other all day, but Helen apparently couldn't keep the grin off her face as they held each other's stare.

"Everyone's gone for the night, Guv. Is there anything else?" She moved inside, closing the door behind her.

Helen stretched out her legs in front of her and crossed her ankles. "I was just reading Uniform's report on the Whiting clan. They all have alibis, apparently. They're in the process of checking them out. Any more luck on Sandy's romantic antics?"

She shook her head as she stood in front of her. "Finding the car that hit him might be even trickier. I've asked Davies to check out the repair garages in the area."

She scolded herself. She didn't want to talk shop now. Placing her feet either side of Helen's crossed ankles, she continued to move up her long legs, watching the expression change on Helen's face as she got closer to her torso.

"What are you...?" she started to say. "Someone might..." she tried again.

She stopped moving, their bodies only inches apart, placing a finger over Helen's lips to stop her from continuing with her admonishment. When she replaced her finger with her lips, her kiss was gentle, teasing at first, until Helen reacted.

She smiled to herself as Helen threw caution to the wind and pulled her closer. Thoughts of being caught in a compromising position with a junior officer must have slipped her mind.

With a press of her crotch onto Helen's thigh, she began to gently rub against the firm flesh below. There was dampness between her thighs.

Helen's response was an immediate move to Kate's trousers. She stealthily undid the buttons and zipper. Slipping her hand inside, she lowered her thigh just enough to cup her hot centre.

She wrapped an arm around Helen's neck and buried her hand in her hair while pressing harder against the hand between her thighs. She rushed towards her orgasm, pulling away from Helen's swollen lips to conceal her moan against Helen's neck as she came.

When she pulled back to look at Helen, she saw only desire in her darkened eyes, a small grin of accomplishment on her lips. As much as she wanted to reciprocate, she knew better than to push her luck. She was just about to suggest meeting up later when a wiggle of Helen's fingers brought a fresh wave of spasms, making the words catch in her throat.

Hearing the giggle in Helen's voice as she asked "What's up?" made her act fast. Grabbing Helen's fingers, she stepped back, allowing her to force two of Helen's fingers inside her. The shock on Helen's face made it all worthwhile as she adjusted her posture for the best position.

"Wiggle them all you like now!"

The challenge set, Helen began slowly thrusting her fingers inside her. She groaned in pleasure once more as the pads of Helen's fingers massaged her G-spot with each thrust.

She frantically slipped her hand inside the waistband of Helen's trousers, quickly finding the wetness she wanted. Using two fingers, she circled Helen's clit with every thrust Helen made inside her.

Those searching fingers quickly brought her to orgasm once more. Their kisses were frantic as they panted through their pleasure. Helen's hips began to twitch desperately against her fingers, signalling she was close. Keeping her fingers firm, she felt the release in Helen's body and cradled her firmly as it shuddered.

"I'm not sure I can walk after that," she whispered, her voice a little husky.

"Are you trying to put me in an early grave or just get me fired?" Helen replied, blowing out a breath.

She pulled away and asked the question that she had originally come in to ask. "Would you like to meet up later?"

Helen moved forward, using her free hand to remove damp hair from her face. "I can't. I have to visit a sick relative."

She raised her eyebrows at Helen's statement to hide her disappointment. She had been hoping for a replay of last night. "Nothing serious, I hope." Her mind drifted back to the phone call Helen had received. She was relieved it wasn't Helen that was ill.

Helen ignored the question as she quirked an eyebrow and said, "I think I might need a lie-down."

Releasing a giggle, she spotted the tissues on Helen's desk. They were probably for distraught victims on the worst days of their lives. Freeing her hand from Helen's underwear, she sucked on her own moist digits, relishing the taste of Helen as she looked directly at her.

Helen's eyes narrowed as she leant forward, capturing her lips as soon as the fingers had left her mouth.

"We shouldn't be doing this." Helen leant back on her desk with her free hand.

She felt a sudden sense of bewilderment. *Is this how she breaks it to me, with her fingers still inside me?* Her face must have exposed her concerns.

"Here, I mean," Helen quickly added. "We should definitely be doing this, just not here."

Relief flooded through her. "Thank God, because I really like doing this with you." She gently removed Helen's hand from inside her underwear.

Backing away, she buttoned up her trousers. She stepped to Helen's side and then moved closer, softly kissing Helen on the lips. "Good night, Guv."

She winked as she backed away, then turned towards the door. She closed it softly behind her.

CHAPTER 14

SPOTTING KATE'S CAR IN THE small driveway, Helen parked outside the vacant house next door. She'd been curious to see where Kate lived on her first visit. Now she was just thinking up excuses to return. Walking towards the front door, she felt the flutter begin to rise in her stomach as her mind drifted to what had transpired last night in her office. Kate Wolfe could easily become someone who could make her rethink her priorities. That thought alone scared and excited her at the same time.

"A domestic goddess too, I see?" Helen grinned down at the gloves covering Kate's hands.

"Am I late?" Kate asked as she pulled back a glove to look at her watch.

"No. I couldn't sleep. Kept thinking about our arsonist."

"Oh!"

As Kate followed her into the kitchen, Helen noted the disappointed tone her single-word response.

After tossing her rubber gloves onto the worktop, Kate picked up her mug. "Tea?"

Helen's response was swift. Shaking her head, she stepped towards Kate and took the mug from her hands, placing it back on the worktop. She kept her eyes on Kate's as she lifted her hand to cup her cheek. "To be honest, I just wanted to see you. Alone."

She moved closer still, bringing their lips together, releasing a barely audible groan as they moved against each other. She had been mulling over ways to catch the firebug, but she was also unable to stop thinking about Kate.

Helen felt her shirt being grasped, bringing their bodies firmly together as they settled back against the worktop. Their kisses soon became heated as their bodies melted together.

Kate pulled away from her lips. "If we don't stop soon, I'll be forced to take you upstairs again."

Helen groaned at Kate's words. She continued to leave lingering kisses down her neck. "You can't say things like that to me now."

As she breathed in the fresh floral scent from Kate's hair, she knew she was acting like an infatuated teenager, but she didn't care. It had been so long since she'd woken up thinking about something other than work. Or, worse, Julia. Kate was a breath of fresh air in her tired life. She certainly wasn't like any other police officer Helen had met before, and she liked that, more and more each day.

Reluctantly, she stepped back from Kate, seeing the flush of desire on her cheeks and neck. Looking up to meet her gaze, she could see the passion mirrored in Kate's darkened eyes too.

Glancing up at Kate's injury, she was glad to see some of the inflammation had subsided.

With a breath, Helen tried to slip back into work mode as she remembered what else had brought her to Kate's door so early.

"Okay. I got the latest fire report through. They found a beer can with fingerprints and DNA right next to the garage. They're trying to match it to the cigarette butts they found at the house on Morley Lane. I'm betting it's at least one of the Whiting lads. The fingerprints are already confirmed as Kyle Whiting's. We had his fingerprints on file from before."

"I thought all three had alibis for when the fires were started," Kate queried.

Helen released a long breath, annoyed that the uniformed officer hadn't been clearer when he reported back to her. "Well, it turns out two of them alibied each other. So, basically, two of them, Curtis and Kyle, don't have solid alibis. With the image you pulled off the CCTV, we've got enough for a warrant to search their place. Just waiting for it to come through."

"Sounds promising…Guv," Kate smirked as she stepped forward, encroaching on Helen's space. She slipped her hand inside Helen's jacket, and the familiar warmth of a hand tracing the line of her body made Helen shiver. Her raised eyebrows did nothing to deter Kate as she pressed her lips against hers. It took only a second for Helen to react, lips parted as arms wrapped around Kate's torso, pulling their bodies together once more.

———◆———

She was tired of clicking her heels while they waited for the search warrant to come through. The tape measure she had found earlier in her garage was burning a hole in her pocket. Jotting a quick note on a Post-it to let Helen know she would meet her outside, she walked into Helen's office and watched her on the phone for a moment. She could see the buzz in her eyes at the thought of catching the arsonist, closing one half of their case. It looked good on her.

Helen met her gaze. She was smiling, sparkling even. She stuck the Post-it on Helen's desk, waiting for a response.

Helen read the note, nodding.

She quickly made her way outside. Taking the tape measure out of her pocket, she did a quick check of the car park before squatting down out of sight. Drawing out the tape, she held the end against the ground as she checked the height of the bumper on PC Kirk's white Subaru Impreza. It was a wild idea, but she couldn't resist checking. It was like a chicken pox itch she just had to scratch regardless of the fallout, although in truth she hoped to do this particular act discreetly. Her disappointment was instant: the height was all wrong. Kirk must have had some custom work done and not recently, by the faded look of the bumper. She even checked the back and side to see if there was any change. It was still too low. Unfortunately, this wasn't the car they were looking for.

A whistle behind her made her jump up in fright. Standing, she could see Kirk standing next to the driver's side of his car. He was stony-faced as he glared at her. They had had very little contact since the evening in the pub, and the thought of him being close to her made her skin crawl. She could easily imagine him pulling the wings off flies when left to his own devices, just to see them suffer.

"Now, what could you possibly be doing down there, *Virginia*?" Kirk sneered.

Deciding it was best to try and defuse the situation, she tried to play it down and said, "Uh, nothing. Just thinking. Doing a bit of research."

Kirk pressed his key fob, unlocking his car. Opening the driver's door, he threw his bag onto the passenger's seat before refocusing his attention on her.

"With a tape measure?"

"Oh!" She casually threw the tape measure in the air a few inches, catching it easily. "Yep." She didn't bother to bluff an excuse, not that she had one anyway.

Kirk stood inside the open door on the driver's side, resting his hands along the top of the door and the roof of his car. "If I didn't know any better, I'd say you were checking the height of my car bumper."

"Just getting an idea of the type of car we're looking for. Don't worry, you're off the hook. It's the wrong height." She tried not to let her disappointment show, but she knew she'd been unsuccessful by the grin on Kirk's face.

"Is that what they teach you down there in London? You're wasted up here. Maybe you should get a job in professional standards."

She bristled at his inference that she was a turncoat. "Fuck you!" she threw at him as he secured himself in his car.

Kirk lowered his driver's side window. "I tried that already," he mocked before putting his window back up. The ignition fired up, and he quickly reversed out of his space, revving his engine a little too much as he glared at her through the windscreen.

Standing her ground, she smiled back at him. She almost wanted to send him over the edge, to force his hand. If he ploughed towards her, she had options. There were cars on either side of her. She felt confident she could clamber over either one to get away if she had to.

Kirk made the first move, speeding forward, turning his wheel at the last minute to stop perpendicular to the space he'd been parked in, forcing her to step back.

She saw the laughter on his face as she caught her breath. He gave her a quick one-finger salute before pulling away.

"Making friends?" Helen said, walking towards her as she stood in an empty parking space, her head turning towards Kirk as he drove towards the exit.

It took a second for her to find her voice. "Not exactly." She wondered how much Helen had seen of her interaction with Kirk.

"You two should just get a room,"

She tried to hide her distaste for Kirk as she watched him push his way out into the line of traffic outside the station. "There's not enough alcohol in the world to make that happen."

"Maybe you should give him a wide berth for a while,"

She stared at the passing traffic, waiting for her annoyance to dissipate. After a few minutes, she had a clear view across to the pavement on the far side of the road. "Hey, is he on our list?" she asked, watching the taxi driver who had taken her home the other night help an elderly woman put her shopping into the back of his car.

"Who?" Helen asked, as she looked past Kate.

"Taxi man," she said fiddling with the tape measure in her hands.

"I don't think so. Was he on the list of registered drivers of the possible cars?"

"What's his surname?" She asked, pulling out her notebook.

"Walters."

She made a note to check him out later.

"We have our warrant," Helen said, brandishing the folded papers. She pulled out her keys and walked to her car. "I've called for backup to meet us there."

She nodded as she got into the passenger seat. She was a little apprehensive about this search. She didn't want Helen to think she wasn't up to the job, but she was nervous in case she got hurt again. It wasn't so much the injury itself; it was more the fear of it happening again, not to mention the twisted anger she had seen in Paul Wilson's face as he lunged at her with a knife.

Helen filled the silence that had developed between them. "They retrieved the car from the quarry; it matches the description of Jarvis's car. The boot opened as they were landing it. No body inside."

She felt the guilt gnawing at her insides. Jarvis wasn't coming home anytime soon. "Oh!" She busied herself with stashing the tape measure in Helen's glovebox.

"It'll take Forensics a while to go through it, although it doesn't look like it was down there very long. Looks like it was hotwired, apparently."

She looked out of the window, unsure of how to reply to this latest instalment. She hated the thought of letting Helen down. A warm hand on her thigh brought her back to the surface.

"I, erm…wondered if you'd like to come around for dinner tomorrow, as we're off duty. I'll probably be on call, but hopefully it'll be a crime-free night."

She smiled at Helen's request. "I would," she said, grateful for the change of subject. They made their way to the outskirts of Warner. "Can I bring anything? Wine?"

"No. Just yourself."

Dreading the answer to her next question, but she needed to know. "Did you find anything when you looked around the quarry yesterday?"

Helen sighed. "No, nothing."

CHAPTER 15

DRIVING THROUGH THE SANFORD ESTATE, Helen was surprised by the striking resemblance it had to the inner-city, rundown areas of back home. The only difference was that they had better views up here. The estate had all the main components: the renowned fly-tipped household furniture, cars with flat tyres, once-grassy community spaces now turned into barren mud patches.

She pulled up outside the Whiting house and waited for the two patrol cars to arrive before pulling her keys from the ignition. Looking in her rear-view mirror, she spied the edge of the stab vest she had put on the back seat earlier.

The deep barking of what sounded like a large dog made Helen look around. She hoped it didn't belong to the Whitings.

Biting the bullet, Helen reached back and grabbed the jacket. She pushed it towards Kate. "I need you to put this on."

"What? Are you serious?" Kate replied, as she held up the vest.

"Yes. I am. I can't have you being injured again." Helen realised how stupid it was, considering how the vest didn't cover anywhere Kate had been injured so far, but she continued to push. "It's just a precaution. Uniform will have them on too."

Kate frowned back at her. "Exactly. They'll think it's stupid."

Helen settled a hand on Kate's thigh, getting her attention. "Wear it for me, then. Please."

Kate's frown disappeared. Her eyebrows threatened to leave her forehead. "Is that an order?" she asked with a grin.

"Yes. I'm sick of filling out paperwork for your so-called exploits, regardless of how honourable they are."

"Yes, Guv."

Kate slipped off her jacket, throwing it in the back. Pulling the vest over her head, she tightened the Velcro straps around her middle. She made a show of adjusting them several times under Helen's scrutiny before finally murmuring, "Happy?"

As she got out of the car, Helen probably didn't do a good job of suppressing a grin. Walking over to the huddle of uniformed officers, she gave brief instructions on what they were looking for before pulling out the warrant and heading for the front door. With no doorbell for Kate to take her frustration out on, she decided to knock instead. Hearing movement beyond the door, Helen mentally prepared herself.

The door opened, revealing a mature, slim woman in faded jeans. Her long shirt had several of the top buttons undone, exposing an ample chest. The word *brassy* came to mind.

"Maria Whiting?" Helen didn't wait for an answer. "We have a warrant to search the premises." She held aloft the paperwork.

Maria Whiting's face soured as she looked back at Helen. For a moment, it looked as if she was going to slam the door in their faces. It wouldn't be the first time. Grabbing the paperwork, Maria Whiting sighed and stepped aside as stampeding feet made their way into her home.

Helen was just about to follow them inside when a blur of a figure sped past her. She turned on her heels and watched Kate immediately take off, after what looked like one of the Whiting clan. Which one, she couldn't say as he frantically zig-zagged between parked cars, Kate hot on his tail. Helen instinctively wanted to call after her but managed to restrain herself. Instead, she decided to keep an unobtrusive eye on her while Uniform checked the house.

But before she went in, she watched Kate, beginning to gain ground as the two running figures made their way across a field to a small playground. Kate managed to grab onto the jeans of the slower of the two, slowly reeling him in. Unfortunately for the Whiting lad, his low-slung jeans started to slip down his body, exposing his boxer shorts and impeding his progress. Now close enough to grab, Kate launched her attack, landing on top of him as she brought him to the ground.

Helen's ringing phone broke through her concentration. Pulling it from her pocket, she answered it without looking at the number. An unfamiliar voice echoed in her ear, the monotone informing her that he'd just sent a report over on initial findings from Sandy's trolley and Rutland Lane. Her mind popped back into focus. She'd heard something about silver paint flecks. "Sorry, could you say that again?"

She ended her call, relieved to see that Kate was heading back to the house with her bounty. Helen simply shook her head in Kate's direction. "You should have let Uniform handle it," she said mildly, not wanting to tear a strip off Kate for simply doing her job.

Studying the man in the handcuffs, Helen estimated his age to be around eighteen. With no tattoos visible on his neck, it had to be the youngest brother. "Curtis Whiting?" Helen queried looking at the young man as he fought hard to avoid all eye contact.

"Guv, we've got something in the garden," PC Davies called from the front doorway.

Helen followed Davies through to the back of the house, and was greeted by the sound of next door's dog as she entered the rear garden. The muted sound told her it was inside the house. The terrified ten-year-old in her was absurdly grateful. Looking around, she could see the small half-fenced mud plot was littered with car parts in various states of decay. The officer continued through the garden towards a small distressed wooden shed at the boundary line.

"What's under here?" Helen asked as she passed the tarpaulin-covered lumps lining the fence on the left.

"Car engines, Guv." Looking back inside of the shed, he continued, "We found some bagged-up clothing in here. It stinks of petrol."

Helen walked over to the doorway of the shed, spotting the almost translucent, red-and-white-striped carrier bag on the floor. Crouching down, the odour of petrol and smoke filled her nostrils. Using a gloved hand, she carefully moved around the denim and cotton materials. Finding a label in the neckline of a top, she turned it over. It read: *Medium*. That didn't tell them anything as all three brothers were similar in size, although the younger one, Curtis, was definitely the scrawniest.

"Okay. Bag it up, get it to Forensics." They needed to find out which Whiting brother the clothes belonged to.

Looking up, Helen scanned the shady inside of the shed, which, in contrast to the garden, was pretty empty. The side opposite the grimy window housed a number of empty shelves made from single strips of narrow timber held up with right-angled, metal brackets. A lonely red plastic beer crate and a scrunched-up black bin bag were the only things that occupied the worn plywood floor. Why was it so empty compared to the rest of the garden?

"Guv!" PC Davies called as he stepped back from the shed.

Helen stood, turning to see what Davies was staring at. "What's up?"

When she reached the side of the shed, she saw the object of his curiosity: wedged between the shed and the fence was an olive-drab metal petrol canister, a jerrycan, the kind you might pick up from an army-surplus trader, perfect for transporting an accelerant with which to start a fire.

"Get that to Forensics too, for fingerprints."

"Yes, Guv." Davies stretched, allowing a gloved hand to pull the can free from its hiding place

Helen took it from him. Shaking it, she felt the swish of liquid inside. As she unscrewed the top, the overpowering smell filled her nostrils. "Petrol." Satisfaction seeped through her. It was all coming together. "Maybe they can match that to the accelerant at the scenes."

Turning back to the house, she saw Kate standing outside the back door, an expectant look on her face. She walked towards her, unable to resist teasing her.

"Have you cuffed him to a lamppost?"

Kate smirked. "Uniform are searching him before taking him down the station. Anything?"

"Petrol-soaked clothing and a jerrycan hidden behind the shed. We also found some beer cans in the rubbish, same brand as the one found at the fire."

Kate nodded, exposing a brief grin before looking back at the house. "Anyone else at home?"

Helen shook her head. "No. Get Uniform to pick up Kyle. He's a mechanic at Len's Garage."

"Guv," Kate replied.

Aware of Maria Whiting lurking nearby, Helen discreetly called Kate to one side. "While you were on your morning jog around the estate, the crime scene techs called; they found paint flecks at the scene on Rutland Lane and on Sandy's trolley. Silver, apparently. They're sending the report over."

Kate nodded. "Great. The most popular colour there is. It should help to narrow it down a bit if they can get the exact colour, I guess."

"So ungrateful." Helen shook her head as she walked back inside the Whiting house.

CHAPTER 16

HELEN TOOK THE LEAD IN the interview room, reminding Kyle Whiting that he was under caution before introducing them both. Kyle had a sneer on his face that she wanted to smack off the moment she set eyes on him. He had a strong facial resemblance to Curtis, despite their four-year age difference. But although he was sitting slumped in his seat, she could see his body shape was bigger. His arms, stretched across his chest, were as oily, from working at the garages, as his clothes. She could just make out a small grouping of tattooed stars on the right side of his neck.

"Would you like a drink, Mr Whiting?" she offered as she pulled a pen from her paperwork.

Kyle Whiting seemed surprised at the question. Annoyance quickly surfaced. "No. I need to get back to work."

"Of course." Helen's voice kept her voice calm and unhurried as she shuffled though her paperwork and placed a piece of paper in front of Kyle. "Mr Whiting, we're investigating a number of arson attacks in the area over the last couple of months. Each of the fires was started with an accelerant in the form of petrol." Helen looked up, meeting his gaze. "For the benefit of the tape, I'm showing Mr Whiting a list of dates. Can you tell me where you were on the dates shown here?"

Kyle picked up the sheet of paper. "Working, out with mates…who knows?" He shrugged his shoulders before pushing the sheet away.

"We'll need the names and contact details of friends who can confirm your presence on these dates." Helen paused for a moment, taking the time to straighten the sheet of paper in front of Kyle. "Let's start with the most recent date, the thirteenth of March, Monday. That's four days ago. Where were you between the hours of ten and midnight?"

"At home," Kyle said smugly.

"Can anyone confirm that?" Helen asked, knowing that Curtis would be his alibi.

"Mum. Curtis."

Helen nodded. "On the night of the thirteenth, there was a fire at the garages off Green Lane. Do you know where that is?"

"No," Kyle said as if bored by the question.

"You've never been there?" Helen confirmed.

"No," Kyle repeated, frustration evident in his voice.

"At the scene of the fire, we recovered a beer can. For the benefit of the tape, I'm showing Mr Whiting a picture of a can of White Hart Lager." Helen pulled a photograph of the beer can from her file and placed it on top of the first sheet of paper. "We found some of the same brand of beer at your home when we searched it earlier today. Do you drink that brand of beer?"

"No comment."

Helen used her pen to point at the picture. "On this particular beer can found at the scene, we found your fingerprints."

The muscles in Kyle's jaw clenched several times, no doubt as the realisation set in. "No comment."

"When we searched your home, we also found some clothing hidden in the shed. For the benefit of the tape, I'm showing Mr Whiting a photograph of some clothing." Helen placed the photograph on the table for Kyle to see. "Do you recognise this clothing?" She used her pen to point at the photograph of clothes recovered earlier that day.

"No." Kyle pushed away the photograph of the jeans and long-sleeved T-shirt.

"They're with Forensics at the moment. I already know they have petrol on them." Helen left the photograph on the table, pulling out another one to join it. "For the benefit of the tape, I'm showing Mr Whiting a photograph of a petrol can we also found hidden behind the shed." Helen placed the photograph of the can in front of Kyle. "Do you recognise it? We're checking it for fingerprints, so we'll know if you've handled it."

"No comment," Kyle repeated, the smug look now gone from his face.

"Do you have access to petrol at the garage you work at, Kyle?"

Kyle glared at the table, reluctantly nodding his head.

"For the benefit of the tape, can you verbally answer the question please, Mr Whiting?"

Kyle slumped back in his chair again. "Yes," he hissed.

Helen turned the screw. She could see the tension on Kyle's face. "Would you be willing to give us a sample of your DNA to eliminate you from our enquiries?"

Kyle's brow knitted together. "What?"

"We've swabbed the beer can for DNA to see who was drinking from it. We just need something to compare it to. It could help to eliminate you."

Helen knew it was pretty impossible to tell exactly when that can had been placed at the scene, but this obviously hadn't occurred to Kyle yet. His reluctance to discuss anything with the duty solicitor was actually working in their favour for once. She knew he smoked; she'd heard him ask for a smoke earlier. Maybe the cigarette butts found at the house fire belonged to him too.

Kyle avoided the looks from his solicitor. "No!"

Realising she was getting nowhere, Helen decided not to go any further. Curtis was the one she needed to talk to. "Okay, Mr Whiting, thank you for your help. We'll be holding you until we can confirm your alibis for the dates in question. I'll send in a uniformed officer to take some details. Is there anything you want to tell me before we interview Curtis?"

"No comment." But Kyle flinched at the mention of his brother's name.

Helen cracked a small smile at his words. "Interview terminated at 3:35 p.m." The look on Kyle's face said it all. Curtis was the weak link. Helen gathered up the photographs before leaving the room with Kate close behind her.

Standing in the corridor, she studied Helen's calm exterior. She had enjoyed seeing her work over a suspect, admired her perception, the way she knew just how hard to push someone.

"What do you think?"

Helen held the file close to her chest as she leaned back against the wall and said, "Well, it's pretty obvious Kyle is trying to cover for his little brother. I'm just not sure why he's setting fires in the first place."

"But Kyle does have easy access to petrol from the garage," she offered.

"I know, but he seemed genuinely surprised about his fingerprints being on that beer can. I don't think he would have made that mistake, and the image on the CCTV looks more like Curtis, don't you think? Smaller build, longer hair."

She had to agree. Having seen them both in person, Curtis was the more likely candidate from the CCTV image.

In the second interview room, the atmosphere was very different. The smell of perspiration hung in the air. Curtis was slumped forward over the table, head buried in his folded arms. A different duty solicitor was seated next to him, pen and notepad at the ready. Maria Whiting sat behind them, her back to the wall, away from the table. As Curtis was under eighteen, she was acting as his appropriate adult. She just hoped that she could hold her tongue; she'd heard her shouting at the uniformed officers earlier.

A subtle vibration made its way through the table. Looking to one side, she caught the glimpse of Curtis's leg working overtime as it bounced on the ball of his foot.

Helen began in her calm tone, reminding Curtis of his rights and introducing everyone before explaining that he was here to answer questions in relation to a series of arson attacks in the area. She began laying out the groundwork as she had with Kyle, providing him with a list of dates when the fires had occurred before asking Curtis what he had been doing on the date of the most recent fire. Everyone in the room could see the nerves literally leaking through his skin as he reluctantly glanced up at Helen's gaze.

"Don't know," he said in a jumpy voice before looking back at the table.

She caught the sneer on Maria Whiting's face as she sat behind.

"Where were you between the hours of ten and midnight?" Helen questioned.

"Out with friends."

Pushing a pen and paper in front of Curtis, Helen continued in a composed manner. "Can you write down their names for me so we can confirm that you were with them at the times in question?"

"I…" Curtis hesitated a second, looking back at his solicitor. "Can't remember who was there."

"He said he was out with friends; what more do you bloody want?" Maria Whiting piped up.

"Mrs Whiting, please, you are here to observe, not to answer for your son," Helen growled before focusing her attention back on Curtis. "What sort of phone do you have, Curtis? Is it one of those new smartphones? Do you know they have GPS on them? We can usually pinpoint exactly where you are when they ping off various telephone masts in the area."

She noted Helen's change of method, how she left space for Curtis to squirm.

"Do you know where Green Lane is, Curtis?" Helen continued.

He flashed a quick look in Helen's direction before staring back at the table.

She tried not smile at the realisation. Helen had him. The guilt was in his eyes as he tried to look away. His hands leaving lines of moisture on the surface of the wooden table as he moved them back to his body in a protective manner.

"No." Curtis shook his head.

"Are you sure? There are some garages there, some used, some empty. There was a fire there on the night of the thirteenth of March."

His hands shook as they covered his face. She couldn't understand why he didn't just spill. Then it would all be over.

"We found a beer can at the scene." Helen pulled the photograph from her file. "For the benefit of the tape, I'm showing Curtis Whiting a photograph of a beer can. We found some fingerprints on it. You were kind enough to provide us with yours when you came into the station. If they're a match, we can place you at the scene. Do you understand what that means, Curtis?"

Maria Whiting rolled her eyes as she glared at the back of Curtis's head.

Hands still covering his face, Curtis said, "Yes." The mumbled words made their way through his trembling fingers.

"Doesn't mean he did anything." Maria's shrill voice filled the room again.

"Mrs Whiting, please. This interview is with your son. Don't make me request a replacement."

Helen's tone was fierce, but who could really blame her? Maria was just sticking up for her son, but right now, she was also undermining Helen. Looking back at Curtis, she saw that he was close to caving in. Helen just needed to push a little more.

"As you know, we searched your house earlier today, Curtis. We found the clothing you hid in the shed. For the benefit of the tape, I'm showing Curtis Whiting a photograph of the clothing we found bagged up in the shed." Helen pulled the photograph from her file, placing it on the desk for Curtis and Maria to see. "Do you recognise these clothes, Curtis?"

"They all wear each other's clothes," Maria bellowed again.

She glared at Maria Whiting, who strained her neck to see the photographs over Curtis's shoulder.

"Mrs Whiting, if you interrupt again, I'll be forced to ask you to leave. Do you understand?"

She noticed Helen didn't bother to inform Maria that she had just implicated all her sons in the crime. But even with her limited experience, she knew that teenage boys could be territorial about their clothes. Turning back to Curtis, she could see that he was chewing the inside of his cheek as he looked at the photographs. Helen just needed to put the final nail in the coffin.

"We have an image of you on CCTV, Curtis, wearing that exact top. We can swab it for DNA if we have to. We know they're yours. For the benefit of the tape, I'm showing Curtis Whiting a CCTV image." Helen placed the final photograph on the table, like a triptych.

Curtis looked up. "I didn't kill him."

She tried not to move, waiting for Curtis or Helen to continue, Maria looked totally lost for words.

"Didn't kill who, Curtis?" Helen queried.

"The old guy, in the house," he said quietly.

Helen waited a couple of seconds before asking her next question. Her restraint as she waited for Curtis to fill the silence was impressive.

"What house is that, Curtis?"

"The empty one on Morley Place, at the end."

"Can you tell me what happened, Curtis? At Morley Place?"

"I go there sometimes, to get away. It's been abandoned for ages. I could smell something as soon as I went inside. He was hidden by some boxes, but I saw his foot poking out."

"You found the old man there, for the first time, that afternoon?" Helen confirmed.

Curtis's nod was barely noticeable. "Yeah, but he was already dead. Must have crawled in there and died. I just wanted someone to find him. He was starting to smell bad."

She resisted the urge to butt in and ask the obvious question about making a phone call. Maybe he was a possible suspect. He could have hit Sandy and then tried to cover up the crime. She'd glanced at his record earlier. He'd been given a street caution for possession of cannabis seven months ago. Nothing car related. According to the DVLA, he didn't even have a provisional licence, but that didn't mean he couldn't drive. She was just about to voice her question when Helen beat her to it.

"Do you drive, Curtis?"

Curtis shook his head, frowning. "No."

"Not even illegally? Most lads your age can't wait to get behind the wheel," Helen continued.

She saw him clench his jaw, just like Kyle. *Must be a family trait.* She saw the anger burn in his eyes.

"I'm not interested in cars anymore. That's Kyle's thing, not mine," Curtis screamed before covering his eyes with his hand.

Anymore? After knocking over Sandy or something else? She made a note to check out all the cars the Whitings had access to.

"I don't blame you there. It's just a way to get from A to B for me. Can't understand why people are so fascinated by them; we'll come back to that later." Helen cleared her throat. "So, you were at the house on Morley Lane on the afternoon before you started the fire?"

Curtis nodded.

"I need you to verbally answer the question please, Mr Whiting?"

"Yes, I was there."

"Was there anyone else with you?"

Curtis just looked at Helen, unable to formulate words, his face blank.

"We have a witness that heard voices at the house in the afternoon."

Curtis's lips formed a straight line for a second before speaking. "No. I was just talking to myself."

"Our witness heard shouting, Curtis, not just talking," Helen clarified.

"I was angry."

"What were you so angry about?"

"Just stuff," Curtis mumbled reluctantly.

"Tell me what happened later, when you went back to the house on Morley Lane."

Curtis closed his eyes as she spoke. "I waited till everyone was in bed, took the can of petrol from behind the shed. Then I walked back to the house where the old man was. It was quiet. I sat there for a while, smoking. I didn't want to burn him. It just—it didn't seem right. You know?" He looked almost hopeful as he said it. Like he was just hoping someone would understand what he'd done. "He was already dead. I just wanted someone to find him. So I made sure the fire was away from him." Hope faded and was replaced by a look of pride. He'd set a goal, and he'd achieved it. She could kind of understand why he'd be proud of his actions. Well, almost.

She felt Helen nudge her foot under the table. Out of the corner of her eye, she caught Helen's glare urging her to take notes. She quickly made some bullet points on Curtis's actions as Helen continued.

"Tell me about the fire at the garages off Green Lane."

To her relief, Curtis seemed remorseful. He wanted to talk, set things straight. Looking past Curtis, she could see Maria Whiting had her head in her hands.

"I—I thought they were abandoned. I didn't mean to hurt anyone."

"I know that, Curtis. I just need you to tell me what happened that night."

Curtis held his head in his hands as he spoke. His tone was soft. "It was late. My brother was drinking beer in the back garden. I was in the shed. He went inside for something. I ran off with the beer before he came back. I heard him shouting as I went up the road. I just wandered around. You know? Just walking." He shrugged. "Ended up by Green Lane. One of the garages was open. There was no one around, so I went inside. There were some aerosol cans on a shelf. I just wanted to see if they popped when they went up. Like fireworks or firecrackers or whatever. You know? I was just—I just wanted to know. There was a petrol can in the corner. So I poured a little bit around them, and lit it."

Knowing that most arsonists stick around to see the fruits of their labour, she went for it. She knew she was butting in, but she couldn't stop herself. "Why didn't you stop that man from running in and getting hurt?"

"I wanted to, but then a couple of his mates turned up. There must have been something else in there. It spread so quickly. The garage next door went up before I could do anything."

"Other than the petrol you used, you mean," she said louder than she intended to.

Curtis ducked his head back into his folded arms.

Helen placed a hand on her arm, fixing her with a stare. "Could you get Curtis a drink?"

"Sure." She took the hint. She knew she'd fucked up, pushed too hard.

"For the tape, acting DS Wolfe is leaving the room."

She quietly closed the door behind her, asking the uniformed officer waiting outside to organise a drink for Curtis. Reluctantly, she headed back to her desk to be productive in some other way. Picking up Karen Hill's case file, she swallowed hard as she read through it. She made a note to inform Helen of her findings.

Disappointed with her lack of self-control, she began to work through the list of potential hit-and-run cars. After numerous phone calls, the list had been reduced to a grand total of thirty-three cars, none of which had any links to the Whitings that she could see. Her shoulders slumped at the high number still on the list. Seeing the taxi driver's name was still on it, not once but twice, she contacted the DVLA. The woman on the other end of the phone was very helpful. Sensing a bit of light at the end of the tunnel, she made notes as she replaced the phone in its cradle.

"Kate."

Stood in the doorway of her office was Helen, her face expressionless. Before she disappeared back into her office, her nod beckoned.

She made her way across the room. She was fully expecting another bollocking. Helen was already seated behind her desk now. She pushed the door closed behind her. She didn't want everyone to hear how shit she was.

"Curtis has admitted all of the fires. CPS is happy," Helen announced. "He's just finishing his statement. I don't think there was any real intent to endanger life."

The grin on Helen's face helped to ease her fears. "And Sandy?" she asked.

"No." She shook her head. "It's not the Whitings. I believed him when he said he only found Sandy at the house the day before he set the fire. He just wanted him to be found."

"Why didn't he just make a phone call?" she queried.

"Who knows?"

She let out a satisfied breath, relieved that they could close at least one of their cases.

"I just spoke to Curtis's mother; she said his father had disappeared recently," Helen sat back in her chair, blowing out a breath as she rested her head back. "Ran off with another woman. A couple of weeks later, the fires started being reported. Maria came home from shopping one day to find that his father had just packed up and left."

"Shit." *Maybe Curtis just wanted his dad to come back. Not that she could relate to that, having never known her own father; but she knew how it felt to lose someone.*

"Apparently, the shed was his dad's domain. He cleared it out when he left. Curtis started hanging out in there after that."

She waited a few beats before trying to excuse her behaviour in the interview room. "Guv, I'm sorry about earlier. I still have a lot to learn about interviewing suspects."

"Forget it. Everyone has their strong points. If it wasn't for your work on the CCTV, we wouldn't even be in this position."

"We make a great team." She winked, grateful for Helen's words once again. "See you tomorrow." She turned to leave but stopped before taking a step, remembering her news. When she turned back to face Helen, she caught a familiar smile.

"So, Taxi Malc has a new car, silver Hyundai Solaris, which is a possible for the hit-and-run." Although it was more 'hit and take' in Sandy's case. "His old car was a silver Prius, again a possible, which, so Malc told the DVLA, had apparently been crushed in a scrapyard outside Manchester. But he has yet to produce the V5C part of the log book to them."

Helen leant forward in her chair. "Malcolm Walters, he's a pretty quiet guy, never in any trouble, as far as I know. More importantly, why would he do it? What could his motive have been? No skid marks. Drinking maybe? That would put the kibosh on his taxi business. Could it be as simple as wrong place, wrong time? How many have you managed to narrow it down to now?"

She rolled her eyes. "Thirty-something." The infectious smile on Helen's face made her do the same. "And there's nothing back from the garages about repairs yet."

"What about Sandy's squeezes?"

She noted her choice of word, pursing her lips in reply. "Uniform is checking out the alibis for Frances Moody's sons for the time of Sandy's murder." She took a breath for the next bit of news. "According to the medical report, Karen Hill was two months' pregnant when she committed suicide."

Helen nodded, a thoughtful look on her face. "We're getting closer," she said and stood as if to emphasise the point. She moved around the desk to reach for her. She felt the warmth of Helen's fingers as they trailed down her arm, interlocking with her fingers. "Now, don't be late tomorrow. 6 p.m."

She used her thumb to rub the side of Helen's hand. "I'll be there."

CHAPTER 17

As she made her way down the darkened path towards Helen's hidden-away home, the uneven footing made her keep her eyes on the ground. The glint of the smooth cobbles was highlighted by the light outside Helen's house. She frowned at it. Helen must have turned it on for her benefit, like luring a moth to the flame. She had been looking forward to having Helen to herself all day.

She was surprised by the detached house's grandeur. It had some age, much like the police station, but she hoped it hadn't suffered the same crude modernising. In front of the large wooden door, she reached out to press the doorbell, then realised it was a pull mechanism. She pulled it briskly twice.

"It's open."

She pushed on the door. "Hello!" she called as she dropped the catch on the front door before closing it.

"In here." Helen poked her head into the hallway.

"That's very trusting, considering there's a murderer on the loose." She made her way down the hallway, past several closed doors.

"You're the only angry doorbell ringer I know."

"What?" She reached the kitchen and looked around, surprised by how large the room was and by the abundance of professional equipment that occupied the space.

Helen glanced at Kate, a grin on her face. "I've had the pleasure of witnessing several angry doorbell pressings over the last couple of weeks."

"I see."

She placed two bottles of wine to the side as she took in the sight of an off-duty Helen Taylor: dressed in jeans, a loose-fitting, blue-checked shirt, and with thick socks pulled over the bottom of her jeans, she looked very sexy. Kate licked her lips in anticipation. "I'm trying to figure out what's worse: being called Virginia, or being known as the angry doorbell presser."

Helen turned to face her, wooden spoon in hand. "Tough choice."

Blowing on the spoon, she stepped across the room closer to her. "Taste this," she said and offered the spoon up to her mouth.

Locking her gaze with Helen's, she hesitated for a second before tasting the offering. "Wow!"

The unmistakable creamy coconut flavour of korma filled her mouth, a light spicy citrus edge cutting through the buttery aftertaste. "That's—"

Helen beamed at her reaction. "Good?"

She nodded her approval. "That's amazing. I can see why you have all this fancy equipment now."

"Not all coppers live off takeaways, you know."

"I can see that," she responded.

"How's the head?"

"Hard, thankfully," she replied, brushing over the topic, even though she had actually spent most of the day in bed, resting up.

Helen held her ground in front of her, and leaning forward, she captured her lips in a soft kiss and mouthed, "Hi."

She wanted more, she grabbed Helen's shirt, pulling her closer, bringing their lips together with slightly more force. Helen leaned in, deepening the kiss.

"Hi," She replied as she held Helen's eyes for just a moment before Helen pulled away. Her attention refocused on the saucepan. It was an opportune moment to catch her breath.

"Don't feel too bad about the doorbell thing. Richards was a bread strangler."

"A what?" The bottle opener was on the worktop. She'd overheard plenty about her predecessor in the office, but nothing relating to his bread proclivities.

"When his wife was pregnant, she'd give him a shopping list of things he needed to pick up before he went home. We'd end up stopping off when we were out and about, when he bought French bread he'd squeeze the life out of the baguettes, looking for the freshest one."

She sniggered. "Well, you've got an eyebrow thing going on, so people in glass houses, and so on."

Helen turned to her, a worried look on her face. "What eyebrow thing?"

"You know that arched brow thing you do?" Her voice had turned tight as she plucked out the cork with a little too much elation. "When you want someone to tell you more. You used it on Slim Jim and several other unsuspecting individuals." *Including me.*

Helen checked the rice in the steamer and smiled over at her. "I said you didn't need to bring anything."

"I know, but my mother always said to never turn up empty-handed if someone's going to the effort to cook for you." She looked around, taking in the adjoining room with a dining table. It was warm and homely, but with a refined edge compared to her rustic cottage. "This place is amazing. To quote someone I heard recently, 'It's very you.'" Spotting the two wine glasses on the side, she filled them both and took a quick sip of her own to calm her nerves.

Helen looked across the room, cocking an eyebrow at Kate's words. "Thanks. It's a work in progress. There's still a lot to do. When I bought it, I had to do a lot of work before I could even move in: leaky roof to fix, new ceilings, new flooring and plastering. Would you like a quick tour?" She turned down the heat under the saucepan.

"Yeah." She put her glass down on the worktop before turning to face Helen, who moved into the hallway and stood outside the closed door facing them.

"Now, this room has yet to be finished. Parts of the timber panelling had to be taken off to repair some damp around the fireplace."

Helen opened the door and switched on the light, revealing a partially clad room. The naked light bulb exposed the bare walls scattered with areas of pink plaster. Fresh floorboards were visible near the fireplace on the far wall. There was warm ochre timber panelling on the opposite wall with a built-in bookshelf. This was going to be an impressive room when it was finished.

"Wow! This panelling is beautiful. Is it oak?" She ran her hand along the surface. The moulded detail and craftsmanship were both very tactile under her touch as well as aesthetically pleasing to the eye.

"Uh, yeah. I think so. I've got to get a joiner to make up some new panels to match the ones that were damaged."

She nodded, fascinated by the original workmanship as she followed Helen back into the hallway, where Helen hovered at the bottom of the stairs.

"Upstairs is a bit more finished, but that will have to wait. I think dinner's ready."

She attempted to help as Helen moved around the kitchen like a Tasmanian devil, decanting their meal into self-serve bowls, plucking naan breads from the oven. She did her best to stay out of her way as she collected the wine glasses, taking them to the dining table.

Setting the bowls on the table, Helen took her seat and said, "I don't want to talk shop, but just to keep you in the picture, I had to field a few phone calls today on our case."

"Sandy?" she questioned, frustrated that Helen didn't actually get a day off. *The price of rank.*

Helen nodded. "They wanted to know what progress we'd made and when we'd be making an arrest for his murder now that they know he's not just a tramp."

"What did you say?"

"Well, I said we hoped to be making an arrest in the next couple of days. We still had some background work to do on possible vehicles and their owners and a few leads from Sandy's past."

"And did that satisfy them?"

"For now. Anyway, enough of that. Help yourself," Helen said with a wave of her hand. "So, what made you become a police officer?"

She paused for a moment before speaking, suddenly not hungry anymore. An uneasy feeling filled her stomach. Her head was thick with images she'd struggled to forget. Blinking away the moisture in her eyes she began her story. "When I was a child, my best friend was abused by someone her family trusted. It was before all this grooming stuff was so widely understood. Anyway, he got away with it, and I—I couldn't understand how he didn't get sent to jail. I knew it was wrong." Reluctant to say more, she realised she needed to change the subject.

Helen nodded. "Justice can be hard to come by sometimes. I'm sorry. It must have been very confusing for you back then. You were a child. I mean, it's understandable why people decide to take things into their own hands sometimes." Helen slowly put down her fork, resting her hands on the table.

She held her tongue, trying to hide her surprise at Helen's words.

"Drink drivers are my Achilles heel. I worked a case years ago—a businessman mowed down a woman and her two grandchildren on a crossing in the middle of the day, killed two of them outright. The youngest died later in hospital."

She considered how many times Helen must have had had to bite her tongue and just accept her hands were tied when it came to doling out real justice. "What happened to the driver?"

"Shitbag barrister got him off with just losing his licence for eighteen months and a two-year suspended sentence. Criminals can buy their way out of prison these days. But, then, they're not the ones that have to go and tell the families that their relatives are dead, are they?"

Unsure of exactly how to tackle that subject, she just kept quiet, nodding her agreement.

"Sorry." Helen picked up her fork again. "So, are you still friends?"

"No." She reached for another piece of naan bread. She wasn't ready to tell her everything yet. It was too soon. "What made you move here from Manchester?" she deflected.

"My foster mother moved to just outside Warner when she retired. A few years ago, she started developing Alzheimer's. I got a transfer out here; she sold her house and we lived here for a while with a nurse, but it got too much. She lives in a care home now. She was diagnosed with breast cancer three months ago…"

"I'm sorry. I didn't mean to pry." Putting down her fork, she reached across the table for Helen's hand.

Helen met her eyes. "It's okay. I was taken into care when I was six. Luckily, I was fostered about four months later. One of the fortunate ones, when you think of the kids we come into contact with."

That explained Helen's continued personal phone calls. And why she had been called out to the fire scene. Curiosity prevented her from filtering her next words before they left her mouth. "Why were you…?" She let the question hang.

"My mother was a drug addict. She fell off the wagon one too many times, and Social Services took me away." Helen took a sip of her wine.

She swallowed hard as she studied the woman opposite her. She was so impressive. Regardless of her bumpy start, Helen had built a great life for herself. *Was that what drove her?* She noted that Helen hadn't even mentioned her father. She decided to shelve that question for another time.

"Julia was like the mother I never had. She was warm and kind. I owe her everything. Looking after her now is the least I can do."

"That must be a great comfort to her." She realised too late what she had said. Maybe Julia didn't even recognise who she was anymore. Hastily, she tried to repair the damage. "She must be very proud of you, what you've accomplished, I mean," she said.

Helen grinned as she took another sip of wine. "The irony is, Julia never wanted me to join the police force. She wanted me to become a teacher or doctor, neither of which appealed to me. I knew from an early age that I wanted to make a difference in my own way."

She was speechless. The guilt she felt ate her up all over again. She hadn't been honest with Helen on so many levels. She didn't even know where to start to make it right. *Was making it right even possible?*

"Would you like more?"

"No, thank you. That was wonderful."

Helen smirked at her. "You're most welcome. Shall we move somewhere a bit more comfortable? Bring your wine with you." Helen stood. Grasping her own glass, she approached the wood-panelled doors on the right side of the room.

She was surprised to see the doors disappearing into the sides of the walls, exposing the large sitting room beyond. It was cosy with dimmed lighting and plump sofas either side of a large fireplace.

"Wow! That's amazing." She looked in awe at the doors just poking out of the ends of the walls as she moved into the room.

"Shall we finish our tour?"

"Sure." Putting her glass down on a small side table next to the door that looked like it led back into the hallway, she turned the knob, but nothing happened.

"Uh, sorry, I keep forgetting. That door's locked, I'm afraid. Julia's hidden the key somewhere. I still haven't found it yet."

"Oh." She turned to see Helen only inches behind her. The ends of Helen's mouth quirked up in a smile as she placed her glass on the side table next to hers.

Helen reached out, placing her hand on Kate's arm. "So, how are your injuries healing?"

"Maybe you should inspect them and find out," she challenged, grinning as the raised eyebrow appeared on Helen's forehead.

"Maybe I will."

Helen moved closer, forcing her back against the door. One hand roamed up the side of her neck, while the other moved to caress the side of her face. Helen held her gaze for a long moment before moving forward, pressing their lips together. Her response was immediate: she ran her tongue along Helen's bottom lip before slipping it inside. Their kisses quickly became ardent. The guilt she felt from their earlier conversation faded a little as Helen's lips evaporated any clarity of thought, but the gravity of her lies were beginning to weigh her down.

The weight of Helen's body as she pressed against her was exhilarating. She slipped a hand beyond the waistband of Helen's jeans. Her fingers gently skimmed over the surface of the underwear she found. The pads of her fingers found the damp patch between Helen's thighs, forcing a moan of approval to escape her lips. She knew she was just as wet. The interplay between them during their last exchange in Helen's office had been a little unbalanced. She took action to rectify that. Turning her body, she quickly switched places with Helen, pressing her firmly against the door. This woman had a way of making her feel so hot with the slightest of touches or looks. Now she was on fire for her.

She dropped to her knees and slowly removed Helen's jeans and underwear, depositing kisses along the exposed skin as she edged towards the small mound of curls at the apex of her thighs. Her hands ran up the inside of Helen's thighs. Glancing up, she met hooded eyes before focusing on the glistening folds in front of her. Slipping her tongue between them, she got a taste of Helen's excitement. Using her hands, she parted Helen's swollen lips, exposing her fully as she pushed her stiffened tongue inside, exploring her completely.

Her focus moved further up as she found Helen's hardened clit, she swirled her tongue around it several times before sucking it into her mouth. At the wobble in Helen's legs, she moved her hands to a more supportive position on either side of her hips.

The raspy moans coming from Helen were driving her crazy. Helen buried a hand in her hair, holding her in place as she pushed her hips forward, thrusting herself deeper into her mouth.

"God, Kate I…I might collapse."

At that declaration, she pressed Helen firmly against the door, making Helen come against her mouth with a hearty cry.

Helen's back slipped down the locked door. She landed on her haunches. Her legs felt wonky. "Jesus!" she managed as she caught her breath.

Kate remained kneeling on the floor in front of Helen, watching as she rested her head back against the door.

"I didn't realise I was going to be dessert," she sniggered as she pushed against the door, managing to grab Kate's hand to ease her way forward.

"That's what happens when you don't provide any." It was all Kate managed to say before Helen crushed their lips together. Her lips instantly surrendered against Helen's insistent tongue.

The flavour of her own juices, mixed with korma, dominated her senses as she consumed Kate's mouth. She frantically undid Kate's trousers and knelt in front of her. She wanted to feel her. She couldn't wait any longer. Groaning at her own success, she quickly pushed them down, underwear and all, exposing Kate's body to her greedy eyes. She dipped a hand between Kate's thighs and quickly found the wetness she sought, coating the ends of her fingers.

Moving forward, Helen's body pressed against Kate's pushing her onto the rug covering the floor.

"Lie back," Helen whispered as she kissed her way down Kate's neck. She watched from her high position as Kate adjusted her body below. As

Kate settled back, she reached forward, slipping off her boots before pulling off her trousers and underwear.

A groan escaped Kate's throat as Helen settled on top of her.

Helen was in no rush for this to end. She wanted to savour every second of it. She pressed the lower half of their bodies together as she hovered above Kate. She ran her hand under Kate's T-shirt, feeling the tightness of her stomach muscles as Kate tensed, seeking release, pushing her hips forward. Inspecting a little higher, she found a lacy bra. She cupped her right breast feeling the hardened nub of the nipple beneath. It made her mouth water at the prospect of putting her lips on it. She pushed up Kate's T-shirt and kissed a trail to the delicate bra she had exposed.

Kate pulled at her T-shirt to assist Helen's exploration, releasing a gasp as soon as Helen latched onto her nipple. As she moved down Kate's body, Helen left a trail of cool skin in her wake. She gave Kate's bruised hip attention next as she circled it with kisses.

Helen moved lower, gently blowing cool air over Kate's moist, hot lips, as she continued to tease her mercilessly. She grinned as Kate thrust forward in the hope of gaining some contact.

Helen pulled back for a few seconds before slipping her tongue between Kate's moist folds, lapping at her ample juices. Hearing Kate's groans of approval brought a smile to her lips as she made her way to her now-swollen clit, sucking it firmly into her mouth, assaulting it with her tongue. Helen used her hands to spread Kate's legs wide in preparation for her next move: She replaced her mouth with keen fingers so that she could move her body above Kate's once more. Focusing on Kate's breasts, she quickly sucked a hard nipple into her mouth as she plunged her fingers deep inside Kate.

Kate's hips were out of control, thrusting in time with Helen's relentless searching fingers.

Helen pulled her lips away to place kisses along Kate's jaw and neck.

"I love how wet you are," she whispered. Helen could feel her own orgasm surface for the second time as she rubbed her hot centre along Kate's thigh. Her fingers continued to pump into Kate as her hips rotated furiously.

It sent her climaxing first, pushing against Helen's fingers with what must have been her last ounce of energy as she came with a shudder.

The vibrations around her fingers sent Helen over the edge. She came against Kate's firm thigh, collapsing on the floor next to her.

Kate's hips continued to flinch under Helen's gentle touch. Her fingers were still inside as she nuzzled into Kate's neck, satisfied for now.

CHAPTER 18

As she stood at the window sipping cold water, the foxes frolicked through the dark gardens below. The red glow that covered the younger cubs was missing on the larger fox; it was darker in colour, black maybe. She wondered if they suffered the same fate as black sheep, ostracised family members. Was that what she was? Forced out of her job, distanced from her family? Now that she had been parachuted into an unfamiliar environment, she felt even more alienated.

"Kate?" a voice called in the distance. "Marco?" the voice continued, now with the addition of light footsteps.

"Polo!" she replied.

"Marco?" The voice was closer this time.

"Polo!"

Arms wrapped around her from behind as Helen cuddled up to her. "What are you doing out here?"

"I was thirsty. Then I saw the foxes in the garden. There's a black one. Have you seen it?"

"I know. He's been coming through here for years. They come through from the fields behind the pub."

Helen's arm snaked around her. Her hand plucked the glass of water she'd placed on the windowsill. She watched as it was returned as few seconds later half its contents now missing. Turning she faced the warm-bodied water thief behind her.

"Are you pulling rank on me, Guv?"

"Who, me?"

Helen's feigned look of innocence needed some work, she reached up and stroked the side of her face with the back of her fingers. It took her a second to realise that Helen was naked. This woman was beautiful, warm, caring; she was perfect for her in so many ways. Why did she have to meet her now?

"What are we doing here?" she asked in a quiet voice.

"Well, if you're requesting diagrams and instructions, I'm not sure you need them after last night."

"No. I mean—" Her sentence was cut short as Helen swooped in, capturing her lips, preventing any further question of their situation.

Helen pulled back for a second and said, "We're having fun. Seeing where it goes, aren't we?"

That was true of their situation, but Helen only knew half the story. She was falling for Helen. Hard. "Yes. But—" She tried again, unsure of what she actually wanted to admit.

Helen ran her hands up the sides of her body. Slipping them under her T-shirt, she quickly found her breasts, caressing them softly as Helen found her lips once more.

"You have a very persuasive argument," she managed to say between kisses.

"I know," Helen said with a grin as she took her hand, leading them back to the bedroom.

Snuggling deeper into the pillow, as she heard the soft padding of bare feet on floorboards. She wasn't ready to get back to reality just yet. She wanted this dream to last a little longer. With the addition of movement on the bed, she felt a smile develop on her face. A warm body enveloped hers, covering her exposed back where the sheet had slipped. A knee slipped between her parted thighs as Helen stretched over her to whisper in her ear, "We need to get up now, Rip Van Winkle."

"Are you sure?" she murmured. Her voice felt raspy from sleep. Warm lips fell upon her neck, bringing her to life. She turned her body, forcing away Helen's knee as she settled on her back. "You know, when you're the boss, you get to set the rules. No one will have the balls to ask why you're in…" She stopped in mid-sentence with a grin. "I was going to say 'late', but I mean on time in your case."

Helen rested her upper body weight on her arms as she looked down at her.

She toyed with the sash of Helen's robe. "You smell so good." She carefully untied the knot, allowing the robe to fall open.

"We don't have time for that now," Helen said with a grin.

"We don't?" She reached into the gown, and Helen's body tensed. Slipping her hands around Helen's waist, she pulled their bodies together. "Are you sure?" she whispered before their lips met in a crush. The feeling of skin-on-skin contact was invigorating.

She used all her strength to flip them over, giving herself the upper hand, then devoured Helen's lips as her free hand tugged at the robe, exposing her naked body fully. Slipping a knee between Helen's thighs, she parted them. One way or another, she would be first into work this morning. Removing her attentions from Helen's lips, she moved down her body, gently nibbling at warm, pert breasts as she kissed her way towards her target. She pushed Helen's thighs further apart and settled her body between them. With her thumbs, she separated Helen's outer lips, exposing her hot centre.

The break in contact must have made Helen come to her senses. She started to sit up.

"We… I—"

She took Helen's clit into her mouth

"Oh, fuck!" Helen collapsed back onto the bed.

She moaned her approval at Helen's expletive as she continued to swirl her tongue around the hardening nub. A cool hand made its way into her hair as Helen thrust herself forward, encouraging her to press harder. A flood of juices met her lips as Helen's gasps and groans continued to fill her ears.

Helen's back arched off the bed with a final thrust as she came. She went with the movement, holding on to drain every last drop of pleasure from her before easing off, allowing her to catch her breath.

She gently kissed her way along Helen's thighs, across her stomach, sending Helen into a lethargic state of torpor. Realising Helen had drifted off, she stealthily climbed out of bed, covering up Helen before tiptoeing to the bathroom for a quick shower. Helen continued to doze.

"I'll see you at work," she whispered before depositing a final kiss on Helen's lips. She chuckled to herself at the thought of being the first to arrive at work, regardless of her slightly underhand approach.

CHAPTER 19

THE OFFICE WAS ALMOST EMPTY when she got there. *Great!* Hardly any witnesses to even see her arrive before Helen. Settling at her desk, she found the file from the crime scene techs that Helen had left for her. Sipping her customary morning cup of tea, she read through the file. The paint residue found on the trolley was in the process of being tracked down to a manufacturer. So far, all they could say was that it was silver. Turning to the list of contents that had been found in Sandy's trolley, her eyes stopped halfway down.

> *KPG 17: Photograph—Figures seated around a table, unnamed, blank on back.*
>
> *KPG 18: Photograph—Unnamed male and female, blank on back.*

Evidence of Sandy's fancy woman, maybe? She flipped through the rest of the file. Unfortunately, copies weren't included. She needed to get a look at them to confirm who Sandy's last lover had been. Last love. All in all, Sandy had had a pretty sad life. She imagined him feeling unfulfilled in his professional life, and having to run away from a fraud investigation resulting in discontent in his personal life too.

She knew she was projecting her own feelings on the case. She didn't even know Sandy, but she did know what it felt like to be discontent with parts of her life.

There was a photograph of the scene of the incident and the location of where Sandy's trolley had been found in relation to the road. Someone had thrown it a distance, down a banking, away from the road, no doubt hoping it wouldn't be found. They had gone to such lengths to hide the body, but not his belongings. Why? Panic, maybe? If so, it was the first sign of that.

After her conversation with Helen the other day, the lack of skid marks stood out to her like a beacon. Did it show intent? Maybe Rutland Lane wasn't the location where Sandy had met his end, just where his stuff had been dumped. She picked up a pen to made a note to ask Helen about it when she arrived. Her head filled with the image of Helen lying back on the bed, her dressing gown in disarray as she wrote the note.

Looking through more photos, she saw that a small piece of silver plastic had been recovered from the right-hand side of the road. According to Forensics, it was possibly from a lower bumper, or skirt, from a vehicle.

The lack of skid marks still bothered her. Had the driver been so intent on hitting Sandy that there had been no shock factor as they had knocked him for six? Maybe it wasn't premeditated, but it surely showed intent.

The sharp sound of the swinging blind on Helen's office door across the hall drew her attention from the paperwork. Getting up, she quickly made Helen a cup of tea as a peace offering.

Tentatively knocking at her half-open door, she could see that Helen was already on the phone. As she placed the tea within her reach and backed away, she spotted the raised eyebrow and pursed lips aimed in her direction.

Helen placed her hand over the mouthpiece as she looked at her. "Don't run off," she said, keeping her voice low.

She held her position near the door in case she needed to make a quick exit, casting a gaze out towards the main office. She was grateful that it was busy, preventing Helen from being too verbal about this morning's delay tactics. The clunk of the receiver being replaced made her look around.

"So," Helen said, leaning back in her chair as she looked over at her. "What have you got to say for yourself? Blotting my perfect attendance record." A hint of a smile was evident on her face.

"Are you reprimanding me, Guv?"

"Somehow, I get the feeling you'd like that."

"Depends what you had in mind." She held Helen's gaze for a moment before remembering that she had work-related questions to ask. She cleared her throat. "Did you see the photographs on the list of contents from Sandy's trolley?"

Helen quickly sat more upright in her chair. "I did. They should be back in the evidence lockup now."

"I'll go and take a look. Might be the lover he had at the time he disappeared."

"And how are we doing on the car?" Helen pressed.

"Should be able to narrow down the search by the end of the day."

"Good. Use Davies if you need to, and keep me informed."

Sorting through the evidence, she eventually found the photographs at the bottom of the box. She turned them over in her hands. They were both aged and crumpled from constant viewing and storage. The first was a strip of black-and-white photos from an old passport booth, the kind you used to find in shopping centres, filled with kids on the weekend taking silly photos. She moved towards the light to get a better look. There he was: a youthful Sandy, his dark hair slicked back, exposing his happy face as he looked at the figure next to him.

The young woman must have been sitting on Sandy's knee, ducking down to get in the shot with him. She looked directly at the camera in the first picture. She was beautiful, her blonde hair draped around her shoulders, strong cheekbones framing her face. In the second and third image from the strip, her head was turned to look at Sandy. Their mouths were caught in mid-flow. They must have been talking. In the final image, they were captured in a passionate kiss, eyes closed, leaning towards each other. It was a bittersweet image considering they were possibly both dead now, if the secretary's information was accurate.

The second photograph contained the same woman. This time, she was one of a number of figures at a restaurant, but she was easy to spot, her hair up in fancy twist. It had the look of a works night out with the mixture in age ranges; the seasonal decorations hinted at a Christmas celebration. They were all sitting down the long sides of a table, raising their glasses as the photograph was taken. The empty chair could have been for the photographer maybe.

Looking closer, the woman on the far-left nearest the camera looked a little like the secretary she had visited the other week. She had the same mole on her left cheek. This was a new line of enquiry to follow; she needed to get the secretary to take a look at the photos. Maybe she could identify the woman with Sandy in the photo booth. Signing out the evidence, she headed for Helen's office.

"Guv, I think we need to talk to the secretary again. I'm betting she can identify the woman in Sandy's life." She offered the photographs to Helen.

Spreading the bagged-up photos on her desk, she noticed the half smile on Helen's face as she picked up the picture containing a happy Tommy Sandwell. If anything, it made her more determined, not only to find the person who killed Sandy, but also to hold onto what was right in front of her. Who knew what might be around the corner?

"Get Davies to go. She knows him. I need you working on that list of suspect cars. I want you here if we are actually able to make an arrest today." Helen gathered the photos and handed them back to her.

"Yes, Guv." Taking the offered photos. She wanted to ask Helen if she was sure, but she knew better than to question Helen's orders, and she had already given her an explanation, even if that explanation seemed a little hokey; there definitely seemed to be more going on. She had to wonder if Helen was protecting her again, but from what?

———————◆———————

Helen strode over to Kate's desk, noticing that she looked uncomfortably hunched over as she checked through a huge pile of printouts. "I just got a call from Davies. The woman in the photos with Sandy is definitely Karen Hill. She was pregnant when she committed suicide, right?"

Kate fiddled with her printout, frantically trying to fold it back into shape. "Yeah. Not long after Sandy went missing."

"That's a pretty good reason not to go back. Maybe it was his baby."

"She had a husband." Kate flicked through her notes. "Erm, yeah, here." She pointed to the note. "Survived by her husband, Martin Hill."

"The secretary said Martin Hill was in the photo too at the restaurant," Helen clarified. "He's hidden behind one of the other people, but he was there. She thought it was a little odd that he was there as it was a management do, really. Is he on our list of car owners?"

Kate scanned the list. "No." Looking up at Helen, she continued, "Maybe our guy isn't even on the list." Kate dropped the paperwork back on her desk. "They could be from anywhere, and could have dumped or burned the car out—anything" She hunched her shoulders, letting out a long breath.

Helen actually liked this spark of frustration; it meant she cared. She lightly gripped Kate's shoulder. "Okay, okay. Let's see if we can find this Martin Hill and what kind of car he drives."

"Yes, Guv."

Grateful she still had some control over Kate, Helen headed back to her office.

———◆———

Helen resisted the urge to slam down the phone in frustration. The thought of another meeting at the care home drained her spirit. Fatigue was the only thing that prevented an outburst. Slumping back in her chair, head pointed up towards the ceiling, she closed her eyes and worked up the strength to drive out to The Oaks.

"Hey. Bad news?" Kate asked softly.

The familiarity of the voice eased some of the tension in her head as she recalled the memories they had made last night. She felt a sense of arousal as Kate leaned against her side of the desk. Her nearness was enough to feel the butterflies begin to take flight.

"Maybe." Helen let out a long breath. "I have to go to Julia's care home for a meeting."

"What kind of meeting?"

"They're trying to move her to a hospice because she's refusing any more treatment for her cancer." Her shoulders sagged with the weight of her situation. She felt helpless.

"I'm sorry." She was moving further along the desk but then stopped when her thigh brushed against Helen's. "What time do we need to be there?"

It took a second for Kate's words to register. "*We?* You don't need to be there."

"I know, but you're exhausted. Let me help. I could drive you. When you're finished, we could pick up some dinner on the way back."

"Any news on Martin Hill yet?" Helen asked, briskly changing the subject. Leaning on Kate wasn't something she wanted to start doing, considering she wasn't going to be around forever.

"Not yet. He was one of the line managers in the Sandwell biscuit factory. He stayed in the area for a few years, then nothing after he sold his house. It's like he disappeared off the face of the earth," Kate replied, her annoyance evident.

"Or changed his name," Helen mused as she considered Kate's earlier offer. She obviously wanted to help. "Shouldn't you be a little fatigued after our antics last night?"

"What can I say? I must have more stamina." Kate grinned.

Helen's attempt at a raised eyebrow did nothing to temper Kate's statement. Maybe she was becoming immune; she couldn't have that, not yet. "Oh, really?" Helen rose to the challenge and, standing upright, she slipped her right leg between Kate's, pressing her thigh against her centre before wrapping an arm around her body. Glancing through to the large office beyond hers, she was pleased to see it was empty. She bent to whisper in Kate's ear; the smell of her musky perfume was intoxicating. "We'll see about that. Later."

Kate gasped at the contact. Helen grazed Kate's cheek with her lips. "And I still haven't forgiven you for this morning," Helen said, eyebrow raised again.

Kate feigned innocence, deliberately knitting her brow as she spoke. "You mean for saving your dignity and arriving separately."

Helen purposely kept a blank face. "I mean the dirty tactics you used to tarnish my early-bird track record."

"Oh, that! Well, I was just using my skill set."

"I see. IT guru, domestic goddess and... what should we call that?"

<hr />

The final shards of daylight were fighting a losing battle with the darkness as they drove out to The Oaks care home. Helen looked across at Kate, whose face was lit up by the dashboard instruments.

"You didn't need to do this, you know."

"I know, but I wanted to." Kate flashed a quick smile at Helen before placing her eyes back on the road.

"Slim doesn't think you're good enough for me," Helen blurted out. The fatigue was loosening her tongue a little too much.

"Is that right?" Kate snapped. If there was animosity between her and Slim, surely it should be on Kate's side after what happened with his weaselly sidekick. "Bastard! And I bought him a bloody Mars bar the other day." Kate thumped at the steering wheel as if to emphasise her point.

Helen grinned. "You did? When?"

"When I picked up the wine the other day. He was hanging about outside the shop. I threw it at him as I went by."

"You threw it at him?" Helen repeated, clearly trying not to laugh.

"He still freaks me out. I didn't want to have to talk to him."

"I was about to say that he doesn't know you like I do." Helen reached across and placed a hand on Kate's thigh. "Thank you for driving me."

Kate softly covered her hand with her own. "No problem. How did he know?"

"He saw the way I reacted when you got hurt the other day, figured it out." She thought they had been careful, apart from the time in her office, but the less Slim knew the better.

"Will it be a problem, him knowing?"

"No. He won't say anything," Helen replied and changed the subject. "What were you talking to Kirk about the other day?" "Talking" was a loose term for their *tête-à-tête*, but Helen wanted to know the depth of the problem between the two of them.

"In the car park?" Kate clarified. "How much did you hear?"

"Well, I heard his parting gesture."

"I was checking the height of his bumper," Kate replied. "I know it sounds bad."

Helen wasn't sure if she should laugh or reprimand Kate for her actions. "You thought he was the driver that hit Sandy?"

"No. Not really. I just wanted to be sure. His car was one of the types that fit the bill. It was more of an experiment, really. And he's really creepy, don't you think?"

Helen knew better. Kate's intention was to wind up Kirk, especially after his attempt to grope her. She herself had no warmth for Kirk or his volatile nature. There was a reason he hadn't been promoted in his twenty years of service.

She didn't like the way he seemed to be fixated on Kate, which only spelt trouble. She needed to get on top of the situation and scolded herself for not having that quiet chat she'd planned after the incident in the pub. Seeing the care home come into view, Helen felt the familiar ache in the pit of her stomach, although she felt a little less nauseous having Kate next to her.

"I do, and he definitely has misogynistic tendencies when he doesn't get what he wants, which in this case, was you." Helen sighed, resigned to the task at hand. "You can park on the left."

Kate pulled the car into a space at the side of The Oaks.

"Where are you going?" Helen asked as Kate exited the car with her. She wasn't ready for her to see Julia, certainly not in the state she had seen her over the last couple of visits. Maybe another day when she'd had time to lay the groundwork for their meeting.

"I'm not waiting out here. It's freezing. I'll just wait in reception. I've got some stuff to look through while you're busy."

"What stuff?" Helen questioned.

"Just IT guru stuff," Kate said with a grin. "The elusive Martin Hill will not defeat me."

———◆———

Stumbling along the corridor, Helen tried to rub away the sting that still smarted across her right cheek. It was the shock that hurt more than anything. Julia had never lifted a hand to her in all her life. She had seemed on edge as soon as Helen had entered the room, so different from the other day. Her sense of humour had dwindled first—not that she'd been particularly effervescent in that area to start with. But Helen couldn't remember the last time she'd seen her so angry and confused; she was fading away right in front of her.

"Hey," Kate offered in welcome as she made her way through the darkened hallway into the bright reception area.

The bright light must have allowed Kate to see her puffy, reddened eyes. She tried to avoid eye contact as Kate stood there, looking ready to embrace her, to wrap her in her arms. Helen kept a little distance between them, locking her gaze onto the carpeted floor below her feet.

"Let's get out of here," she replied. She could hear how low and defeated her voice sounded. The last thing she wanted was to break down in the reception area.

"Hey," Kate tried again, reaching out for Helen's shoulder, squeezing it gently.

Helen felt the dam begin to break again at the gentle prodding and covered her eyes with her hand as the tears began to flow. She was quickly pulled into Kate's arms as her body began to shake with emotion. Comforting arms wrapped around her, pulling her against Kate's body.

"What happened? Does she have to move out?" Kate asked softly.

Gathering herself, Helen stood back, allowing a little space between them. "No." Spotting the balled-up tissue offering in Kate's hand, she wiped her nose with her thumb and forefinger. "I popped in to see her after. She told me off for not tidying my room, and slapped me. She thought I was somebody else. Someone called Caroline."

Kate let out a breath. "I'm sorry." She rubbed Helen's back as she held her against her own body. After a few moments, Kate released her grip. "Come on, let's get you home." She grabbed her laptop with one hand while the other still held the small of Helen's back and she led them to the exit.

Helen walked out of the building and stopped by Kate's car. "I know it's her illness, but...I've never seen her like that. She's never raised a hand to me before." Lost for words, Helen threaded her arms around Kate's waist, the warm, firm body making her grateful again that Kate had come with her.

The drive home was too quiet. Helen wrestled with her feelings. Julia had been such a powerful woman in her prime; it was hard to see her in her current state.

"Shit! Sorry, we didn't stop for any food," They were pulling up outside Helen's house.

Helen sat back in her seat. "It doesn't matter. I'm not really hungry."

"Me neither," Kate said.

"What? Kate Wolfe without an appetite? Somebody call a doctor!"

"I know it's hard to believe."

Helen still felt a little shaken. "What about if I said I had some leftovers?" Kate turned to face her, a spark of interest just visible on her shadowed face.

"Leftovers, you say?"

"Maybe with a glass of wine?"

"Sold." Kate pocketed her keys before getting out of the car.

Once Helen had placed the leftover pasta in the oven, she excused herself to shower and change, leaving Kate to choose a bottle of wine and cut some bread. She needed a minute away from the eggshell treatment she was getting. It was obviously a new experience for Kate to see Helen in such a state. In truth, Helen had never felt so tired and useless.

Supper, like the drive home, was equally quiet. Helen pushed the remainder of the food around her plate before finally giving up. "Have you finished?" she asked, glancing up at Kate. She hadn't realised that Kate was already looking at her.

"Yeah."

Helen picked up the pasta and headed into the kitchen. She scraped the plates to within an inch of their lives, cringing at the high-pitched sound. Moving towards the sink, she felt powerless as the plates slipped from her hands, the shards crashing into an untidy pile in the sink.

"Fuck!" Helen yelled, gripping the edge of the sink, staring at her handiwork.

"Here, let me." Kate moved towards her.

At the sensation of Kate's presence next to her, she stretched out a hand, preventing her from getting any closer.

"No!" It was intended to prevent her from coming to harm, not to threaten her in any way, but Kate flinched at the anger in Helen's voice.

Stepping backwards, she held up her hands in surrender. "Wow, you're harder to comfort than a velociraptor."

A warmth cut through Helen, releasing some of the tension in her head. She looked up, meeting Kate's gaze. There was a familiar glint there. "A velociraptor? Do you have a lot of experience with taming ancient avian-dinosaurs?"

Kate slowly dropped her hands. "Not a lot, but I hear they can be a little bitey when they're in pain." Kate held her position, making no effort to move closer.

Helen kept her gaze firmly on Kate. "I see."

"Maybe I should go. Let you get some rest."

Helen blinked at her words. She was pushing away the one person she felt totally comfortable with.

"No," she said and quickly moved towards Kate, unaware that she had backed off so far. It took several steps to finally reach her. "I'm sorry. Please, stay with me tonight."

CHAPTER 20

In Helen's dining room, she checked the computer she had left running overnight as she sipped her tea. A search for Malcolm Walters was working on the problem from the other end, a bit of a chance, but Walters's internet footprint might yield the clue they needed.

But the data the search had turned up was surprising; nothing on Malcolm Walters dated back more than twenty-three years, around the time that Martin Hill disappeared. Surely that was too much of a coincidence.

"Hey, I think I know why we can't find Martin Hill. Malcolm Walters is Martin Hill. You were right; he changed his name."

"Show me," Helen mumbled around the last bit of her toast as she entered the room.

"Okay, yesterday I did a number of searches on Martin Hill and there's nothing after he sold his house in 1991."

"Right." Helen sucked on her fingers.

"Last night, I thought I'd try it from another direction. So, I did a search on Malcolm Walters—"

"Why Malcolm Walters?"

"That stuff about the missing logbook, and having his old car crushed— it just seemed a bit too convenient, so I thought it was worth checking. There's nothing before 1991. No birth certificate, marriage certificate, nothing."

"Have you got Martin Hill's DVLA photograph?" Helen asked.

"Not here; it's on my desk over the road."

"Okay. Let's go." Helen said, her hand snaked around Kate's waist as she kissed her neck. Pulling away, Helen asked, "Does Malc have a gun licence?"

"I'll check." She hastily closed her laptop.

Helen turned off her car engine and sat looking at the stone farmhouse in front of them. It was hard to believe that the person they had been looking for had been right under their noses the whole time. The DVLA photographs confirmed it. Helen definitely felt that she was losing her grip, professionally. Looking across at Kate, she thought maybe personally too. Kate would be leaving before she knew it, and then what? Helen didn't do long distance; she'd tried it once before and didn't like it. It only took a couple of months for it all to fall apart. Was that how it would be this time? She knew the longer it went on the harder it would be when Kate's secondment was over, but there was something between them, something she hadn't felt for a woman in a long time. How could she just walk away from that?

"Ready, Guv?" Kate enquired, concern evident in her voice.

Helen glanced in the rear-view mirror, spotting the front of the marked police car parked just around the corner. She wondered what was going through the man's head right at this moment. She knew he would have spotted their car as it made its way along the exposed country road. Apart from his property, the road was a dead end. Was he the type to be loading up a shotgun to take them all out, or would he end it all before they got the chance to arrest him? Or, as she hoped, was he going to come quietly?

"Yeah," Helen replied, more sounding more confident than she felt. Watching Kate make a grab for her door handle, she reached across, placed a hand on Kate's arm, and said, "Can we be a little careful with this? Just because he doesn't have a licence doesn't mean he won't be armed."

Kate turned to look at her. "You know me, Guv. Careful is my middle name."

But Kate's quip had fallen on deaf ears. Helen frowned. She needed this to go well, and not just for Kate's safety. She liked a case to be trussed up like a turkey with all the questions answered, even if it was just to justify her own curiosity. Kate must have read the tension on her face as her tone changed considerably.

"I promise I'll be careful."

Relieved, Helen felt the pressure in her head reduce a notch or two. "Maybe I should do the talking, just to make sure."

No doubt this was exactly why interdepartmental relationships were frowned upon, to say the least. It worried her how much Kate put herself out there to be hurt. She wasn't cautious enough. It surprised her a little, considering she usually worked in inner-city London, where you tended to get streetwise pretty quickly, just as Helen had in Manchester.

"Spoilsport," Kate threw over her shoulder as she exited the car.

"Your body will thank me," Helen said to the grin on Kate's face.

Helen shot Kate a deliberately sideways look at the lack of a doorbell. Amused by the snubbed look on Kate's face, she mumbled, "Unlucky" before knocking on the wooden door in a rhythmic tune, as if to make up for it.

There was immediate movement beyond the door, heavy footsteps headed in their direction.

Malcolm Walters opened the door wide. Helen noticed there was no look of shock or fear in his eyes. Dressed in black jeans and a grey shirt, he looked tired, as if he hadn't slept in days, the way old people do. Heavy bags bulged under his eyes. She prayed Kate would keep her word as she focused her attention on the large mug in Walters's hand, knowing Kate would like to make a grab for Walters, slapping the cuffs on him, before even introducing herself.

"Morning, Malc," Helen said, keeping her tone even. She noticed a slow smile of relief cross Walters's face as he stepped back into his house, leaving the door wide open. Helen quickly stepped forward to enter the house, thus preventing any kind of standoff.

Kate was swiftly on her heels. Their path was cut short as they all bunched up in a tiny oblong-shaped kitchen. Helen looked back round through the doorway through which she had just entered, trying to get an idea of the layout of the house. She nodded for Kate to check the other downstairs rooms. Walters lived alone as far as they knew.

Malcolm Walters took a seat at the small square wooden table pushed up against a wall, which took up a third of the small kitchen.

"I've been expecting you for the last few days. I knew you'd find me."

Helen leant back against the short row of kitchen units that lined the long wall opposite the table. "Why didn't you hand yourself in, or run?" she questioned calmly.

Out of the corner of her eye, she saw Kate return, shaking her head. There was no one else here. Kate remained standing awkwardly in the doorway. There was no room for her to stand comfortably in the room without crowding them. She noticed Kate nod towards the wood-panelled back door behind Walters, no doubt worried he'd try and escape. Spotting the handcuffs in Kate's hands, she shook her head, hoping she got the message. The fear of another knife attack had left her a little jumpy; Helen had seen it in her eyes at the Whiting house.

"And go where?" Walters finally answered. "There's nothing for me now, hasn't been for over twenty years. I just wanted a little time to sort things out." He placed his now-empty mug on the table in front of him.

"Where's the car? The silver Prius?" Helen clarified.

"In the garage out back. I was going to burn it out, but I couldn't see any point."

"Can you stand up for me please, Malc?" Helen straightened up, preparing for her speech. She thought for a moment that she should let Kate do the honours, but something inside her told Helen that this would be her last big case. Figuring there would be many more on Kate's horizon, she continued. "Malcolm Walters, also known as Martin Hill, I'm arresting you on suspicion of murder. You do not have to say anything, but it may harm your defence if you do not mention when questioned something that you later rely on in court. Anything you say may be used in evidence."

Helen pulled her cuffs from her pocket, slipping them onto Walters's limp wrists.

Taking her cue from Helen, Kate pulled out her phone. She asked the person on the other end to search the garage.

"Take a seat," Helen said, stepping back.

Malcolm Walters let his cuffs clank on the stripped wooden table top as he struggled to clasp his hands together in front of him. He sat quiet for a moment before speaking.

"I felt a sense of relief for the first time in years that night. It was finally over."

Helen felt Kate's gaze on her again. Giving her the briefest of nods encouraged her further into the room. Kate pulled her notebook from her jacket pocket to record whatever Walters had to say.

Helen looked back down at him. She didn't want him to spill it here; she wanted him to say it all on tape. She needed to get him back to the station as soon as possible, but she also didn't want him to clam up.

"What made you wait so long?"

Walters toyed with the mug in front of him. "Believe it or not, I didn't realise it was him until a few months ago." Walters looked up at Helen as she took his mug from the table, placing it in the sink behind her. "I couldn't believe it. I mean, what are the odds? Both of us washing up in the same town."

Helen knew exactly how he felt, like a piece of driftwood on an abandoned beach. Warner certainly hadn't been high on her list of places to live and work; necessity had brought her here. As hard as it was to think about, she knew that responsibility would be over soon; it was out of her hands. After Julia's departure, would she really want to stay in a town where everyone knew everyone else's business? It had provided her with a more sedate, warm environment when she needed it, but what about in a few months? She could see her life drifting away from her if she stayed in Warner.

Davies's footfalls heading in their direction broke the silence that had fallen between the three of them.

"Guv!" he called, poking his head through the doorway.

Kate moved to one side, allowing Helen to pass her by.

Davies spoke in a quiet voice, unaware that Walters had already all but confessed. "We found the Prius covered up in the garage. The front end's all smashed up."

Helen nodded. "Okay, call the crime scene techs to collect it and process the house."

She walked back into the kitchen and looked at him. "Let's get you to the station."

Helen walked along the corridor. Kate was waiting outside the interview room, and as she walked over, Kate drained the last dregs of her drink.

"He's refused a solicitor," Kate told her. "Said he just wants to make a statement." She threw her empty can in the bin next to the vending machine.

"Clear his conscience, more like." Helen reached for the door handle. Kate was right behind her.

In the interview room, Walters was sitting facing the door, and Helen stood there for a moment before taking her seat. Unlike Curtis Whiting, Malcolm Walters looked calm; resigned to his fate. He'd obviously had plenty of time to accept, and maybe even justify his actions, at least to himself.

Kate sat quietly, checking her notes as Helen introduced everyone, noting the fact that Malcolm had refused a solicitor, reminding him that he could change his mind about that at any time during this interview.

Malcolm Walters's response was to fix his lips in a straight line, nothing more.

"Malcolm, we need to establish your identity. Can you tell me your real name and why you changed it?"

"I changed my name from Martin Hill when I moved away from Glazebrook in May 1991. I wanted to set up a new life, make a fresh start."

Helen noticed that Malcolm's shifty eye contact with her. She wondered if it was from shame for what he'd done.

"I still couldn't escape my past. I loved Karen. I loved her so much. I didn't know she was…" Walters's lips trembled as he covered his mouth with his left hand.

Was what? Having an affair? Pregnant? Suicidal?

"Your wife, Karen Hill, was having an affair with a co-worker at the Sandwell biscuit factory?" Helen clarified.

"Yes." Walters's words were garbled behind his hand as he wiped at his nose. He lowered his head making a visible effort to gain control of his emotions.

Helen waited a few beats, then asked, "How did you find out about the affair?"

"I saw a note he'd left for her. He'd slipped it under her desk blotter, but part of it was sticking out." Tears started to bunch up in Walters's eyes. "It said how happy he was that she was pregnant; he couldn't wait to be a father. I didn't even know she was pregnant then. We'd been trying for a while, but we hadn't…"

A lump formed in her throat. She looked away. Walters tried once again to harness his emotions.

"When did you find out she was pregnant?" Helen asked in a small voice.

"She told me later when she didn't have a choice, I guess. I wish—I wish she hadn't… Because she…"

Helen focused on her paperwork as Malcolm Walters roughly wiped at his eyes. Normally she was capable of keeping her emotions in check during interviews, but lately she was struggling to keep them under wraps. Hardening her thoughts, she focused on the fact that she would never get to shoot the breeze with Sandy anymore because of what Walters had done that night.

"It's a terrible feeling when you realise you're not enough to make someone want to live, that they think they would be better off dead."

Helen swallowed hard. The room was silent except for Walters's continued sniffle. She risked a sideways look at Kate, who fiddled with her pen, her gaze locked on the table.

"She stepped in front of a train a month after Tommy Sandwell disappeared." Walters's voice had become unevenly pitched.

Helen waited for his breathing to regulate before moving on. "Can we talk about the night Tommy Sandwell died?"

Walters nodded, seeming relieved at the change of subject. "It was a Tuesday night. Late. I was on my way home after dropping a fare off on Spencer Street."

Helen mentally pictured a map of the area, noting the proximity of Spencer Street to Rutland Lane, just around the corner. "Take me through the events of that night," she said more firmly.

"I saw him stumbling as he crossed the road in front of me. All I could think about was what he'd taken away from me. Everything he'd destroyed. Me. Karen. The baby. That could have been my baby. I wouldn't have—I could have—she didn't even need to tell me it wasn't mine. We could have been happy if not for him. But no. He had to have what was mine. He had to take it—take her—and it destroyed us. Destroyed her. My beautiful, beautiful Karen." He wiped at the tears in his eyes, but he didn't stop. "So

I saw him, and knew who he was, and I just couldn't stop myself. I couldn't stop seeing everything he'd taken. So, I just put my foot down."

That explains the lack of skid marks on the road.

Helen wanted to confirm the road name, but let him continue. "How did you know it was Tommy Sandwell?"

"I'd seen him knocking around the town for years, but like most people, you don't really look too hard at tramps." He laughed, the empty hollow sound of someone with no hope. "We're all too scared of catching something, I guess."

Helen waited patiently for him to continue, refusing to comment on Sandy's social status.

"I heard him arguing with another guy a couple of months ago. I already knew he was called Sandy, but this other guy called him Tommy. The more I looked, the more I thought it was him." He half smiled for a split second. "He still had that bandy-legged walk."

Helen tried to recall any memories of Sandy's walk. Nothing came to her.

"When I saw him right in front of me, I couldn't stop myself." He covered his mouth with his hand, stifling his words. "After—after—afterwards, I put him in the boot and drove around. I had no idea. I just—I just didn't know what to do with him. Then I remembered the house on Morley Lane. I'd passed it a few times driving round. I knew it was empty."

"What did you do after that?" Kate queried.

"I got roaring drunk. Whisky. Lots of it. Then I—" he sighed heavily. "Then I drove around some more. Stupid, I know, but I'd already done the worst I could do, so what else did it matter? I drove out onto the old quarry road." He chuckled bitterly. "Hit a deer or something. At least I think it was. Bloody thing had run off before I could see."

"And the new car?" Helen asked.

Walters let out a breath.

"I thought getting another car the same colour was a good idea. Thought it would buy me some time. Thought someone might notice if I stopped working altogether."

"I need you to write all this down in a detailed statement," Helen said.

Walters nodded. "Then can I go to my cell?"

Helen walked out of her office, a warmth spreading through her at the sight of Kate still hunched over her desk. The empty office allowed her to be more vocal.

"Hey, leave that till tomorrow. You've got thirty minutes until you're officially late for dinner."

Kate looked up from her paperwork. "So, what did Walters need to sort out so badly?"

"He wanted to make sure the sale of his estate went to a children's charity."

CHAPTER 21

HELEN GLANCED UP AT THE clock on the wall. "You're late!" she yelled from the kitchen at the sound of her front door closing.

"Sorry. I stopped off to get a bottle of wine."

Helen was grateful she'd had time to shower and change before Kate's arrival. She'd wanted to wash away the day's events. Interviewing Walters had been difficult, but thankfully Sandy's case looked pretty simple now that they had all the pieces. She felt more relaxed in her domestic environment. Washing up the last of the breakfast crockery, she dried her hands on the tea towel. At the sound of Kate's footsteps, she pushed behind her ear some stray hairs that had escaped her ponytail.

"You smell good," Kate whispered in between kisses to the side of Helen's neck.

"I thought you were going to say the pizza smells good."

"That, too, of course."

She took the freshly cut pizza to the table in the adjoining room. As she took the seat opposite Kate, she noted the dark circles under her eyes, her deflated disposition. She tried to focus on her food. Was Kate tiring of her already?

Helen looked up from her second slice of pizza, remembering her earlier phone call. "The crime scene techs matched fibres found on Sandy's clothing to Walters's car boot. And blood found in the boot is a match to Sandy, so it looks pretty cut and dried."

"That's good news." Kate wiped at the pizza juice on her chin.

She saw a glimmer of satisfaction in Kate's eyes. Her appetite subdued for the time being, she pushed her plate away, wiping her hands on the napkin. Helen didn't like not knowing what was going on in Kate's head. She rose and put some distance between them, escaping to the kitchen.

Kate handed her the final plate, wiping her hand on the tea towel. The distance was in her eyes, the same worry she was sure she had seen over the last couple of weeks. She thought it had been the case getting to her, but with the case closed now, she wasn't so sure anymore. Of course, there was still the missing architect to deal with.

Tossing the towel on the worktop, she spotted Kate's barely touched wineglass on the side. "Not drinking? I thought you'd be celebrating after today."

Kate smiled as Helen's gaze landed on hers. "Just tired, I guess."

Helen wanted to push for more, but almost feared Kate's answer. If she was losing interest in whatever it was that was going on between them, she was about to find out. With two cases closed, she hoped to be spending a little more social time with Kate before her sabbatical was up. But she needed to clear the air before that could happen.

"What's wrong? Are you okay?" Helen said softly as she averted her eyes, focusing instead on the two fingers she used to push aside Kate's hair to get a look at the healing cut on her forehead. She couldn't bear to look into Kate's eyes as she said the words, in case she saw something she wasn't quite ready for.

"It's nothing, really. Family stuff."

Helen allowed her gaze to travel down to Kate's once more. She saw exhaustion and something else that she couldn't quite put her finger on. A hand circled her waist, pulling their bodies closer. Kate's eyes slowly flickered closed as her lips pressed gently against her cheek. Helen smiled as the warm lips slowly made their way to her own. She willingly turned her head to speed up the process, capturing Kate's lips.

Helen took control slowly, moving her across the room while battling passionate kisses as their tongues collided.

Slipping her knee between Kate's thighs, she forced them apart and pressed Kate back against the kitchen wall. Her hand softly caressed the seam of Kate's trousers before she slipped it beneath the waistband and found soft cotton underwear. She began with gentle caresses before adding more pressure and stroking the material above Kate's clit, her touch slow but relentless. The blush on Kate's cheeks told her know exactly how worked up she was.

Kate groaned. "God! You're going to make me come right here if you do that much longer."

Helen kissed the soft skin of Kate's neck. Her pulse throbbed just below Helen's lips. "Well, that's something we should definitely explore."

Helen reached down. Taking Kate's hand, she pulled her along as she made her way through the house to her bedroom.

———◆———

She released her hand from Helen's and stood behind her, circling Helen's waist, feeling the warmth from her back against her body as she began working on the button and zipper of Helen's jeans. Once the waistband loosened, she skimmed a hand over the underwear, gently cupping the mound beneath her fingers.

A groan escaped Helen's lips. Remembering how Helen had nearly undone her in the kitchen, she slipped her hand beneath her underwear. Helen rolled her head back, leaning into her as fingers traced the line of her lips. She gently parted them.

Two fingers wound their way between Helen's moist lips, and she found the pool of wetness at Helen's entrance. Circling the area, she bathed her fingers before slowly moving up to the hardened clit.

Helen gasped, her breathing coming faster. Using her free hand, she skated over Helen's taut stomach and up to her firm breasts, softly pinching at a nipple before pushing her bra up. It released Helen's breasts to fall into her warm palm. In the short time since they had moved from the kitchen, she'd managed to turn the tables on Helen.

Her breathing fell into Helen's rhythm, her body rising and falling in time as her hands and fingers continued their exploration.

Helen leant back against her firm frame for support, her body twitching, her cry guttural, as the orgasm ripped through her. She held her firmly as the strength slowly returned to her limbs.

Helen managed to turn around to face her. "Playing me at my own game."

"I don't know what you mean," she managed through her chuckle.

"You will. Trust me, you will."

CHAPTER 22

HELEN PICKED UP THE ENVELOPE that had landed on her doormat. It was handwritten, addressed to DCI Helen Taylor, although it looked unofficial, with no postmark.

She walked into the kitchen to make some tea, then worked her finger under the sealed flap. *What the hell was this thing?* There were thick papers inside the envelope. She unfolded them but was unable to contain her enquiring mind and opted to look at the last page first to find the sender's name. She frowned at the name: *Lexi Ryan*. It didn't ring any bells.

Reading the final paragraph, she couldn't believe her eyes.

> Please believe me when I say I didn't intend for any of this to happen and certainly not to fall in love with you, but I did, and I can never regret that. I just can't. You're too special to me to ever regret a single moment I spent in your company, in your arms, or that you'll spend in my heart. I know you will feel it is your duty to find me, and I don't blame you for that. What we have, or had, was the best thing that ever happened to me.
>
> Love always,
>
> Lexi Ryan

Scanning further up the last page, she saw the bewildering confirmation: Kate's name, written with an explanation that she was the Lexi who had signed the final paragraph. What the hell was going on? She had seen Kate—Lexi—whoever she was—only a few hours ago. She picked up her phone and scrolled through her calls, settling on Kate's contact. Her finger hovered over the call button a second. But then it went straight to answerphone anyway. She didn't leave a message. Kate had obviously left the letter. Maybe she should read it first before speaking to her.

The penetrating sound of her phone ringing made her jump. It almost slipped from her fingers.

"Taylor," Helen said into the phone, her voice tight on autopilot.

"Guv." Davies cleared his throat. "We've had a report of a fire at DS Wolfe's home. They've found a body."

Helen placed a hand on the work surface to steady herself. What the fuck is going on here? Visions of last night filled Helen's head.

"Guv?" Davies repeated, obvious concern in his voice.

"I'm on my way," Helen garbled as she rushed upstairs to get dressed.

———◆———

When Helen arrived at the scene, the remains of the cottage were barely recognisable as the place she had visited only recently. Blackened walls surrounded gaping ruins. The upstairs was completely absent from the rest of the structure. It looked like a tooth cavity, the kind of fire that people don't just walk away from.

Remains of furniture were being dampened down by a fireman in the empty driveway next door. It didn't make any sense. The body couldn't be Kate's. She'd been in Helen's bed until a couple of hours ago.

Helen saw Kate's vehicle in the small driveway as she climbed out of her car. It seemed to have escaped with only minor damage, mainly from debris falling onto it. Helen attempted to blink back several tears as she approached the house, figuring Kate must have driven back home to get changed before work. Why couldn't she have just worn yesterday's clothes or even borrowed something? None of this had to happen.

She'd been drawn to Kate from the first moment she'd met her, teased her relentlessly, and fighting her growing feelings. Now it was as if someone had turned off the sun. She had just started to see her future in a different light, but that was over. She couldn't do this anymore. Life was too short to be this mentally exhausted and lonely. Her life was empty now, and just getting emptier. *When Julia finally…* She didn't want to finish that thought, but she knew there would be nothing for her here after Julia was gone. Taking a calming breath, she walked towards Kate's driveway. The last time she'd been here, things had been so different.

Helen steadied herself with her left hand to the boundary wall, for the second time that morning. She recognised the uniformed officer immediately—Davies. Rather him than the obnoxious Kirk. She could punch Kirk's lights out right now, repay him for all the horrible things he'd said to Kate over the last few months. Avoiding the looks from the firemen securing their equipment, she focused her attention on Davies.

"Guv, the body's been taken to the morgue."

The leaden tone to Davies's voice was not lost on her. He, like Helen, had spent the most time with Kate during her secondment.

"Any idea what the FIO thinks so far?" Helen tried to keep things professional. If he lost it, she would too.

"Accident, he thinks. Said there was a power cut in the area last night, something to do with renovation work on the substation. He, er…he thinks she fell down the stairs with a lit candle. That's how the fire started—found wax on the carpet at the bottom of the stairs. Next to the body."

Helen busied herself putting on latex gloves as Davies's voice trailed off. "What time was the fire reported?" she asked, still unable to believe what he was saying.

"Around six. Neighbours are away." Davies pointed to the house at the opposite end of the short row. "The middle house is empty. Farmer across the valley reported it. Said it was well alight."

"Six?" Helen repeated with a frown. Hadn't Kate still been next to her in bed at that time? She hadn't looked at the clock when Kate left. Why did she leave so early? How could the fire start without anyone being there? How else could Kate's car be in her driveway now? Surely Kate hadn't rushed into the cottage while it was ablaze. Nothing could be that precious. Nothing was worth that kind of risk. She'd seen Kate's recklessness first-hand, but surely this was a step too far. Why would she have a candle if the house was already on fire? Nothing made any sense.

Davies lifted the police cordon for Helen to enter. She ducked under and approached the front of the blackened building. The front door was open, hanging by one hinge at an awkward angle. Pushing it open a little further,

Helen entered. Faced with the silhouetted remains of a stairwell on her left, she swallowed hard. Was this where Kate had met her end? It couldn't be. Something wasn't right. It just didn't add up. Debris covered every inch of flooring, making it difficult to walk through the scene. Turning around, she'd seen what she needed to see.

———◆———

When Helen returned to the station, she secured herself in her office to try and make sense of recent events. She avoided calling her superiors to discuss the passing of a fellow police officer; no doubt they would be on her case soon enough. Helen couldn't face hearing from Dr Nicholls or Graham Brown, spouting updates. She still firmly refused to believe what everyone else took for granted. Pulling out the letter she had received that morning, she rearranged the pages back into their rightful order. There had to be another explanation.

Dear Helen,

Firstly, I'm sorry to have to tell you this all by letter, but the situation was taken out of my hands. As you have probably figured out already, I've left the area, I regret the untidy mess I was forced to dump on your doorstep. I wanted to tell you the truth on so many occasions, but the thought of seeing the disappointment in your eyes stopped me every time. I know you'll feel angry with yourself for not seeing it coming, but please don't blame yourself for what I've done. I've brought this all on myself and ruined any kind of a future I wanted with you. Please believe me when I say that. It was killing me keeping all this from you, but I was trapped in a plan of my own making. I know most people would probably say that if they could go back and change things they would, but, in truth, I wouldn't change a single moment I spent with you. I've never fallen so hard or fast for anyone ever before. Please give me a chance to explain my actions before you dismiss me from your life.

As with most stories, this has a beginning, so I'll start there. The person you have come to know and hopefully care for over the last few months is not Kate Wolfe but an impostor. I thought you'd spot it the first day we met, but I guess I was lucky, making the crash landing as I did at the fire scene.

The answer I gave you when you asked me why I became a police officer is true except for one fact: the girl in question was my younger sister, Leah. I never really knew my father. He ran off with a work colleague when I was two, just before Leah was born. Which left only my mother. She was more than enough to make up for any loss we incurred at his departure. She was a wonderful woman, creative in so many ways at keeping us occupied as kids, including using her first love—music. She played the piano beautifully and encouraged us to study music. Unfortunately, my mother fought a losing battle with me. Computers had already captured my heart and my imagination.

My sister, on the other hand, wanted to learn the guitar. Although Leah was taking lessons at school, my mother searched out a local musician/tutor to give my sister additional lessons to further her talent. By doing this, my mother set in motion a string of events that changed all our lives forever.

She found in the local paper a musician by the name of Paul Stone, who was offering private lessons. Over the next few months, my sister's guitar skills improved a little, but there were more worrying signs that I started to notice. Like her withdrawing from the world. She lost her appetite, stopped being the happy-go-lucky ten-year-old she had always been. I'm ashamed to say this went on for some time before she had the courage to confide in me. I was her big sister; it was my job to protect her. I failed. When I think about the things he did to her now, I feel physically sick.

Stone was questioned by the police on the strength of Leah's admission, but this was twenty years ago, a time when policing was different. Stone had a number of other young music students that vouched for him. So, with no real proof, it was Leah's word against his. Leah began to clam up, retreating into herself as the police began to lose faith in the investigation when there was no corroborating evidence.

When puberty hit, self-harming and depression kicked in. She was institutionalised at the age of sixteen after trying to commit suicide for the second time.

Left to our own devices, my mother and I grew apart. My one vice was computers. I became a hacker of sorts while my mother turned to alcohol. She couldn't forgive herself for bringing that man into our lives. Our family began a slow-motion implosion. I sought solace at university in an effort to bring order to my life. I'm ashamed to say I avoided going home, not wanting to be sucked in to my mother's despairing world.

I visited Leah when I could; her health fluctuated to the extremes over the years. She always had fresh drawings on her walls, the same distinctive pattern or image. I wasn't sure what it was or what it represented to her; she often avoided answering any questions I had regarding the image. During a particularly lucid visit, I risked asking the question again. She told me it was the pattern from a ring. A ring that was on the hand of the man who touched her and made her do things.

A few weeks later, she'd deteriorated once again. She suddenly seemed frantic, despairing. Before she let me leave, she made me promise to make sure I stopped him from doing it to anyone else. I wanted to soothe her. I needed to, Helen. I needed to help her then as I'd been unable to help her when we were children. So I made the promise.

I promised my baby sister that I would never let that man harm another child as he'd harmed her.

Two days later, she was dead. She'd hanged herself.

Twenty-eight years old and she'd never lived, never. He took her whole life from her.

And everything became so crystal, so perfectly clear to me then. I couldn't protect her when she needed me. The least I could do now was make the man who ruined her life pay for what he'd done.

Finding Stone was easy. He'd moved away to escape the stigma of being questioned for child molesting, but he'd stuck with music, opening his own tiny shop near Reading. I became his student for a while—changed my name of course—just in case he recognised my surname.

Do you know what the scariest part of it was?

He seemed normal. Completely and totally fucking normal. There was not one single thing about him that told the world what a monster he was. Not one. I hacked his life. Nothing. During my lessons, I noticed there was no ring on either hand. So, I did some more digging into his previous residence, the one he'd lived in when he was teaching Leah. And I found something I'd never known. He'd rented out a room to a student.

A student called Richard. Richard Jarvis. Studying architecture.

I started my search for Jarvis that very day. What choice did I have? And let me tell you, finding him was easy. He was just outside Warner. Forty-three years old, single, working as an architect at Dalton & Weeks. I hacked into his computer, finding nothing at first. Then I dug a little deeper.

He was careful, I'll grant him that. But that didn't stop me. I found his collection. Collection. That makes it sound like something everyone would be proud of? Like great works of art or sculptures or music. But it wasn't like that, Helen. Do I need to go into detail of what I found? Do I need to tell you how despicable, how offensive, how degrading...how sickening that collection was? How young those children were? I don't, do I? You'll know.

I thought this would be enough. I could drop an anonymous tip to one of the police hotlines and they'd find it, and he'd pay—I'd have fulfilled my promise.

Life's never that simple, is it?

The next time I looked, it'd gone. Vanished. Poof. And even I couldn't trace it. There was no way the police would. No way he'd finally get what he deserved. He had to pay, Helen. You can see that, right?

I had to pursue him. Had to. This wasn't just about Leah anymore. There were hundreds of images and films in his "collection". And no one else knew about them. No one else was going to help them. Or give them the chance of a future that Leah never had. Maybe—just maybe—I could give them something Leah could never find again. Hope.

I orchestrated a meeting with him, claiming I was putting out feelers for drawing up some plans for a self-build project.

I felt nauseous when I saw the ring on his right hand. I even commented on it. He told me it was a family heirloom. Leah's drawing had been surprisingly accurate. Sickeningly so. And every time it glinted in the light, I wondered how many times Leah had stared at it. Had she stared at that to stop herself from looking at his face? His body? To stop herself from thinking about what he was doing to her? Or making her do to him? How many other girls were tortured by the image of that ring?

The questions just constantly zipped around and around in my head. And I had to make them stop. I had to make this right.

The question was, how? Now that I had found him, what could I do to make it right? I thought about it for days. The evidence on his hard drive was gone. Leah was gone. How could I get the kind of justice my sister deserved all these years later? Without Leah around to point the finger, I realised that there was only one way: I had to get him to admit what he'd done. So I hacked into his alarm system, got to know his routine. Then, one night, I broke into his house to confront him. I had no idea what his reaction would be, or mine if he actually admitted the truth of it all to me.

Nothing had prepared me for his rage when he knew he'd been found out. Although I didn't physically touch him, you could say that my mere presence incited the accident that killed him. I just wanted to talk. I swear it. I just wanted to talk to him, to tell him who I was, and what I knew. I just wanted to get him to admit the truth of it all to me so that I could take his confession to the police. To get him punished. To get Leah justice. But as soon as I said my name, he went crazy. He knew who I was, and he started coming at me. He was so angry. I knew he was going to kill me if he got his hands on me, but I couldn't move. All I could think was that this was the face that had abused Leah. This was the monster that had killed my sister when he stole her innocence. And I froze.

It was his own effort to get to me that started it all off. It seems so trite now. So underwhelming. But he slipped. That's all. Just a slip. But when he fell, he hit his head on the steps in his kitchen.

He was dead as soon as he hit the ground.

I know now that I should have just left without doing anything more, but I panicked. I felt trapped. If Jarvis was found dead, I felt sure it wouldn't take long for the police to be at my door, considering how quickly I'd found him. I thought he'd be on someone's radar.

So I did the only thing I could think of. The most stupid thing in the world, as it turns out, but I disposed of his body and car. I knew from his emails that he was going away to a conference and took advantage of the extra time it gave me before he would be noticed as missing.

I thought it was a reasonable plan. No, I actually thought in my panic-addled brain that it was a good plan. But that wasn't all that went wrong that fateful night, Helen. Not by a long shot. Because there was also what happened to Kate.

Although I played no part in the death of Kate Wolfe, I was present at the scene of her death. She was out jogging at night and was hit by a car. It was an accident. She was just in the wrong place at the wrong time.

When you interviewed Malcolm Walters, he said he got drunk and drove around for a couple of hours after dumping Sandy's body. I don't even think Malcolm realised that he'd actually hit a person rather than a nocturnal animal. But the timelines and location all match. I just wish I could've seen the licence plate number to be able to give you certainty.

I couldn't just leave her there, sprawled across the road. After dumping Jarvis's car in the quarry, I took her to her home. Again, there was no plan. None. I didn't even know she was a police officer until I saw some mail at her house. Dr Nicholls will no doubt discover that Kate died months ago, her injuries consistent with being hit by a car, the same type of car that killed Sandy.

The fear of what would happen when a police officer was found to be missing or dead forced me into making yet another panic-induced, stupid decision. I took her place. I hacked into the database, changed a few of her personal details to match mine. I thought six months in a small town would be uneventful, a good place to hide out if there was any fallout about Jarvis's death. But, as we both know, it was anything but.

I deceived you and many others, including Kate's mother, for which I'm truly sorry. I'm making no excuses for my actions; I have only myself to blame. I tried not to involve you, Helen. I tried to stay away from you. I truly did. I fought my attraction, fought my feelings for you. I wanted to save you from the fate that no doubt awaits me. But in the end, I just couldn't. It was all too strong. I had to touch you, to feel you, to know you. I needed to see that smile, hear you laugh, and hear you call me Virginia. Every time you called me Kate, I was equal parts elated and cringing. Because I knew it was an intimacy I craved but one I didn't deserve. I just wasn't strong enough. What I feel for you...it's everything. Everything.

I hope in time you can forgive me for what I've done. I know I was wrong. I know it. But it was an accident. I realise my words will mean nothing to you know, but it's the truth.

As I sit here and write this, I realise I'm no better than Malcolm Walters, considering how I've manipulated those around me to my own ends.

I know that I've incriminated myself in writing this letter and that there is every possibility that you'll come after me and no doubt catch me. You're an outstanding police officer, and an even better person. You deserve someone every bit as amazing as you are.

This may sound like an empty gesture coming from me, but I've loved being with you over the last few weeks. If I had to pinpoint the moment I fell in love with you, I would have to say it was the very first time you trapped me in my car when we were going for lunch. It still brings a smile to my face when I think about it.

Please believe me when I say I didn't intend for any of this to happen, and certainly not to fall in love with you, but I did, and I can never regret that. I just can't. You're too special to me to ever regret a single moment I spent in your company, in your arms, or that you'll spend in my heart. I know you will feel it is your duty to find me, and I don't blame you for that. What we have, or had, was the best thing that ever happened to me.

Love always,

Lexi Ryan

CHAPTER 23

LEXI RYAN LOOKED AT THE Polaroid of her mother and sister. The dusky light penetrating the room allowed her to just make out their features. They looked carefree as they both laughed at the large cake in front of them. Her sister's tenth birthday had been the last time she could remember them being happy. That Polaroid camera had been her favourite gadget at the time. In the low light, she could just make out the birthday card on the table in the background. Lexi had made it for Leah. She remembered writing *double figures at last* inside. Who could believe now how much the two-year age gap had meant between them back then?

Tears pricked Lexi's eyes. If she needed a reminder of why she had done all this, the looks on their faces were all she needed to see. Jarvis had taken so much away from her, but it seemed he wasn't finished yet. Now she had to lose Helen too.

A more detailed look at Jarvis's house could had saved her from all this. She recalled the moment she had seen the tiny camera on her final sweep of his house; finding the server, reviewing the footage of that night, she'd struggled to contain her rage. If she had found that camera earlier, she could have prevented a whole string of events.

Not Kate Wolfe's death. No, there was nothing she could have done to prevent that. She would still have been killed, and Lexi might never have met Helen—even if Helen did hate her guts right now.

She felt terrible for hiding Kate's body for so long, depriving her loved ones of the truth, of their chance to mourn the loss of their beloved daughter. Every email, every message, every recorded *I love you* from Kate's mother had gnawed at her soul. But once she'd set out on that road, there was no turning back. Keeping Kate's body in a fridge in the garage wasn't the best idea, but there had been few options at the time.

Lexi felt a shiver as she remembered the grinding of bones as she carried Kate to her car that night. She knew now that she should have just dumped his car on the nearest bit of coastline, but she was too scared of being seen, caught on CCTV, ironically. It was all too easy to blame Jarvis, but she knew that she had been the one to set these particular wheels in motion.

Lexi tucked the photograph in her pocket as she thought about the task at hand. What could she really expect from Helen? She'd broken the law. Talked herself into her bed. And lied to her the whole time.

Helen was a good police officer, trained to bring people just like her to justice. Nevertheless, she had to roll the dice. She couldn't leave without a sliver of hope.

Lexi knew she could very well be setting her own trap, but she'd still be there regardless. She was clinging to the hope that time would be a healer in what she had done. She trusted—no, she hoped—that Helen would see that she wasn't a terrible person, she hadn't meant it to go so badly wrong. She was just trying to keep a promise. Trying to right a wrong. To get a little justice for Leah—she deserved that at the very least. She would do anything to go back all those years and prevent her sister from ever meeting Jarvis. We all have a duty to protect the ones we love. She was merely performing that duty belatedly.

She hoped the connection she'd shared with Helen was strong enough for her to at least hear her out. To give her a little time to explain face to face how hard it had been for her to continue with the deception, especially as she began to fall in love with her. She needed Helen to know that more than anything.

Lexi thought back to their first meeting at the police station after the fracas at the house fire. Helen had been firm but fair despite Lexi's stupidity. She'd been physically attracted to Helen from the very start. Combined with her keen acumen and sense of humour, the attraction had drawn her in so easily. She wasn't sure how many people Helen shared her playful side with, but Lexi felt honoured to be amongst them. All the teasing, 'the alphabet game'—she'd walked right into that one. She recalled the fear in

Helen's eyes after the scuffle with the knife. Lexi had never had that kind of connection with anyone before. She wanted that in her life.

She wanted Helen.

———◆———

Helen crossed the road from the pub, having been dragged there to pay her respects at the loss of a fellow officer. In truth, she'd lost much more than that. The letter she'd received two days ago was playing on her mind too much for her to spend time with her colleagues. She needed to be alone.

She walked down the short path towards her house. She hadn't realised how dark and desolate it looked. It had been such a good investment at the time, overshadowing all the negatives that she now saw in the darkness. How had she been so stupid to fall for a total fraud? Beautiful? Yes. Charming? Certainly. But still a fraud regardless of the circumstances.

Helen knew that if any inconsistencies were found after the post-mortem, they would be swept under the carpet. The chief constable could never let it get out that there had been an impersonator in their midst, even if she had helped solve several crimes along the way. Kate Wolfe would be notched up as a promising officer taken before her time in a terrible accident, her past indiscretions forgotten. Maybe that was best for all of them. Including Helen.

A sharp pain emanated from her chest at the thought of never seeing Kate—no, Lexi. She would never see Lexi again.

How could she have gotten it so wrong? She knew how to read people, didn't she? Not this time, apparently. Somehow, Kate had slipped right under the radar.

Flicking on the hall light, Helen threw her keys on the small table in the hall before walking towards the kitchen. Just because she wasn't in the pub didn't mean she couldn't have a drink. Walking past the door to the sitting room, she saw the flash of a lamp turn on. Freezing in her tracks, panic rattled through her. She was unsure of what to do next.

Her colleagues were less than two minutes away. But a lot could happen in two minutes. Helen frantically rummaged in the inside of her coat until her hand rested on the handle of the extending baton. The other hand gripped her mobile phone. She quickly brought up the directory. Before she could select a number, a familiar voice broke the silence.

"Don't call anyone. Not yet. Please," Lexi's voice pleaded from the dimly lit room.

"What the fuck? What are you doing here? I thought you'd gone." Helen struggled to hide the anger from her voice. She hadn't anticipated seeing Lexi ever again, never mind right now—in her own house. She heard movement as Lexi came into view, framed by the doorway. She released her grip on the baton but kept it in easy reach. After all, she didn't really know this woman at all.

"I couldn't leave without seeing you first."

Helen stood still. Not moving. Not speaking. What was there to say? *I love you but I don't even know you? Yeah, that should be a good place to start.*

"You found the key?" Lexi asked, her tone sounding hopeful. Helen saw the dark circles under Lexi's eyes as Lexi trailed her fingers along the edge of the door; it had been locked on her last visit, the key missing in action. It was the same door they had made love against only a few days before. Things were so different then, but as she now knew, they had already begun to crumble as soon as Jarvis's car had been discovered in the quarry.

Helen nodded reluctantly. "Found it in a pickle jar in the fridge." She decided not to mention the fact that she had spent the previous night sleepless and had scoured the house for the misplaced key, as if it would somehow allow her to make sense of the recent events that had blown her world apart.

"I know I'm probably the last person you want to see right now. I just wanted a chance to explain."

Helen looked at the floor, unable to meet Lexi's eyes. "Didn't you already do that in your letter?" she spat out. She knew deep down that there had been something troubling Kate—no, Lexi—before the fire. She'd even offered to help at one point, but she couldn't get her to open up. Helen reluctantly looked up, meeting Lexi's gaze.

"I'm so sorry. I wanted to tell you face to face, but I—I guess I thought you might arrest me."

Helen pushed, "Shouldn't I?"

Lexi looked down at her hands. "Probably, but I couldn't do that to my mother. I'm all she has left."

Helen let out a breath. Not only was Lexi guilty of unlawful burial, concealing a death, impersonating a police officer, and possibly murder, she was also a terrible daughter. *Daughter*—that word resonated with her. What about the real Kate Wolfe's mother? She'd never really know how her daughter died. But that wasn't all she was. Whatever the truth of Richard Jarvis was, Lexi had believed that he was the man who had abused her sister. The vague details in Lexi's letter haunted Helen, and she'd never known Leah Ryan. How hard must it have been to be in Lexi's position? Knowing he was out there, still torturing children. Still ruining lives. Never facing justice or punishment of any kind for his crimes. Never having to face the consequences for the children and families he destroyed. What would she have done in Lexi Ryan's position?

It was the question Helen kept coming back to. Over and over again. What would she have done had she been face to face with the man she believed had done all that?

"You're a good hacker, I'll give you that." Helen's voice went bitter. Even she could hear it. "Much better than your file suggests."

Lexi's brow knitted in confusion.

Helen felt the venom in her mouth as she spoke. "Hacking into the police database, changing Kate's details to be ready for when you took her place, then changing them again before you left. Very tidy."

"I'm sorry for all the deception. I wasn't trying to hurt you. I never wanted to hurt you. If there was any other way I could have changed it, I would have. Please believe that. The last thing I ever wanted to do was hurt you. I hated lying to you. I hated it. I wish—oh, I wish so many things now—but most of all I wish you and I had met under different circumstances. Not like this, where everything has just spiralled…"

Helen rubbed her eyes, hoping to clear her mind of the conflict she felt. She knew she should arrest Lexi. She had a lawful duty to report a death, but somehow she couldn't bring herself to do it. Helen had checked her story as best she could in the short time she had spent at her desk—when she wasn't at the scene of the fire or trying to console Kate's family. There was indeed a young girl called Leah Ryan who had claimed to have been abused by a man just as Lexi's letter had said, daughter of a single mother and sister to a Lexi Ryan. She'd even managed to find Richard Jarvis's previous addresses from the DVLA. He was resident at a London address the same time as Stone, but was it enough? Did it really justify what Lexi had done to Jarvis, let alone the real Kate Wolfe? And then there was the web of deception she had spun. Self-defence could be very difficult to prove. People never walked away with their lives intact.

"I let my guard down with you. I trusted you."

"I know. I'm sorry." Lexi stepped a little closer.

The movement made Helen look up. She didn't like being on guard around this woman. They had been intimate on so many occasions, it didn't feel right. Seeing Lexi up close, she could see she'd changed her hair: it was shorter and dyed raven-black. She was back to being Lexi, at least according to her arrest record from when she was a teenager.

Apparently, young Lexi had gone off the tracks a little in her youth. Computer fraud wasn't the crime of choice for most kids in the nineties, but it seemed that Lexi knew computers inside and out. Her file had Lexi labelled as a reasonably high-profile hacker at one point.

In the short time Helen had known her, she had grown to care for this woman, maybe more than she wanted to admit to her face. Helped by the support Lexi had shown over Julia, it was obvious that Lexi cared for her too. It was hard for her to comprehend how that person could be responsible for two deaths.

Lexi stopped in her tracks, probably at the grim look on Helen's face. "What happened between us was real."

"Bullshit. I don't even know you, Lexi. I knew Kate. I—I cared about Kate."

Lexi shook her head. "I know you think that, and I get it. I do. But nothing between us was a lie. When I touched you, Helen, that was real. When you touched me, that was real too. Every time I made you laugh, when I drove you crazy, or let you trap me in the car and let you beat me to lunch. That was all real." She stepped closer, then stopped again. "I love you, Helen. That's real. I didn't intend to hurt you or for any of this to happen. When I found Kate and discovered she was a police officer, I couldn't see another way out without creating a major investigation."

Helen nodded. "We're pretty strict about our fellow officers being killed."

"I know. It was meant to be so simple." Lexi blew out a frustrated breath. "Just ride out the six months up here, then disappear on my way back to London, no one any the wiser." She smiled sadly. "But then I met you." Lexi made a move to touch Helen's arm, then looked back up into Helen's eyes, "I fell in love with you. The last thing I wanted was to implicate you in my mess."

Helen tried to shrug off Lexi's words. She didn't need Lexi trying to ingratiate herself, or to rekindle what they had. Wasn't she just trying to save her own skin? An unwelcome thought occurred to her: was Lexi here to tie up loose ends? Helen was the only one who knew the truth. Knowing she wouldn't let any discrepancies fall through the net, maybe the letter was just to keep her quiet till Lexi could finish her off.

Lexi's voice broke through her train of thought. "I've got the missing footage from Jarvis's house. I wanted you to have it."

Helen frowned, her suspicions awakened. Why would she give it to me? Has she doctored it using her infamous IT skills, like the Curtis Whiting image? Helen balked. Except she hadn't doctored that CCTV picture. Lexi had actually put her skills to good use. Curtis was guilty, and he fully admitted it. Lexi had been the facilitator to close the case and not just that one. Sandy's case too.

"Here." Lexi held out the memory stick for Helen to take. "I only found out about the CCTV inside the house when I went to put something back after..." Lexi trailed off again. "He slipped and fell, hit his head on the steps in his kitchen. I didn't touch him, I promise you. Please take it."

Helen reluctantly took the offered stick.

"I need you to know I didn't kill him. It was an accident. I told him who I was, and he went mental."

"He knew you?" Helen queried.

"My name, yes."

A frown crossed Helen's brow. Why would Jarvis know the name Lexi Ryan? Unless he had good reason to remember it; her detective brain was just getting into gear. She needed to know the sequence of events to somehow justify Lexi's actions. "Tell me about Kate Wolfe."

Lexi swallowed hard. "I had nothing to do with Kate Wolfe's death. I just found her body. I honestly think Malcolm Walters did it, after he ran over Sandy; he said he went out drinking, remember?"

Helen nodded.

"On his way back home, he said he thought he'd hit an animal with his car. She was out in the middle of nowhere, jogging, dressed in black. I don't think he knew what he'd done."

Helen recalled Waters's words during his interview. He thought he had hit a deer, even felt bad about it. "You saw it. Why didn't you call for help?"

Lexi shook her head. "I heard it. His taxi radio whistling in the background. He got out of the car, but I don't think he even saw her. When I got to her, she was already dead."

Helen frowned. "Whistle? Is that why you looked at Kirk's car?"

Lexi nodded.

"Where did it happen?" Helen questioned.

"On the road to the quarry."

"When you were dumping Jarvis's car," Helen clarified, piecing it together.

Lexi nodded her confirmation.

"You hotwired his car?" Helen asked, curiosity getting the better of her.

"No. I had his keys. I pulled off the casing just to make it look like it."

"You knew about the power cuts?" Helen queried.

Lexi nodded. "I didn't know what else to do with her body. A neighbour told me about the power cuts, even brought me around some candles one night. I thought it would be a way out of it all." Lexi looked down, avoiding Helen's gaze. "Not that I really wanted a way out. I knew it would be the end of us, and I didn't want that. I never wanted that, despite what you must think of me right now. But I was out of time. Kate's mum was threatening to visit. I couldn't put her off anymore."

"And now what? You're running away from it all?"

Helen's words were cutting.

"I'm going away because I have to, not because I want to." Lexi pulled a slip of paper from her pocket. "I'll be at this place two months from today." She held out the paper for Helen. "I meant what I said earlier. About being in love with you. I know you might never be able to forgive me for what I've done. And I wouldn't blame you if that was the case. I truly wouldn't. But…" She took a deep breath. "But if there's any way you could forgive me…maybe give me another chance. A chance to prove myself to you. To show you that it was really Lexi all along that you were with…well, I'd really like that."

"I—" Helen was about to give Lexi her answer now, save her wasting her time.

Lexi cut her off. "I'll be there at 1p.m. if you want to meet."

Helen made no move to take the piece of paper. Could she really have any kind of relationship with this woman? Memories of Kate flashed through her mind. She had been difficult from the start. Even so, it hadn't prevented Helen's attraction to her. Then she got to know Kate. They worked well together. She'd even stepped in, preventing Helen from getting hurt at a cost to herself. Then there was the filming of the house fire to collect evidence. Why would she do all that? Was she just playing a part? Who was the real Lexi?

Lexi moved towards her, pushing the slip of paper in her hand before clasping her own hand around Helen's. Leaning forward, Lexi brushed her lips along the side of Helen's face.

"Was it worth it?" Helen asked as Lexi turned to leave.

Lexi stood facing the door, as the question hung between them. "No. I always end up losing someone. First my sister, then my mother, and now you. I just wanted him to admit what he'd done to Leah. Now I'm not sure any of it was worth it."

Helen nodded, fighting off her feelings of sorrow for Lexi and her shattered family.

Lexi closed the door quietly behind her.

CHAPTER 24

HELEN SAID HER GOODBYES TO the small group of stragglers that remained at Julia's wake. Due to the long drive from Warner and Julia's home town of Ledbury, many of the attenders had already left. It had been Julia's wish to be buried next to her sister Ellen in Burniston, just outside Scarborough, which meant Helen now had a three-hour drive home. She'd been surprised to discover that even after her diagnosis, Julia had had the presence of mind to outline the service she wanted—right down to the people she had wanted to be invited. Helen had dutifully contacted all requested parties; some were friends of Ellen.

Julia had frequently visited Julia's only sibling. Ellen had died two years earlier; cancer was in their genes. With neither of them having any offspring, this was the end of their family tree. Of course, in Julia's case, she'd housed many children over the years, a few of whom had made the journey today. It warmed Helen's heart to think of the number of lives Julia had changed over the years. As she walked to her car, her mind pitched back to the card attached to the arrangement of white tulips she'd spotted while surveying the funeral flowers. Lexi had obviously been keeping tabs on her, or Julia at least.

On her way home, she detoured to The Oaks; she'd put it off for too long. It was time to clear the decks. She still had the same knot in her stomach as she walked into the reception. She remembered back to the time Kate, or rather Lexi, had been with her, when she'd insisted on driving her.

She'd felt so comforted by her presence, even more so as she fell asleep in her arms that night.

Blinking away the image, she informed the receptionist that she'd come to pick up Julia's belongings. She was quickly whisked away to a storage room. The receptionist picked up a clipboard from the shelving and scanned the paperwork. Julia's room had obviously been reoccupied in the last week. They certainly didn't hang around.

Helen felt terrible for not coming earlier. She had wanted to be the one to clear out Julia's room. But, no matter how much time you had to come to terms with an expected loss, it was still a curveball when it actually happened. Julia had been the only constant in Helen's life, apart from her job. Julia had picked Helen up and put her back together as best she could after Helen had been removed from her so-called mother. She'd given her everything she could.

Looking around at the names neatly written on the boxes surrounding her, it reminded her of an evidence locker. Julia's life had been reduced to a box on a shelf.

"I just need your signature here." The receptionist handed her the clipboard.

She signed against the space marked with an X and took the offered boxes, one stacked on top of the other. "I'm sorry for your loss."

Helen simply nodded before walking away. It was so different being on the other side of those words. The emptiness they held for her now. She hated to think how many times she'd used them in an effort to comfort family members. She had never comprehended how truly meaningless they were.

———◆———

Helen reluctantly put down the rag she'd been using to stain the newly installed shelving in the front reception room. Whoever was at the door was pretty persistent. She hoped it wasn't someone from work feeling sorry for her again. She'd taken the standard bereavement leave offered, then extended it—twice. Every time she thought of going back, a cold feeling settled in her stomach. She needed time to think. Lexi's lies still weighed heavily on her shoulders.

Opening the door, she was faced with a thin elderly man who looked vaguely familiar. "Hello," she offered, reluctant to let him in without knowing his reason for calling."

"Helen Taylor?"

"Yes."

"My name is Emmet Walker." He handed her a business card. "I was Julia Chamberlain's solicitor. I've been trying to contact you over the last few days."

"Oh." There had been several phone calls, but Helen had been avoiding answering them, worried that she'd get roped back in to work if she actually answered. "Come in."

She stepped aside, closing the door behind him. Her head had been so filled with funeral plans and Lexi's ultimatum that she'd had little time to think of anything else. Any thought of Julia's estate had completely slipped her mind.

"Thank you."

"Please." Helen gestured for him to follow her through to the dining room. "Would you like some tea?"

"No, thank you." Emmet Walker set his briefcase down on the table before taking a seat. "Julia came to me a little over two years ago to finalise her will, just after her sister's death, I believe."

"I see." Helen took the seat opposite. She couldn't imagine Julia having a hidden fortune to bequeath to anyone, not after her care home costs. Helen had paid for the funeral; it was the least she could do considering everything Julia had done for her.

"I won't take up much of your time. I can see that you're busy. In short, Miss Taylor, you are the sole beneficiary of Julia Chamberlain's estate."

Helen looked down at her dirty hands and paint-streaked clothes.

Emmet Walker pulled a wad of paper from his briefcase. "Along with all Miss Chamberlain's worldly goods, most of which I believe are in storage at the Secure Store near..." He checked his paperwork. "Great Holcomb, you are also bequeathed all monies in Miss Chamberlain's accounts, which, after any final bills, adds up to just over twenty-two thousand pounds."

"Okay." Considering how long Julia had been resident at The Oaks, the amount was shocking.

"And, of course, the Scarborough property: flat 15a, Seaview Terrace, Scarborough."

Property "I'm sorry?"

"It belonged to Julia's sister, Ellen."

Helen stared at him blankly as the words began to sink in.

"Julia was the sole beneficiary of her sister's will, and you are now the sole beneficiary of Julia's will."

To her surprise, Emmet Walker pulled a set of keys from his briefcase and placed them on the table in front of her.

Although she hadn't taken Julia's last name, they were family, and now she was the last of the line. She was alone for the first time in her life. There was nothing left for her now in Warner. She couldn't just go back to work as if nothing had happened, of that she was certain. With Kate—no, with Lexi—she'd had a glimpse of something, something that had set her world on fire. If she stayed, she'd wither up and die, consumed by her own loneliness.

It was down to Helen to change that. She needed to put herself first for once. With no work colleagues or family to question her decisions, there was no fear of suffering their disappointment. Julia had been a precious lifeline for her over thirty years ago when she'd first come into her life. She'd given her a chance when her own mother was incapable of caring. Now Julia was doing it all over again. She owed it to her to make the most of it. The money she'd bequeathed would tide her over till she settled in somewhere else, at least. With no ties to anyone or anything, she was finally free to decide where exactly this opportunity would take her.

CHAPTER 25

Two Months Later

Lexi gripped the rail at the end of the pier. The bitter costal wind made the metal feel like ice in her hands. The sound of a police siren in the distance made her stomach begin to churn. She quietly regretted her romanticised, if not stupid, idea of meeting at the end of a pier. She frantically looked around. There was no escape except for the harsh sea below.

She had been both dreading and looking forward to this meeting in equal measure since the night she'd left Warner, convinced that it wouldn't go the way she wanted. Would Helen see a future with her after what she'd done? The guilt Lexi felt had congealed over the last two months, reduced to a hardened lump in the pit of her stomach.

Considering Helen's recent loss, who knew if she was even going to appear? She knew how hard Helen would have taken the death of the only woman she could call a mother. When Lexi had read the news, she could only think of her need to comfort Helen.

The sky was full of blustery grey clouds, darkening to the horizon. Lexi always liked this place, even on the worst of days.

Risking a quick look back to the seafront, she saw the police car speeding along the front, the siren now turned off, lights still flashing.

"They're not here for you."

Lexi turned fully to see Helen holding two takeaway hot drinks. She looked good, fresh-faced, the dark circles that had laid heavy under her eyes all but gone. She even showed a hint of a grin at Lexi's obvious anxiousness. Helen's casual approach eased some of the butterflies frantically moving around Lexi's stomach.

"Really?" she asked, seeking further confirmation.

"Really. I got you a hot chocolate," Helen replied, offering one of the cups.

"Thanks."

Lexi reached for the drink with both hands. The warmth from the cup instantly brought her fingers back to life. Near the shoreline over Helen's shoulder, two police officers were exiting one of the shops with another figure in tow.

Helen turned her head, following Lexi's line of sight.

"They're picking up a guy called Paul O'Brien. I recognised him when I got the drinks. Disappeared when he was released on bail from Manchester over a year ago. I had to look at his ugly mug on a poster in the station every day for months."

Lexi was genuinely impressed by Helen's attention to detail. She looked across at Helen's profile. Her hair had gone wild in the wind, but she looked calm and relaxed. As she gazed out to the horizon, she wondered what Helen was thinking about.

"Always on duty, huh?" Lexi offered, she felt heat of desire rise to her cheeks despite the cool breeze.

"Not anymore," Helen answered, mirroring Lexi's position as she looked out to sea, resting her forearms on the handrail.

Lexi swallowed hard, trying to hide her surprise at Helen's news. She struggled to meet Helen's gaze, unsure of what she would find waiting for her. Resentment for pushing her into an untenable situation, maybe. "What?" she asked in confusion.

Had Helen really thrown away her whole career because of the difficult position she had put her in? Lexi had had no idea that she would do that for her. Did she truly care for her that much? She didn't need to go that far; she just needed to turn a blind eye. But wasn't that in itself asking too much of her? Before she had a chance to question her about it, Helen made her own request.

"How's your mother?"

Lexi's return to London had been less than satisfying. Leaving Helen behind had been hard, added to the guilt she carried for what happened in Warner. The relief at finally getting the justice she deserved for her sister had never really materialised. Informing her mother of her actions, how she had kept her promise to Leah, had had little effect on her mother's continued decline, almost as if there were nothing to stay around for, not even her surviving daughter. Lexi shrugged off the parallels that her life had with Malcolm Walters.

Unsure of what to say, she settled on something middle of the road as she felt Helen's eyes on her. "Same as usual."

"No dramatic recovery?"

Helen's words sounded harsh even as they were swept away by the wind. Tears stung Lexi's eyes. Had it been a mistake to meet up? She managed to look away, preventing Helen from seeing the tear slip down her cheek.

"I'm sorry, Lex. I didn't mean that."

Lexi hastily wiped at the tear with her coat sleeve. "It's fine." She felt the cavernous hole open around her feet: first her sister, then her mother's continued determination to end her life by her own hand, all because of one man's selfish actions. Lexi knew she'd done some terrible things, but surely it wasn't comparable to what he had done. How many other lives had he ruined over the years? Now she could add hers to the list. She had thrown away the chance of being happy with someone.

Placing her drink on the decked floor, Helen stepped closer to Lexi. "No. It's not fine. Come here."

Helen pulled her into her arms. The familiarity was almost painful for Lexi. What if this was the last time they'd be together? She couldn't let that happen, not without a fight. It took a few moments for Lexi to regain control of her emotions. She kept her face pressed into Helen's shoulder as she spoke. "I wasn't sure you'd come today."

"When I saw you that night in Warner, I wasn't sure I'd be here either. I missed you."

Lexi felt her own smile against Helen's cheek. She had waited so long to hear those words. "I've missed you too." Her whispered words barely scratched the surface of how she felt. She had missed Helen's friendship, the smell of her skin, the long, languid kisses she gave as they made love, even her confidence and constant teasing. "It's so good to see you."

Her arms instinctively gripped Helen a little tighter. The night she had walked away from Helen's house, she'd been sure she had seen her for the last time.

Heavy bootfalls on the pier heading in her direction behind her drew Helen's attention. She pulled back a little to meet Lexi's big brown eyes before she turned to deal with the interruption. She saw only warmth and hope. Any doubt she had at coming to the meeting was swept away by the wind.

"I need to talk to this officer for a minute. I'll be right back. Don't run off." She walked over to meet the uniformed man. After giving him an explanation regarding her intimate knowledge of O'Brien, they shook hands and parted company.

At the end of the pier, Lexi seemed deep in thought as she looked out to sea. Helen picked up her hot chocolate, disappointed that the heat had dissipated. She retook her place next to Lexi, their arms brushing as they both looked out to sea.

"Did you leave your job because of—" Lexi didn't turn to look at her.

"You?" Helen finished for her. "No. You and Julia may have been the straws that broke the camel's back." Helen turned to face Lexi. "But I was burned out when I left Manchester. Warner was a step back for me. Now I need a change." She sipped her drink. After over fifteen years, the stress of working endless brutal cases illuminating humanity's ability to be cruel and little else had taken its toll. She didn't like the perception of life the job had given her, not to mention the lack she felt of any other aspect to it—she had no family or friends outside of work.

"So I took some time off after Julia. And decided not to go back." Helen trailed off, staring at her hands wrapped around the now lukewarm hot chocolate.

"I'm sorry about Julia," Lexi said quietly.

"I was surprised by the flowers. Thank you. They were her favourites." Helen turned to look back out towards the sea to hide the tears that threatened to fall. Julia's death was still raw for her.

"I know. You told me."

Helen let out a long breath, allowing a small smile at the shared memory of their time together.

"Time off suits you. You look good."

Helen turned her body sideways, once more leaning on one arm as she faced Lexi. The attraction Helen felt for her was still strong—magnified, if anything—by their time apart. She had never met a police officer with Lexi's abstract approach to her job, and it had been a refreshing change. Even now, knowing what she did about her, Helen was still fascinated by the person in front of her. She looked as beautiful as ever, although a little tired, maybe. Had she been concerned about their meeting?

"Fancy a walk?" she asked, hoping to keep Lexi for a bit longer.

"Sure."

Lexi nudged Helen's shoulder as they walked along the pier towards the shore.

With all the heat gone from her hot chocolate, Helen tossed it into the nearest bin, holding it open for Lexi to do the same.

She saw the smile on Lexi's lips as she plunged her hands deep into her coat pockets in an effort to warm them.

"What?" Helen asked as they continued walking.

"Nothing. I was just speculating as to whether you would wear that coat all through the summer too."

Helen wanted to tell her that if she had stuck around, she would have found out, but she held her tongue instead. She wasn't here to start an argument. The anger and her dented pride for not seeing the deception coming had taken a while to dispel. A trust had been broken. Helen had tried to put herself in Lexi's position a number of times. Having never been the victim of violent loss herself, it was hard for her to say whether she would have done the same thing. But she had seen people trying to acclimatise to the loss of a loved one at the hand of another. She could empathise with the need and desire for fair justice, not just some lip service from a judge. Although her own upbringing had had its challenges, Helen considered herself all the better for it. She would have gone to the ends of the earth if someone had been responsible for the loss of Julia.

Time was definitely a great healer in this case—time and the fact that Lexi hadn't actually killed anyone. Alongside the CCTV footage Lexi had given her, she'd found enough evidence to corroborate Lexi's version of events. That had been a relief. Much more so than she had anticipated.

"What have you been doing with your time off?" Lexi asked as she ran a hand along the icy steel handrail that ran along the pier.

"I've been keeping busy, working on the house, mainly getting it finished so I can sell it," Helen replied as she tried to tame her hair made unruly by the wind.

"Finished that panelling, then?" Lexi enquired.

"All done," Helen smiled as she recalled Lexi's fascination with the interior of her house. "And you? What are you doing with your time now you're not in the force?"

Lexi half smiled at Helen's question. "Well, I'd only been a copper for seven hours before I got promoted to detective sergeant, so I think I did pretty well." Lexi huffed some breath onto her nails on her right hand before polishing them on her left arm. Her expression stretched out into a toothy grin.

Helen played along. "It must have been a moment of weakness. Or maybe I saw some potential in you."

Lexi nodded. "Yeah, unfortunately, my current boss doesn't quite share the same view as you."

"Really? Well, they obviously haven't seen your full skillset yet."

As they fell into habitual grooves, it felt like the months apart hadn't happened. Upon reaching the end of the pier, she raised a hand to her left, directing them along the sea defences. Lexi followed without question.

"So, where is it you're working?" Helen asked, wondering if it was local to Holme Point, Lexi's suggested meeting spot today.

"At Shield Securities, checking their security," she said, with a hint of irony. "And coding, that kind of stuff. Have you got anything lined up?"

Helen let out a long breath. "I'm not sure I'm employable after being a copper for so long. It's going to be boring working nine to five."

"That's not true, Guv. I'm sure there are lots of things you could do. You could become a private eye," Lexi continued with a little too much excitement.

"Oh God, I'll have to get used to people calling me by my first name again."

Lexi frowned. "It can't have been that long. You must have some friends," she offered.

"Not really. Mostly colleagues," Helen said, quietly feeling a little sorry for herself. In the time she'd had off work, she'd seen only a couple of ex-colleagues. The highlight was her old DS, Richards, bringing around his new baby. He had popped round with some thinly veiled disguise of an excuse, supposedly wanting some advice on a case. She was pretty sure he had expected to see her in pieces, having just walked away from a successful career. Maybe it hadn't hit her yet. She had made a point of waiting until Richards had settled back into work before she'd left her position. Was she being too level-headed? The story of her life. Helen's mind began to wonder at Lexi's choice of location.

"So, you've been here before?"

"When we were kids, we used to stay in Lynmouth, just along the coast, every year during the summer for a couple of weeks." Lexi smiled back at her. "Sometimes we'd come here to go crabbing off the pier."

Helen nodded. She had never seen the fascination in baiting hooks with scraps of bacon to catch the same crabs everyone else caught. She felt sorry for them being pulled out and crammed into buckets for hours.

The wind seemed to have eased a little as they walked along the sea defences. Like the pier earlier, the promenade was almost empty too, no doubt due to the cool weather. Fortified by the familiarity of Lexi's company, Helen broached the subject she had been avoiding since meeting on the pier.

"Lexi, I watched the footage you gave me." She let the statement hang as she waited for Lexi to get her mind around what she had just said.

"You did? Do you think it was my fault that he's...?" The wind concluded her question.

Helen reached for Lexi's hand. "No."

It was a streamlined answer, but it didn't make it less true. Helen recalled the image of Jarvis lying on the floor in his kitchen as Lexi rushed over, frantically checking for signs of life.

"I don't think it was the shock of seeing you that made him fall. I think he was angry at being cornered. From the footage, it looks to me like he was reaching for a knife as he moved towards you and lost his footing on the steps."

Lexi sucked in a hefty breath. "What—?"

The knife had obviously been a shock. She reached for Lexi with her free hand, slipping it inside Lexi's coat. The warmth of her body was refreshing. It felt so long since they'd been intimate. She missed the tenderness between them.

"There's more," Helen continued as she rubbed the back of Lexi's hand with her thumb as if to soften the blow. "We found some images on a computer storage drive when we searched his place again."

Lexi frowned. "You went back?"

"I wanted to see if there was any evidence of what he had been doing. Anyway, after I found it, I went to see his mother. I didn't tell her what we'd found, but I asked her about her son's private life—never married, no girlfriends, or children. She clammed up straight away. I think she knew, or suspected at least."

Lexi rested her back against the railing. Her blank gaze was aimed at the mishmash of beach huts in front of her. "Shit."

Helen had hoped Lexi would see it as good news of a sort—proof, maybe even a little justification, but, still, was it really worth what she'd been driven to do? "With no new information or evidence, the case is still open for now."

Lexi nodded. "I know. I've been keeping tabs on the missing persons register."

Helen focused on Lexi's profile as she waited patiently. Considering how they had parted in Warner, Helen felt the need to say how she felt. The sting of betrayal hadn't totally faded, but her need to have Lexi in her life had grown after her departure. "I've had a lot of time to think since I saw you that night in my house." She took a breath before continuing. "Jarvis was a terrible person. What he did to Leah, and who knows how many others… It's sickening." She clenched her free hand into a fist as she thought about the images she seen at Jarvis's house. "I'm so sorry she didn't get the justice she deserved the first time around. I understand why you wanted to stop him, make him pay for what he did. I've tried to put myself in your position, and sometimes I—I honestly don't know what I would have done. When I think about Julia and her illness, if there was someone, a person responsible for that, I think I'd feel compelled to react, to fight in her corner. To stop them before they destroyed someone else's life."

Lexi's hand was warm as she gripped Helen's a little tighter.

"Lex, I've had a lot of partners before, work partners," Helen clarified, "but when you arrived in Warner, you made me realise what was missing in my life."

Lexi looked up to face Helen, an expression of visible dread on her face.

"I'm not saying I totally agree with what you did, but I understand why you did it, and—I accept it." Helen took a breath as she waited for a response.

The light was beginning to fade as the grey skies above began to darken. Helen hadn't realised how long they had been walking and talking. It was too early for dusk; the weather was closing in.

"Where are you staying tonight?"

It wasn't the response she was expecting. "I don't know. I hadn't really thought that far ahead." Helen let her voice trail off.

"Come home with me."

It sounded like a plea rather than a question or a command.

Helen lifted a hand to cup Lexi's cheek, rubbing the cool skin with her thumb. Exhibiting the briefest of nods, her focus fell to Lexi's full lips, and she moved her hand to the side of Lexi's neck and gently pulled her forward, bringing their lips together. A hand slipped inside her coat, landing on her waist as Lexi's lips parted without dispute.

She quickly pulled Lexi into her arms, the warmth of Lexi's body falling against hers. Over the last couple of months, Helen had often thought of their physical relationship. She hadn't experienced that kind of intense desire with anyone else before. She wasn't sure it would still be there after everything that had happened. But, standing on the promenade, holding Lexi close, she could feel the pull between them.

Lexi's arms tightened around her, waking her from her thoughts. She couldn't resist burying her face into Lexi's hair, breathing in the freshly washed scent.

She'd made her choice. She needed to be with Lexi.

ABOUT CHARLOTTE MILLS

Charlotte Mills was born and bred in the south of England, after studying Fine Art at Loughborough University she has made the Midlands her home for the last twenty years where she lives with her long term partner.

Her career has bridged several different fields including the arts, education and construction.

She began creative writing in 2013, taking the plunge with self-publishing in 2014 with her first book *Unlikely Places*. This was followed up with *Out of The Blue* and its sequel *Latent Memories* in 2016 for which she won a gold medal at the Global EBook Awards for LGBT fiction in 2017.

When she is not writing she enjoys watching films and day dreaming about living in the middle of nowhere without any neighbors in earshot.

CONNECT WITH CHARLOTTE
E-Mail: charlottemills863@gmail.com

OTHER BOOKS FROM YLVA PUBLISHING

www.ylva-publishing.com

REQUIEM FOR IMMORTALS
Lee Winter

ISBN: 978-3-95533-710-0
Length: 263 pages (86,000 words)

Professional cellist Natalya Tsvetnenko moves seamlessly among the elite where she fills the souls of symphony patrons with beauty even as she takes the lives of the corrupt of Australia's ruthless underworld. The cold, exacting assassin is hired to kill a woman who seems so innocent that Natalya can't understand why anyone would want her dead. As she gets to know her target, she can't work out why she even cares.

COLLIDE-O-SCOPE
2nd editon
(Norfolk Coast Investigation Story – Book 1)
Andrea Bramhall

ISBN: 978-3-95533-849-7
Length: 291 pages (90,000 words)

One unidentified dead body. One tiny fishing village. Forty residents and everyone's a suspect. Where do you start? Newly promoted Detective Sergeant Kate Brannon and King's Lynn CID have to answer that question and more as they untangle the web of lies wrapped around the tiny village of Brandale Stiathe Harbour to capture the killer of Connie Wells.

FOUR STEPS
Wendy Hudson

ISBN: 978-3-95533-690-5
Length: 343 pages (92,000 words)

Seclusion suits Alex Ryan. Haunted by a crime from her past, she struggles to find peace and calm.

Lori Hunter dreams of escaping the monotony of her life. When the suffocation sets in, she runs for the hills.

A chance encounter in the Scottish Highlands leads Alex and Lori into a whirlwind of heartache and a fight for survival, as they build a formidable bond that will be tested to its limits.

DELIBERATE HARM
J.R. Wolfe

ISBN: 978-3-95533-368-3
Length: 300 pages (70,000 words)

Ever since Portia Marks learned her fiancée Imma was executed in Zimbabwe, she's struggled with grief. Then a stranger tells her Imma is alive, but he's killed before she can ask questions. To learn the truth, Portia teams with two friends in the CIA. Her search takes her across continents and entangles her in a terrorist plot that will rock the globe. Portia's quest becomes a race against time.

Payback
© 2019 by Charlotte Mills

ISBN: 978-3-96324-125-3

Also available as e-book.

Published by Ylva Publishing, legal entity of Ylva Verlag, e.Kfr.

Ylva Verlag, e.Kfr.
Owner: Astrid Ohletz
Am Kirschgarten 2
65830 Kriftel
Germany

www.ylva-publishing.com

First edition: 2019

Credits
Edited by Andrea Bramhall and Michelle Aguilar
Cover Design and Print Layout by Streetlight Graphics

Milton Keynes UK
Ingram Content Group UK Ltd.
UKHW041320190724
27UKWH00028B/174

9 783963 241253